Tales
of the
Lavender
Twilight

ALFRED P. DOBLIN

Rattling Good Yarns Press
33490 Date Palm Drive 3065
Cathedral City CA 92235
USA
www.rattlinggoodyarns.com

Cover Design: Rattling Good Yarns Press

Library of Congress Control Number: 2024951260
ISBN: 978-1-955826-81-5

First Edition

To my "big brothers" Chuck and Greg,
and to Gary, who inspired
Mr. Picky and continues to inspire me.

The Stories

"The sea rises, the light fails, lovers cling to each other, and children cling to us. The moment we cease to hold each other, the moment we break faith with one another, the sea engulfs us and the light goes out."
~James Baldwin

Holy Communion

John unlocked the door and looked up the street. Tommy was walking slowly in his direction, occasionally touching the rusty iron fence along the side of the community garden for balance. To a passerby, Tommy was a small man moving the way someone nearing eighty would—tentatively as if a slight misstep would hurtle him into Mount Sinai. But Tommy was not nearly that old, having turned sixty-three just last August.

It was the Jack Daniels. Glass after glass. Hour after hour. Year after year. Whoever Tommy might have been had faded into the amber slurry that settled at the bottom of a rocks glass.

John could not picture Tommy as a young man. Had he ever had big dreams? Was there a moment when everything changed, a juncture where Tommy turned down a path that led only to the bottom of a bottle that never quite emptied; Sisyphus condemned not with a boulder but a bottle of Jack Daniels?

This was not like John, to think about why people drink. Drinking was his livelihood. The Crow was his life, a small bar tucked into the West Village that stood like a guard in front of Buckingham Palace—an anachronistic reminder of the past that still silently guarded queens.

The Crow was not famous like The Stonewall Inn which was fine by John. There were no hordes of tourists from Kansas. The Crow was not a brand; it was a life force, deceptive like the silent pauses in a Pinter play, where everything of consequence is revealed.

For decades, gay men left their mark on the place. Before Stonewall. Before AIDS. Before ACT UP. Before TV shows depicting rich, attractive, bitchy alcoholic queers—because you can't call them "gay" anymore, which pissed off John to no end—were considered proof that America, except for Florida, had fully embraced diversity.

John had removed the TV from the bar after one such show became a hit. He couldn't stand watching a room full of gay men not getting the joke—that they were still the joke. Maybe he had become a bitter old queen himself, John sometimes wondered. He was like the parish priest with the little secret who either becomes bitter or alcoholic. John found the perfect alternative by owning a bar.

And why not? The Crow was more church than any place with a crucifix. Each day, from noon to 3 a.m., he and his bartenders, Jose, Carl, and Toby, performed the miracle of the Mass—turning booze into salvation. Not eternal salvation, but long enough.

John would raise the bottles high so all could see and give praise to all who had come to his communion rail to receive. They sat on butt-smoothed wooden stools or leaned against the long oak bar that bore the initials and names of seven decades of gay men who had come before them to that very rail to drink, hands cupping glasses for refills.

One more. Just one more. Hosanna in the highest!

They drank. They drank to celebrate. They drank to grieve. They drank to forget. They drank because drinking was all they could remember to do anymore. In a boozy haze, the face of God would appear just out of reach, and so they came back again and again, hoping to touch it just once.

John understood their need—their need for him and his bar. The Crow was a sanctuary, not unlike the hidden sanctuaries for gay men in the 1950s and 60s. The back-alley darkness of those illicit clubs of the past had given way to the front window where men could pose rather than hide. Police no longer raided The Crow. Two of John's regulars were NYPD. Yet, The Crow was never bathed in sunlight. It was on the wrong side of the street for the sun. And that suited John as much as his bar not being a tourist trap.

"You don't need much light to see people as they truly are," he would say. "Light only complicates things. It's in the dim light of dawn and sunset when everything worth seeing is clearly visible."

At 6'3", John always had an unobstructed view. He turned fifty-four last December, with the build of a former baseball player, which he had been in college. He favored battered T-shirts behind the bar; there were no uniforms at The Crow. The shirts showcased his muscular chest and arms that were well-covered in dark hair. His thick, always well-groomed beard had started turning grey when he was in his mid-40s, and now, was mainly silver, as was his full head of hair which he kept short but not buzzed. His green eyes focused on each customer when he spoke with them.

As for his customers, even the longtime regulars with partners focused on John's bearish face, arms, chest, and hair that teasingly played against the front frayed neckband of his T-shirts. Many a patron of The Crow fantasized about that flirtatious chest hair. John's only soft feature was his voice, which was deep but rarely raised.

John hadn't planned on owning a bar. After college, nothing quite fit. He spent a few years as a banker, then selling real estate, and then with an older friend, now deceased, as a home contractor. That friend left John a sizable amount of cash, and with it, John bought The Crow, not quite sure how to run a bar or even how to make drinks. But he figured it out. There was something about The Crow that lured him in. As time passed, John realized that he had found where he belonged. He understood his customers. They all needed each other.

As he walked behind the long bar, John heard the door opening. It sounded like the bell ringing from his distinct youth as an altar boy at Our Lady of Perpetual Help, calling congregants to worship. John turned around. "You're right on time, Tommy. Jack on the rocks?"

"Yes," Tommy replied as he sat at the right corner of the bar. It was his seat. And while the wooden stool should have been uncomfortable, it was like thick upholstery to Tommy. Warm and familiar, it was as close to home as he could get at this stage of life. He pulled out a jumbled wad of cash—mostly singles—from his windbreaker and placed it on the bar. John never knew where Tommy got his cash, but he always had enough.

John took out five from the crumpled pile. Jack Daniels was on special until 6 p.m. By then, Tommy would be leaving. He would pull himself up with a jerk like a discarded marionette that had suddenly been remembered by the master puppeteer and pulled up into life. It was an effort to move the legs and hands—the legs to go forward and the hands to prevent him from falling to the floor and, once outside, onto the pavement. By 4 p.m., Tommy reeked of the whiskey. He sweated the Jack. He exhaled it. Even at 2 p.m., the potent smell of alcohol and failed promise hovered over Tommy like a cloud. But now, at noon, Tommy was near sober.

"Did you go?" John asked.

"Go where?" Tommy replied, taking that first sip. Once, he would have savored that warm rush. Now, he barely noticed. "Where should I have gone?"

"Davie's memorial," John replied as he began prepping lemons and limes.

"That was today? I forgot."

"It was at 10:30. I thought you were coming from there. I expect we will get crowded soon as the guys come back."

For a second, Tommy looked disappointed at himself for forgetting, but he took a long sip of the Jack, and the moment was lost. "I don't want to go that way. Being found in your bed after four days. I want to go out in a blaze of glory. Something that gets me a spot on the evening news."

"I don't know," John said as he sliced at the limes. "Going to sleep and not waking up seems pretty good. Granted, I don't like the idea of stinking up my apartment, but it's a peaceful exit. I can't believe Davie is gone. I expect him to come in here and sit in that stool, two stools from your left. That was his seat." John looked at the spot where Davie sat nearly every day for the fifteen years John had owned The Crow and for 5 years before then.

"He was an odd bird," Tommy said as he continued to drink. "He always had to sit there. You know he never sat next to me. I thought he was a bit of a snob in his blue blazer and fancy shirts."

John wanted to say Davie didn't sit next to Tommy because he couldn't stand the smell of the Jack and the sound Tommy made as he moved into a deep drunk. Tommy would sporadically make a small, high-pitched sound as he drank through the day. As he squealed "wee," Tommy would raise his right hand and make a twirling motion as if he were shooing away reality before returning to his glass. In another context, it would have been funny. But like all things Tommy, it was just sad.

Davie was the same age as Tommy. Most of the regulars were all about that age, give or take—somewhere between fifty-eight and seventy. Davie was a very regulated drinker. Cabernet. Three glasses that he would make last for hours. He almost never varied. It would take a newcomer to change the pattern, a handsome, too-young man, totally inappropriate, to recharge the aging battery inside Davie. In those moments, John would watch Davie from the other end of the bar. Davie was talkative—he was always talkative—but it would be different when he was lit up by another person. Davie would become curious, funny, and John would find Davie sexy at those moments. He never told Davie. John had made a pledge when he bought The Crow to never get involved with a customer. "It would be like fucking a friend," he would say. "It would never be the same again." It was too late now for such worries. There's nothing sexy about a dead body lying in a bed for four days.

"I'm ready," Tommy said, pointing to the empty glass. John poured a refill and took another five singles from the pile on the bar. As he rang it up in the register, he heard the door open and the voices of many men. Time for Mass.

Jody, Gil, and Ben came in together and sat at the end opposite Tommy, who barely looked up from the Jack. Elliot followed with a stranger, a gregarious man in a tweed sports coat, a half-opened shirt, and a large cross on a chain around his neck. Gene, Frank, Paul, and Charlie entered next. Soon, the bar was full, most were talking about the memorial.

"John, it was very moving," Elliot said as he watched John pour his regular scotch and water. Elliot sold television advertising. He favored bright sweaters that were a little too tight. "I didn't know Davie had been that celebrated as a writer. I knew he made money, but I didn't know he was that respected as an author."

"That's because you don't read anything except the expiration date on a packet of Trojans, duckie," the newcomer in tweed said.

"This is my former friend, Harris," Elliot said with a gentle smirk. "We used to go out to bars together when he drank and didn't live in LA."

"You don't drink?" John asked. "And you're from LA?"

"I know. Even I disgust myself. I'll have a ginger ale, duckie."

"You sound familiar. Have we met?"

"Look at your top shelf." Harris pointed to a scotch.

John looked at the bottle of top-shelf scotch. "You're the owl voice in the commercial."

"Guilty."

"A celebrity. Well, fuck me."

"Duckie, no one as attractive as you should ever say, 'fuck me,' unless they're bending over."

"That's just not a place I'm going to go," John said with a grin. "But the ginger ale is on me."

"Would you pour it over your nipples, duckie?"

"You're a card."

"I'm the whole fucking deck, duckie."

Elliot interrupted, "I hate to stop this repartee, but we're here for Davie, right?"

"You're right, duckie. Davie and I knew each other when we were young and new to New York. He was just starting to write that book that got made into the movie, and I had just signed that damn owl contract. Good times, duckie. Wish I could remember more of them," Harris said raising his ginger ale. "To Davie."

Elliot raised his scotch and water and repeated, "To Davie."

John moved up the bar. Jose, his best bartender, was setting up at the second cash register. The crowd was growing—it wasn't just for Davie. It was a Sunday in early May. Gay men out of hibernation needed to prowl in the city before heading to Fire Island from Memorial Day to Labor Day.

Jody put a red rose on Davie's stool. Jody was a schoolteacher. He taught science, and he looked like a science teacher. Earnest. Pleasant. He had the kind of face you forget even while you are forgetting his name while he tells it to you. But you had to love Jody. There was no other choice. John, reading the mood of his regulars, poured a cabernet and placed it at Davie's spot at the bar.

"Let's have some quiet," Gil said sternly, sounding every bit the Long Island cop he had been for 25 years before retiring and moving to Astoria. "I think we should take a few minutes to remember Davie here, where he spent so much time. The ceremony this morning was about another Davie, someone who moved in a different world than here. I remember the first time he came into The Crow. I was sitting right there," Gil pointed to a spot at the bar.

"And you still are," Ben shouted to general laughter. Ben was the joker. The cut-up from high school who never grew up, the kind of kid even Peter Pan would call immature. "As I recall, you have been pretty attached to your spot. Don't you have pizza deliveries made here?"

"Ha, ha, ha, Mister Smarty Pants. At least I don't have wood splinters taken out of my ass from sitting too long on a stool."

"Ladies," John interrupted, "Let's keep this respectful. And it was only one splinter—and it didn't come from the stool," John added with a wicked smile at Ben as he made a paddling motion with his hand.

Ben smiled. "Bitch."

"In your dreams," John replied, still smiling.

"May I?" Gil interrupted. "Davie would not approve of this kind of talk. Show some respect. He was always polite. I don't think I ever heard him say a nasty thing to anyone here—in twenty years, not a nasty thing. He would always try to diffuse an awkward moment. I remember he came to my rescue a few times when I couldn't keep my mouth shut. And not a word from you," Gil added looking at Ben. Gil had big white teeth that flashed behind the wide lips, and between the lips and the teeth, there had been rumored to have been a lot of pleasure. Like most stories in gay bars, the truth was always smaller than the fiction.

"There's so much I didn't know about Davie," Jody said. "I knew he was a writer, but he never talked about what he had done or whether he was writing anything new. He was kind of quiet about that, even though he liked to talk, he was quiet. Never loud."

"Never drunk," Ben added. "I never understood how you come to a bar most every day for twenty years and never get drunk."

"Wee," Tommy exclaimed from his end of the bar, already disconnected from the conversation. John went over to Tommy's corner and poured another Jack Daniels.

"We all have lives outside of here that we know little about," Jody said. "It's ironic that we all came out of the closet to go into a bar—the same bar day after day."

"Duckie, not a cliché. This isn't West Hollywood," Harris interrupted.

"And it's not a closet," Ben said ignoring Harris. "It's more than that," he added with conviction, surprisingly sounding like an adult. "We can joke. I do it all the time. We can make fun of each other because that's what we were taught to do by the old queens who came before us. Or that's what we thought they taught us. I remember this old guy— probably younger than some of us now—who used to go to Gooch's Lament."

"Christ," Gil said. "I forgot about that place. Lots of show tunes, cheap liquor, and a cute guy playing piano. What was his name?"

"Gino," Ben said. "I had such a crush on him. But there was this ancient guy who would get up and sing the old standards. He wore a thick foundation like he was Joan Crawford, the dead years. And bright red nail polish."

"Jungle red!" a unison chorus spontaneously shouted, a reference to young Joan Crawford's character in the film version of *The Women*.

"Jungle red," Ben repeated. "And he had wicked eyebrows. One day, I don't know why, I started up a conversation. I was probably feeling sorry for myself because some guy had dumped me the night before and I saw the old guy sitting at the bar. He smiled at me, not in a creepy way but inviting. He bought me a cocktail and we started to talk. He told me what it was like being gay in the 40s and 50s. He had known Cole Porter. He knew all the gay men of that period in and out of closets and even—and I mean this literally—some shipping containers off the Westside.

"He was fascinating. The more he talked, the more I realized the makeup was his armor. So were his affectations. It was easier for him to be the stereotype. It's what shielded him from having to confront a lifetime of scars from fights we never had to fight—not that it was easy for us either. But it wasn't the same for us. We fought different battles. Now, when we come to a gay bar— at least bars like The Crow—we don't have to be anyone other than who we are. We're like that Sondheim song: We're still here. We're also the last of a generation of gay men who get the references in the song because we connect through the old guys we met in our twenties to the age of Cole Porter and now to the age of Billy Porter and everything that happened in between. When we're gone, that will be gone."

"Wee."

"Exactly, Tommy," Ben continued. "We're characters here at The Crow. All of us. In a Hell's Kitchen gay bar, we're not characters. We're not even people to 22-year-olds. We're invisible. But here we look out for each other. This is not a closet. This is a living room. Life happens here."

"Here, here," Jody said.

"Queer, queer," Harris followed.

Everyone drank.

"OK, I'm going to tell a secret," Gene said. His normally pale white face flushed. Gene was one of the younger regulars. He would be forty-eight in a month. He had a slight build, a broad smile, and a huge, generous heart that he wore on his sleeve. As a boy, he wanted only two things: to meet Gwen Verdon and to get married. The former was no longer possible, so he focused all his energy on the latter. Many at The Crow said that Gene tried too hard, but John would come to his defense and say Gene was trying, and that was all that mattered and if someone had a problem with that, they had a problem with him.

Like the former ballplayer he was, John understood that just stepping up to the plate took courage. Gene, by John's standards, was fearless in his quest for love. But when it came to drinking, Gene was a lightweight. Two drinks in, and he was already a little wasted and couldn't say anything. Gene was two drinks in.

Gene circled his friends around him and announced, "Davie and I had sex."

Cheers erupted across the bar.

"I'm amazed," Jody said. "You had sex with Davie. I didn't think you had it in you."

"I'll never tell. Well...maybe it was in me and...it was sizable," Gene said, emboldened by the alcohol and Davie's memorial service.

"Jesus, Gene," John said laughing. "This is a family place."

"Apparently, some family members were sleeping together," Ben said. "I think you should change the name of the place, John, to West Virginia."

"As I was trying to say," Gene continued unfazed, "Davie and I had sex. Yes, we did. I want to tell this story because Davie wasn't anything like I thought he would be. He was all buttoned up here, but when we got back to his apartment, he was passionate. Passionate," Gene added for emphasis. He was very animated now from the two drinks.

"We never hooked up again, and it was awkward afterward," Gene continued. "After a few months passed, we started to talk here like nothing happened, which is what we all do when we hook up with someone we see regularly. Davie didn't talk much that one night we hooked up, either. He didn't need to. There was something about his hands. And nobody make a comment," Gene directed at his bar friends, "I'm being serious.

"After we had sex," Gene continued, "we were lying on the bed playfully kissing, and then he started moving his fingers up and down my chest like he was playing the saxophone, and the keys were all over my chest. He was smiling like a little mischievous boy. It was playful but erotic—his fingers were firm and gentle. As he moved them up and down my chest and stomach, I was lighting up inside. I thought this was a man I could get used to. This was my husband. We exchanged numbers. He didn't call. Who knows why? I always wondered if he did that thing with the fingers and the keys with other men. If I was special? I wish I had told him all these years later that it didn't matter that nothing more came of that one evening because that one evening was so memorable. He played the saxophone on my chest."

"First, I never had sex with Davie," Paul said as everyone laughed. Paul was a jock in high school. A jock in college. It made perfect sense that he became a high school football coach. He would brag about his teams like they were his children. They were.

Paul was the only regular at The Crow tall enough to almost look John eye to eye. "We started talking about six years ago," Paul continued. "The Met had a new production of *Tosca* and Davie hated it. Hated it. He was giving John an earful about how horrible the production was and how Tosca should have stabbed the director instead of Scarpia."

"I remember that production," Frank, an avid opera fan, added. "It was horrible."

"I remember that conversation," John said as he went around the bar refilling glasses. "Gene, you said that Davie was always buttoned-up, but he wasn't if you got him started on the things that mattered to him. Opera was his religion."

"I found that out," Paul continued. "I told him I had never been to the opera. In fact, when I first heard him talking about the Met to John, I thought he was talking about the Mets. That's why I sat next to him. I love the Mets."

"Someone has to," Ben said.

"Wee!"

"Exactly," John said, holding up a bottle in Tommy's direction.

"If you're a gay guy, you have to love a baseball team associated with Queens," Paul said.

"Jesus Christ, Paul," John said. "If you're gonna make dad jokes, you might as well impregnate someone."

"Don't look at me," Gene said. He was on his third drink.

"The Mets need love," Paul said, ignoring both John and Gene. "And according to Davie, so did the Met. I think that was the only place he liked being more than here," Paul added.

"You're probably right," said a man who had entered the bar without being noticed. He had been standing there for a few minutes. He looked familiar, but he was a stranger to The Crow.

John spoke first. "You knew Davie?"

"Sorta knew him," the man said, moving closer to the bar. "I'm his brother, Alan. He always talked about this place when he wasn't on a tirade about something at the Met. I saw some of you at the memorial service this morning and I assumed you had to be regulars at The Crow. I wanted to see for myself what this place was all about. What had such a draw for Davie."

"Welcome," John said. "I'm John. First drink is on me. We're just remembering your brother. He sat right over there, nearly every evening." John pointed to the stool with the red rose. "On opera nights, he'd come in late. But he was always here it seemed." John poured a drink and put it down in front of Alan. "Scotch OK?"

"Yes, thanks," Alan said taking the glass. "What did that owl say in that old commercial?"

"Hoot can say no?" Harris said from the far corner of the bar.

"Damn, that was good," Alan said sipping the scotch. "You sound just like the commercial."

"Thank you, duckie."

"This place looks exactly as Davie would describe it. The wooden bar. The initials carved in it," Alan said fingering the carving.

"Davie never signed the bar," John said. "Technically, no one is supposed to carve into the wood, but everyone does after enough time passes. They can't help themselves. Davie never did."

"That sounds right," Alan said. "Davie was such a fastidious person. I assumed he made some of this up and everyone would be in suits drinking martinis."

"Come back after seven," Jody joked. "And after midnight, we put on black ties."

"And jock straps," Elliot chimed in.

Alan looked a little uncomfortable, so John spoke up. "You have to understand that a neighborhood gay bar is a little like a locker room, confessional, and church."

"So many of you came today," Alan said slowly. "Why?"

"Why not?" John replied.

"I don't know. I can't understand why he came here. I could never get him to come out to the Island."

"Maybe you should have come into the city?" John asked.

"I have a family."

"Davie had a family, too," John said pointing to the men around the bar.

"You know what I mean—and I mean no disrespect. But it's not the same."

"You're right, Alan," John said, but he couldn't give Alan a pass. Not today. Not about Davie.

Today, John would speak his mind rather than just make the miracle happen with the raising of the bottles and the distribution of its blessed liquid. "Families are made in different ways, but all of them come from acts of passion. In your world, Alan, it always comes from sex. Here—well, sometimes sex but that's not what makes us family, made us Davie's family. We have a shared passion, not for each other in a way you may understand, but a shared passion to be who we really are. We come here for that. Here. No shame. Maybe a little judgment. But no shame, no boundaries. Just a passion to be who we are.

"The spaces between each stool?" John pointed at the stools lining the bar. "That's where the love is. The affection. The shared memories that we don't even have to say out loud because we all have experienced some of the same things before we got here. Stand between any of these stools, Alan, and you feel that love for Davie. He was loved here. He still is."

"It's a lot for me to take in," Alan said quietly. "Davie and I never quite got each other. I wish we had."

"When did you speak with him last?" John asked.

"About a month ago."

"A month ago," John said so quietly it was almost inaudible. "Davie was dead in his apartment for four days. Four days. I called the police because I knew something was wrong when I didn't see him for four days. I should have called sooner. If I called sooner, he would have been found with more dignity."

"Does that matter?" Alan said, not with anger or scorn but in a pragmatic tone.

"That was his greatest fear," John said. "He told me once he didn't want to be one of those old gay guys who falls or has a stroke or a heart attack in their apartment and can't call for help and they lie there losing consciousness, knowing no one will come."

"We all die alone," Alan said.

"Yeah, we do," John said. "At that last moment, we're alone. But up to that final second, we need to feel not afraid. I pray to God, and I don't know if I believe in God, that Davie did not feel afraid."

"We're all afraid. All the time, we're afraid," a voice from the far corner said. It was Tommy. He was putting all his weight on his hands so he could stand up. His stool fell backwards onto the floor like a sucker-punched fighter who never saw it coming. "We come here because we're afraid of what Davie was afraid of. We don't say it. We make jokes. We look for a lover. Or a friend. And when we don't find him, we find the Jack, ever dependable Jack. Always willing to succumb.

"When I was a boy, my mother would tell me that I should sing when I was afraid. I would sing in my room when my dad would get drunk and start throwing things against the walls and the floor. He started with books or dishes and then moved on to my mother. I'd sit in my room singing quietly all the Irish songs my mom would sing at the piano we had in the living room. She and I would sing before my dad came home or when he was out. I still remember those songs. I'm going to sing one for Davie."

John walked over to Tommy. "That's a real nice thought, Tommy, but maybe you should sit down?"

"I've been sitting for the past thirty years," he snapped.

"But you never liked Davie."

"You don't have to like the living, but you have to respect the dead. All of us know that better than most. How many friends are gone? How many assholes who annoyed us are gone? No one wants even them dead. In my family, we sang at the gatherings after wakes and funerals. It's respect."

Tommy started to sing "Danny Boy." The key was too high. The regulars began to wince at what was to come, but no one wanted to stop Tommy. Instead, Tommy stopped himself. "I can do better. I will start again."

He did, and in a better key. As Tommy began to sing again, the men were surprised by his slightly hoarse Irish tenor. It was not a bad voice after decades of the Jack. It must have been extraordinary once. As he sang, Tommy kept one hand on the bar for balance. He didn't appear to need it.

John wondered if perhaps Tommy had been a singer, one of those young people who arrived in New York with a dream and eventually traded it for a bottle. He looked at Tommy, standing almost erect as his voice, strong and powerful, filled every crevice of The Crow. And unlike his patrons who could never quite touch it, for a brief second as he listened to the closing of the cliched Irish song, John touched what he thought was the face of God. He shivered.

Then there was silence.

Tommy looked back for his stool, his companion on the floor. Someone pulled it up and Tommy sat down, his body returning to its more familiar state. His face was hard to read. The emotion so present while singing had already faded. Tommy stared at his empty glass. He was empty, as well. The last bit of who he might have been poured out in his tribute to Davie. It had filled the air. The traces of his voice still hovered above the bar, slowly dissipating. When it was gone, there would be nothing special left. No refills for an empty man. Tommy needed a drink.

"This is on me," John said as he stood across from Tommy. "So are the rest of them today. You were amazing, you know that?"

Tommy looked up from the glass at John as he poured. Tommy didn't respond. Whatever Tommy was thinking—if he was thinking beyond the promise of an afternoon of free drinks—no one could tell. He lifted the full glass, took a sip, and then faded back into the perpetual twilight of The Crow.

Alan was struggling with his emotions. The song was unexpected. Everything about The Crow was unexpected and unfamiliar. The bar was just like his dead brother. "I wish I had known him better," Alan said. "I was the older one by three years. I always knew he was smarter than me. More at ease with people. And I figured out early on that he was gay. Our mom, during the winter, would call out to us from the kitchen as we came in from playing in the snow, 'cocoa,' she would say, and Davie would reply, 'Chanel.' My mom never quite got the joke. It embarrassed the hell out of me if he did it when my friends were around. It wasn't easy having a little gay brother."

"It wasn't easy being gay," John said, feeling more like himself now.

"I know you're right. But it was hard understanding why he wanted to stay in the city all the time. It's not like I didn't want him to come spend time with me and my family. I did. I just couldn't figure out how to get to know him. That's why I came here after the service. I want to know him. I want to know him."

"He loved cabernet," Elliot volunteered.

"He liked walking in the Brooklyn Botanical Gardens when the cherry blossoms started falling from the trees," Jody said. "Davie would say it was snowing perfume. He loved flowers." Jody picked up the rose he had placed on Davie's stool.

"His favorite opera was *Der Rosenkavalier*," Paul said taking the rose from Jody, looking at it for a second before saying with a smile, "and he never could understand baseball." Paul placed the rose back on the stool.

"His first boyfriend was named Robert," Ben said.

"He once played me like a saxophone," Gene said.

And then the responses came from across the bar, from faces familiar and not so familiar to John. Memories of Davie poured down like rain.

"He loved sunsets. He talked about watching the sky go from gold to deep blue standing in Mallory Square in Key West."

"He wrote early in the morning, even when he had someone in his bed. He would get up quietly and write before dawn."

"He hated zoos."

"Autumn was his favorite season."

"He never ordered spaghetti or linguine in restaurants because it splattered."

"He used to say if Satan exists, he sings Andrew Lloyd Webber songs now and forever."

"He loved chocolate."

"Hershey bars."

"This bar."

"Amen to that," John said. "It wasn't impossible to get to know Davie. It just took an effort. He didn't open up easily, I'll give you that. But when you pried away his shell, your brother was an amazing man. He was worth the effort. If you wanted to know your brother, you should have tried visiting him in his world."

"That's not fair," Alan said. "Families are complicated."

"You're right," John said. "But families shouldn't be so complicated that two brothers can't figure out how to talk to one another. I said this bar is part locker room, part confessional, part church. There isn't much difference among any of those three. You go to get clean in them all. You cleanse your body in a locker room, your conscience in a confessional, and your soul in a church."

Alan was troubled. Not angry or offended. Not moved either. He was like Davie in one way—set in his ways and unlikely to change. In Davie's case, death ended the possibility of change. In Alan's, it was the life he had embraced decades ago, and with his brother dead, there was little point in turning in a new direction. He finished his drink.

Jody walked over to Davie's stool, picked up the rose, and handed it to Alan. "Take it—not as a remembrance of Davie, but of us, his family. We loved him. I think you did, too, or you would not have come here."

"Stand between his stool and the next one," John said. "You will feel Davie. The real Davie. This love between the spaces is all for him today."

Alan walked over to Jody and stood between him and Davie's stool and took the rose. He felt tears started to well up, but he stopped them. He felt his brother and did what he had always done; he turned to go away. As Alan started to move toward the door, he stopped. He had put a packet on the floor next to a stool when he came in and had forgotten about it. He picked it up and handed it to John. "I also came because I found this in Davie's apartment. It was marked to you— 'John at The Crow.' Whatever it is, Davie wanted you to have it." Alan handed the sealed packet to John.

"I don't know what more to say," Alan added.

John fixed his eyes on Alan. John could have said something snarky, but he could see Davie in Alan's face. "Be well, Alan," John said, extending his right hand. "I mean it." He gripped Alan's hand firmly. "Come back if you want to learn more about your brother. We're his family. You're his family. We have someone in common."

Alan managed a half smile, then turned and left the bar.

"Let's have one last toast," John said putting the envelope on the bar. "To our brother, Davie."

Across the bar, "Davie."

Soon afterward, the men started to file out. Not all at once. They had said what they had come to say about their friend. Some would go to other bars. Some to husbands or lovers. Some to the quiet of a book. Some to the loneliness of an empty room. Some would stay at The Crow until the lights in their eyes dimmed like the golden sun setting off the horizon in Key West.

John surveyed the bar covered in empty or almost empty glasses and beer bottles. Jose had gone down to the basement to get ice. There were a few men at the far corner opposite Tommy. They weren't regulars. John could smell the Jack coming off Tommy, who was lost in his whiskey.

John picked up the packet from Davie. He carefully opened one end of the envelope and pulled out a printed document. He began reading:

On the corner of a not-very-pretty street in the West Village, a street where Holly Golightly might have turned a trick, where the past, present, and future mix like rye, vermouth, and bitters into a perfect Manhattan, where old men become young, where young men become, and where all are welcomed at the communion rail, there is a bar and in that bar, there is a man, tall and sturdy, who offers all who would drink, a glass of salvation. His name is John.

John tried to read further, but his eyes had started to blur. This was a story about him and his bar and his buried feelings about Davie—about how sexy Davie looked when he was animated, about how he had wished he hadn't held to his damn code about not getting involved with a customer—filled his lungs like water in the ocean did once when he swam out too far.

John gasped for air. He put his hand on the bar and looked down. It was faint. Barely noticeable. It may have been there for years, for all John knew. And maybe it wasn't him. But he could see the word just to the left of the untouched glass of cabernet. "Davie." He had signed the bar, after all. John let his fingers work the slight grooves in the wooden surface. He began to cry.

"Wee."

Tommy's sound brought John back to his reality. He looked up and saw a young man walking into The Crow. A stranger. The young man looked at the bar littered with glasses and beer bottles and walked up to Davie's stool and the untouched glass of cabernet.

"Is this seat taken?" the man asked.

John rubbed his eyes, took the glass of wine, and drank it in one large swallow. John looked squarely at the young man. "No, this seat is open. He's not coming back."

The Dog Pimp of Columbia Heights

1

Maurice walked out of his apartment on Columbia Heights, turned left, and proceeded to the benches between Orange and Cranberry streets. The heat accosted him like a street preacher hawking salvation. It was in his face. There was no escape. Maurice hated New York in June. The smells were too much for his sensitive nose—a mixture of rotting garbage, urine, and sweat commingled with a splash of Creed. This was Brooklyn Heights.

He and Edgar strolled toward the Fruit Street Sitting Area, two blocks north. It ran just past the end of the Promenade and afforded good views of lower Manhattan and the East River. Maurice would have preferred to have turned right from the apartment and sat near the playground at Pierrepont Place, but Edgar would have none of it.

It wasn't really Edgar; it was George. George had staked out that slice of pavement years ago, and you just didn't work someone else's piece of sidewalk, especially not in the Heights. Here, people still were governed by a certain sense of civility. Every weekday, it was the same routine. At 10 a.m., he and Edgar would walk to the same bench.

Maurice didn't mind being outside or even on display. Hell, he liked being on display, but not like this—just sitting around looking cute. Looking cute came easy—the just sitting—that's what drove him a little Zelda Fitzgerald.

Why couldn't Edgar take him to a park? He could go running in the park, work up a good sweat, and then head to a ridge and roll around until the cut blades of grass pressed against his sweaty, matted hair. Now, that was a good summer's day. And damn, Maurice thought, he would have looked hot. But no, he was stuck with Edgar on a bench in Brooklyn Heights on a scorching day in June, looking out on the water. This was a Stephen Sondheim song, not a life. How the hell did he get stuck with Edgar? It wasn't fair.

Edgar used to teach English at a high school in western Suffolk County. He had taken an early retirement, bought a co-op in Brooklyn Heights before prices rose, and spent his days looking for women.

That's where Maurice fit in. Edgar wasn't much to write home about it. It's not that Edgar was unattractive. Edgar's appearance was extraordinarily unremarkable. His hair was thin, his waist, not so much. He had a thick mustache and bushy eyebrows. The mustache generally carried traces of his breakfast unless Maurice had felt particularly affectionate that morning. Since this was summer, Edgar was wearing tan shorts, a Hawaiian-print shirt, and sandals. He always carried a large book bag. Edgar would position himself on the end of the second bench so he could see the people coming up from the Promenade, and those walking on the sidewalk. Once he spied a pretty woman, he and Maurice would go into action. Maurice was well trained in what to do; Maurice was a Cocker Spaniel.

Who first said, "Love me, love my dog?" It does not matter. Edgar knew the reverse worked even better: Love my dog, love me. Maurice was the bait to lure women into conversation. It was ironic, at least from Maurice's perspective, because after an hour or so in the sun, Edgar was the one who smelled like chum.

The routine went like this: An attractive woman would be seen approaching, and Edgar would start up a conversation with Maurice. Edgar would talk about literature, the weather or a good mutual fund. Occasionally, when emboldened by a rush of testosterone, he would combine topics. When Edgar talked about wanting to update Dickens' *Our Mutual Friend* to "Our Mutual Fund," that was a sure sign that Edgar was trying to conceal the throbbing growth in his shorts. If Maurice was annoyed with Edgar, he would start sniffing at Edgar's crotch at precisely that moment, drawing attention to it. The woman would be embarrassed, Edgar would become annoyed, and he and

Maurice would go home to the air conditioning. Maurice enjoyed those opportunities immensely. He had no sympathy for Edgar getting laid. Edgar had had him neutered.

But generally, Maurice would go along with the act. Women would find a man talking literature to his dog charming. They would saddle up to Edgar like a half-price Prada bag.

They had been sitting for only ten minutes when a lean woman, about thirty-six, jogged up the curved rise of the Promenade's entrance. Her hair was tied back in a ponytail. It swished back and forth in contrapuntal motion to her breasts. Some women were a melody; this one was a Scott Joplin rag.

"So, Maurice, is it too hot for you? I bet you wish you were somewhere cool, sipping an iced tea."

You could do better than this, Maurice thought.

"I know. We could walk to the ice cream store on Montague and buy a sundae."

"What's his favorite flavor?" the female jogger asked. She had taken the bait.

"He likes cookies and cream."

That was a lie. I much prefer strawberry. In Maurice's mind, he rolled out the first syllable of the flavor as if he were an English dowager. *Straw-bury.*

"I love ice cream," the jogger said, stopping. Maurice was fascinated by her breasts and hair.

It took another fifteen seconds before they all stopped moving. This made Maurice slightly dizzy, so he went to lie down at her feet. Edgar was pleased, but Maurice was nauseous.

"I just love Rocky Road," she said with a smile, looking at Maurice.

"I thought joggers always wanted the road smooth," Edgar replied.

That's not half bad, Maurice thought. *Maybe the* Sex and the City *DVDs were helping Edgar's banter after all?*

"You're so cute," the jogger said.

"I try to stay in shape," Edgar answered with optimism.

"I just can't help myself," she said, kneeling to pet Maurice under the chin. She hadn't even heard Edgar. The compliment had been aimed at

Maurice, who tried to feign interest, but he was hot, and her breasts had stopped moving. There was little left to divert him.

"You like Maurice," Edgar said, undaunted.

"Oh, his name is Maurice? Is he French?"

"On his mother's side, I believe."

"How long have you had him?" she asked.

"Maurice and I have been together for eight years."

"That's longer than me and my ex. We never made it past eight months."

"You're divorced?"

"Never married. That was my ex's problem. The only long-term commitment he could make was to his wireless phone carrier. Which explains why his two most dominant characteristics were roaming and rolling over."

Maurice had an itch, so he turned over on his back as if he were listening to the jogger with the now-dormant breasts. He assumed she would scratch his stomach. He was right. *Scratch it, baby. Oh, yeah, just like that. Scratch, scratch, scratch. Work it. Work it. Work it.*

"Oh, how adorable," she said, kneeling over him and rubbing his stomach. Her fingers felt good. She must have just had a manicure. Once she found the itch and worked it out, Maurice stood up abruptly. *Don't get your hopes up, girlie, girl. Women need such little encouragement,* Maurice thought.

"I should be getting on," she said. "I need to get in another two miles before lunch."

"Maybe I'll see you again? I'm here nearly every day."

"Maybe, but I'm just visiting my cousin. She lives over on Willow Street. It was nice meeting Maurice and meeting you..."

She was stumbling for his name.

"It's Edgar."

"Well, goodbye, Edgar. Goodbye, Maurice."

The woman started running in the direction of the Brooklyn Bridge. Maurice watched her ponytail pick up the rhythm. He only could see her from behind, but he imagined the up-and-down motion of her breasts and decided he would remember her as Tits Willow. He yawned and then stretched out on the hot pavement until his paws dug into the crevices of the stone pavers. He was so hot.

"You couldn't have let her pet you a little longer? Would that have been too much to ask?" Edgar whined. "Maybe I could have gotten a phone number?'

That was typical. Blame the dog for the failings of the man. Who was looking to score, huh? Edgar or me? If I had wanted to score, I would have stayed on my back. And if Edgar wanted a woman so badly, why hadn't he rolled over and let Tits Willow rub his belly? The thought so amused Maurice that he let out a yap. Edgar took that as a sign of agreement with his argument and said, "I'm glad you concur."

What a moron. Maurice raised his head and surveyed the scene. Not many prospects at all. A very large woman was approaching. She was sucking down a double-scoop ice cream cone. There was a popular ice cream store at Fulton's Landing, better than any chain shop. The woman was walking up Columbia Heights from the direction of Fulton's Landing. The road was steep, and she was sweating profusely from the effort. Beads of perspiration poured off her face like falling rain. She was winded from the climb, and she belched loudly as she approached Edgar's bench. Maurice knew Edgar wouldn't be interested, but that didn't matter. *There must be some way to keep her by the bench.* Her girth—although Maurice would never body shame anyone aside from Edgar—was blocking out the sun. Between the dripping sweat, the belching, and the instant shade, she was the personification of the opening of Act III of *Die Walkure.*

"Aren't you the cutie?" she said. "Would you like some ice cream, sweetie?" she asked. She leaned over in front of him and started to offer him her cone. The ice cream toppled out and landed on her neck and started to drip down her chest into her damp cleavage. Maurice dove forward, licking madly. The woman was ticklish and started to giggle and fell back on the pavement. Maurice's nose was fully lodged into her strawberry-covered fields. He was yapping and licking, while the woman rolled on the pavement in ecstasy. A crowd started to form.

"Maurice, what are you doing?" Edgar yelled. "Get out of her breasts this very minute. Maurice, please, stop! You're a middle-aged dog. This is not appropriate."

"I can't get up," the woman managed between squeals. She was rolling back and forth. She moved too quickly and squashed Maurice under a thigh. Maurice let out a yelp. He couldn't budge. *Will no one come with the Jaws of Life?* Maurice started to whimper.

"Let me help," someone said.

All Maurice could see was a pair of tan arms covered in dark brown hair. The sun blinded him. There was a muscular shape moving in the sunlight. The stranger lifted the woman up in a single maneuver. By the time Maurice gained his balance, the man was gone. He could see a glistening frame running down the Promenade. He wasn't sure if it was his rescuer, but he knew he would not forget the smell of the man's arms. It was a strong scent, but somehow pleasant. But Maurice couldn't concentrate on that now, no matter how good the memory of it was. Part of the crowd was helping the woman to Edgar's bench; the other part was checking him. There were hands all over his body.

Damn, if only I hadn't been neutered.

Maurice and Strawberry Fields were not the only beneficiaries of all this attention. Edgar, by virtue of sheer geography, was in his glory. He felt he needed to do something to deflect some attention from Maurice and the strawberry-flavored woman. He reached into his book bag and pulled out a moist towelette for the woman, a small plastic saucer, and a bottle of water for Maurice.

Maurice noticed the dish on the pavement. It was blue, cheap, and chipped. It embarrassed him. *Hadn't Edgar ever heard of Fiestaware?* No matter. The water was welcome, even if it was warm and tap at that. Some of the women attending to Maurice responded to Edgar's act of kindness. They started chatting with him.

"You have such a brave little dog."

"Yes, give the dog some water."

"What a cute pooch."

"I hope he's OK."

"Do you have any pâté in there?"

That caught Maurice's attention–he pricked up his ears. He could see a thin, bronzed woman hovering above him. Her legs were shapely and smooth. She had appeared out of nowhere and hovered next to Edgar. She had wedged herself between him and Strawberry Fields.

"I don't think Maurice would like pâté," Edgar said.

Liar. Pâté is my middle name.

"Who the hell is Maurice?" she asked.

Maurice spied the woman's Jimmy Choos with what a lawyer might call willful intent. *If only I weren't dehydrated.* Maurice drank more water.

"Maurice is my dog."

"I wasn't asking for the dog, but for myself," she said.

That was insufferable. Maurice took an instant dislike to her. Edgar was entranced. "I have some fruit in here but no pâté," he said, rummaging through the book bag. He started throwing out oranges and bananas. Strawberry Fields grabbed an orange and started peeling it. Her nails dug into the peel and some juice shot out and hit Edgar in the face.

"I'm so sorry," she said. "I need some electrolytes."

Honey, I think the word is electrolysis or a good waxing, Maurice thought as he looked up her dress. Maurice had no boundaries. To be honest, even an erudite Cocker Spaniel can be a pig.

The bronzed woman moved closer to Edgar. Maurice could see the movement in Edgar's shorts—at first, a slight twitching and then a slight raising of the mast. *Has the whole world gone crazy? What can this woman see in Edgar? And hadn't Edgar ever read* Madame Bovary? *This woman screams high maintenance.*

The crowd was thinning, and Strawberry Fields stood up. She could take a hint. She also took the fruit.

"Thanks for the orange," she said as she headed down Columbia Heights toward Montague, taking the last bit of decent shade with her. By now, the bronzed woman was on the bench, practically in Edgar's lap. Maurice lapped at his water, looking suspiciously at the woman.

"You look so hot, honey," she said. "Do you have a towel in that bag? Let me look." She rifled the book bag and found a small towel, 200-thread-count cotton.

"My name is Edgar," he said to her.

"I'm Sylvia."

Wasn't that the name of a goat in an Edward Albee play?

"Do you come here often?" Sylvia asked as she wiped Edgar's forehead with the towel.

Maurice was beside himself. He didn't get straight lines like that every day. He let out a small whimper. He wanted to let out a loud, billy goat "neyyyhh," but alas, Cocker Spaniels—even smart ones—have their limitations.

"How long have you had the dog?" Sylvia asked.

"Dog?" Edgar responded confused.

"Yes, your dog, Morton."

La Goatessa—that was what Maurice would call Sylvia, he mused. Dehydrated or not, someone was going to have to pay for this slight. Maurice was about to sit up when George and Otto appeared. The commotion over Strawberry Fields had motivated George to walk from his coveted spot to check on Edgar. Otto was George's dog, a miniature dachshund.

George was wearing his HMS Pinafore outfit. He had on a blue cutaway jacket with brass buttons, a horizontal striped T-shirt, a navy neckerchief, white shorts, navy socks, and white patent leather shoes. He was sporting a straw boater. George was seventy-one if a day. New York is full of eccentric old queens. They don't get much notice, so George needed some way of attracting nubile young men who wanted to be pretenders before his throne. Otto was George's Maurice. It was Otto who brought the crowds–he was wearing identical clothing. Every day, George and Otto dressed in matching outfits.

Maurice felt sorry for Otto. He didn't particularly like low-slung German dogs, but even Edgar never made him get dressed up in something so silly. Well, there was that one Mardi Gras in drag, but both he and Edgar had been drinking. But George was cold-stone sober, and poor Otto was walking along the Promenade in little white shoes, a navy blazer, and a boater. There is nothing more ridiculous than a German dog sporting a straw boater—a homburg maybe—but not a boater.

The gold medallion around Otto's neck, a miniature of the one that George sported, clanged against the pavers. It could have been worse. On Ann Miller's birthday, George dressed up like his favorite movie star, and Otto would have to match. The clanging medallion was annoying. The sound of four little tap shoes was insufferable, but oh, could that dog fox trot.

Otto walked toward Maurice. Maurice had to show some interest; it was expected. They sniffed each other like bored men in an East Village dive bar. George sauntered toward Edgar and the young woman. He lifted his boater up in a salute.

"What was all the fuss, Edgar? I heard your dog was licking some woman's breasts. I can see he has good taste."

"Excuse me?" the woman said. "No one licks my breasts. It wasn't me."

"I'm sorry miss. I didn't mean to insinuate that you were easy."

"Honey, I may be many things, but I'm never easy. Edgar, sweetie, who's Captain Crunch?"

"This is George. He sits up by the playground. And this is his dog, Otto."

"He's very cute."

"Me or my dog?" George ventured. He was feeling very spry. It reminded him of an adventure he had once in a dressing room in a Madison Avenue men's store. The gray hair on his chest bristled with excitement.

"You're both cute," she said. She started to stroke Otto under his chin. She was wasting her time, Maurice thought. She was not Otto's type. Otto liked them small, Asian, and with a penis, one not strapped on. That was George's fault; Otto had no experience with women. George was a theater set designer and was working on a production of *Pacific Overtures* when he bought Otto. For the first six months of Otto's life, all he saw was a parade of naked Asian men going through George's house on Remsen Street, which had been nicknamed by the rent boys as the Tea House of George's Moon. So, Maurice knew Sylvia was barking up the wrong bonsai. Otto remained as stoic as a shogun. Sylvia paid no notice to Otto's ennui while both George and Edgar were entranced.

For his part, George liked to flirt. It didn't matter whether it was a woman or a man when it came to flirting. And he was terribly competitive with Edgar, who was terrible at competition.

"You should come over to my bench sometime," George said.

"That's a novel line," Sylvia said, not looking up at George. She was crouched over Otto, but she had managed to rub her right leg up against Edgar's. Maurice felt usurped; riding Edgar's leg had always been his job. "Where's your bench?" Sylvia asked. Her hand stroked Otto's chin while her leg worked Edgar's leg. Maurice had to admit with some admiration that La Goatessa was coordinated.

"I sit up by the playground," George said. "There's shade."

"There's a natural breeze over here," Edgar said.

"Only when you eat too many grapes," George responded.

"I suppose your boy toys find you funny."

"At least my toys don't need to be inflated."

"Maybe I should come back?" Sylvia suggested.

"Please don't leave on my account," George said, trying to be gallant.

"Stay," Edgar added. "George is leaving."

"Don't tell me when to leave."

"I should go," Sylvia said with conviction. She left. Maurice had a new appreciation for George for driving away La Goatessa.

"See what you did? You scared her away," Edgar added angrily.

"I scared her away? Have you looked in the mirror lately?" George asked.

"Oh, that's rich. You probably think that hankie around your neck is attractive," Edgar said.

"It's not a hankie. It's a dickie."

"How apt. Someone should straighten it."

"You think that someone should straighten my dickie? Is that a threat? Someone should straighten my fucking dickie?"

"Someone should straighten that fucking dickie."

"Someone should straighten that fucking dickie?"

"Someone should straighten that fucking dickie."

"Someone should straighten that fucking dickie?"

Edgar had moved closer to George. They began to shove each other, repeating the same profane sentence back and forth, louder and louder, as if they were lines from a David Mamet play. Maurice was concerned. Neither Edgar nor George was in good shape. *If Edgar hurts himself, who would take care of me?* George's boater fell to the pavement, exposing his matted comb-over. George pulled at Edgar's shirt. It had popped open, exposing a mass of Edgar's chest hair and white skin. The glare was blinding. Someone had to stop them before it got out of hand. Maurice did the only thing he could. He walked up against Edgar, raised his leg, and sprayed with all his might. Otto took the cue and did the same on George's leg.

George and Edgar stood stunned on the pavement. George's hair was askew, and Edgar's shirt was torn. Both men were speechless as they looked down at their dogs and their wet legs and realized that Sylvia had departed.

Maurice looked up at Edgar, giving his best lovable look at his master. *Today turned out so much better than expected.*

2

For the next three days, Maurice tiptoed around the apartment on all fours. Edgar was in a mood. The very sight of Maurice angered Edgar. Never mind that he had already made a fool of himself fighting with George—his dog had peed on his leg in public. How do you get past that? His only hope was that all the people who were standing by the bench on Saturday were tourists or from Queens.

Edgar took Maurice out for a walk on Wednesday to test the waters. They got as far as Cranberry Street when a young woman walked past with her small terrier. George smiled at the woman. Her dog sniffed at George's sandals, raised his leg, and sprayed.

The woman was mortified; Maurice could barely control himself. That was more than could be said for the terrier. The dog must have been drinking for days.

On Thursday, Edgar went shoe shopping. He bought machine-washable canvas sneakers. Maurice had to stay in all day. He enjoyed the solitude and the air conditioning. The man in the apartment below had a piano and played show tunes. Sometimes, he would sing. Maurice enjoyed listening. He had always fancied himself on stage, but to date, no composer had seen the same possibilities in Cocker Spaniels that had been successfully mined by singing and dancing felines.

And if that wasn't indignity enough for a musical-theater-loving dog, Edgar hated show tunes. There was nothing musical about Edgar. It was but another cross for Maurice to bear.

By Saturday, Edgar was back to his old self. He preened for an hour in the bathroom, emerging in a thick haze of Aramis. Maurice started to sneeze. Edgar paid little attention. He loaded up his book bag, and at exactly 9:53, they left the apartment. They arrived at the bench at 10 and Edgar pulled out his *New York Times*; Maurice sat under the bench, trying not to sneeze. There wasn't much action on the street. A few joggers, a few seniors—no one was noticing Edgar.

Maurice closed his eyes and dreamed he was in Central Park. There was a brilliant blue sky and a slight breeze. The Great Lawn was lush with scantily clad young men laying on towels and each other. Well-groomed dogs frolicked among the men, Frisbees flew and everywhere Maurice looked were welcoming open containers from high-end food markets. He nibbled from blanket to blanket, from man to man. He nosed by a container and smelled a deeply sensual aroma. He saw the bronzed arm that had rescued him from Strawberry Fields. Was he still dreaming?

Maurice woke up in time to see the muscular frame run by. Maurice sat up and peered from under the bench. He could make out the man's form as he headed up Columbia Heights toward the Promenade. He inhaled the man's fleeting smell. *This is heaven.* Edgar belched loudly. *No, it's Brooklyn. Would no one rid me of this troublesome man?*

Maurice tried to close his eyes, but it was no use. He kept thinking about the bronzed arm and how he missed him because he was sleeping. That could not happen again. As bored as he was, he must come up with something to do. A messiah appeared from the Promenade. Perhaps messiah was an inappropriate description for a Reform Jew from Syosset, Long Island. It was Murray, the Talking Mime. That meant it was 11. Murray always came at 11.

Even in the extreme summer's heat, Murray slathered his face in white makeup and donned a vertical-striped, long-sleeve shirt and black pants. Horizontal stripes made him look fat, while the vertical stripes made Murray look like the oldest employee at Foot Locker. Murray would stand just up the Promenade from Edgar and Maurice and begin his routine. Murray began by pretending to open a window. He would make out the frame of the window with his hands and then start a series of bad Catskills jokes.

"Oy, I wish I could open this window, but it won't budge. It reminds me of my wife on our wedding night. She wouldn't move either. It's a wonder we had the three children. Funny though, none of them look like me."

From the window, Murray went to the door.

"The front door is open because the lock is broken. But I can fix that. I went out this morning and got a dozen bagels and some lox. Oy!"

Murray did to funny what strip miners had done to Kentucky. There were few people around, and none were interested in a talking mime, so Murray approached Edgar's bench. The sweat dotting his cheeks and forehead blotted the white makeup, transforming Murray's face into a large, melted marshmallow in search of two graham crackers.

Maurice played with the sentence: *The schmo is a S'more. The schmo is a S'more. S'more than the greatest love the world has known. I'm on a roll—or a bagel with a schmeer of schmo.*

"Edgar, how are you?" Murray asked. "I heard what happened last week. It's the talk of the Promenade."

"For a mime, you do a lot of talking," Edgar said. He was annoyed.

"I'm a talking mime, you know that."

"It's a stupid idea. Perfectly ridiculous. A talking mime."

S'more than the simple words I try to say to you. S'more, I forget the words, but S'more I'll do for you.

"This is from a human fire hydrant," Murray said, oblivious to Maurice's interior crooning.

"I don't have to take this from you. You want a piece of me?" Edgar threatened.

Oh dear, Maurice thought, suddenly paying attention. *Here we go again.* Edgar was only this irritable when he hadn't had sex in a long, long time. Maurice was trying to remember exactly the last time Edgar got laid. *Was it December?*

"Honey, I was hoping to see you again. And you're here with your dog, Boris."

Damn, La Goatessa was back. Maurice looked up from under the bench and saw Sylvia's waxed stems. She was straddling Edgar like a Schwinn.

"Who's the pasty-faced pastrami?" she asked.

Murray did smell of kosher deli.

The schmo is a S'more with a schmeer. Maurice barked. "Woof!"

"This is Murray, the Talking Mime."

"How do you do," Murray said, offering a gloved hand.

"Talking mime? Is there any money in that?"

"Yes, I do very well at senior centers. The audiences are half-deaf, so they only hear every other joke. I'm a big hit."

"How amusing."

"No, he's not amusing at all," Edgar said. He wanted Murray gone. Edgar was threatened by any competition, even from a talking mime. "Why don't you go on your way?"

Sylvia sat down next to Edgar. "I like it when men get testy," she said as she rummaged through Edgar's book bag, pulling out a bottle of water. "Testy sounds so much like testosterone. Testy. Testosterone. It gets me all excited."

Even Edgar could sense Sylvia was interested. There was something about her mouth— it was on his. She had surprised him with a kiss. Murray made the universal mime gesture for self-gratification and walked away.

Maurice was happy Edgar might finally have sex, but he was stuck now with nothing to do but wait for Edgar to get to second base. And he wasn't even sure if that was correct since he didn't particularly like following sports. *Was baseball the game with the bats, the sticks, or the Zamboni?*

What Maurice felt like was taking a short stroll. Edgar wouldn't notice. He trotted toward the Promenade. There would be no cars. It felt good to be away from Edgar, if only for a few minutes. There was a breeze. And then there was...he could barely speak...him. The guy with the arms was jogging right towards Maurice, the man's body glistening in the sun like the furry Adonis he was. Maurice's legs buckled like he was June Allyson in a 1940s movie. The runner saw him and came over.

"Hey there, buddy. You OK? Are you lost?" The man got down on his knees and began to stroke Maurice. "Did you stray away from your owner, that chubby guy in the Hawaiian shirt? You shouldn't be alone. He must be going crazy looking for you?"

Maurice started licking the man's face. If Sylvia could be bold, why could not he?

"You're a friendly little guy. What's your name?" The man checked Maurice's collar. "So, you're Maurice," he said, looking at the tag. "Or do they call you Morris, like in the book?"

Maurice almost peed. *He reads EM Forster!*

"My name's Danny," the man said, grabbing one of Maurice's front paws and shaking it up and down. "How about you and me look for your owner?" Danny snatched Maurice up in his arms.

I got lost in his arms, and I had to stay. It was dark in his arms, and I lost my way.

This is heaven, Maurice thought. Despite the intense heat, it felt good to be held close by Danny. They started back toward the sitting area where Edgar, no doubt, would be sprawled out like a beached whale. Maurice noticed people were noticing him with Danny, but Danny wasn't paying any attention. Danny was focused only on Maurice, stroking his fur. It wasn't long before they came upon Edgar and Sylvia. She was playing with Edgar's hair, which, fortunately, was still real and attached to his scalp.

"I think you lost someone?" Danny said.

"No, she's right here," Edgar said without looking away from Sylvia.

Damn that pudgy man!

"Your dog. Maurice. I found him on the Promenade."

"He's never done that before," Edgar said, turning toward Danny. "I wasn't paying attention."

"I can see the distraction," Danny said with a smile.

"You should keep him in a crate," Sylvia said as she sat back and took a swig from the water bottle.

I spit in your water. I spit on your mother. I would spit on your father, but your mother was a tramp, so no one knows who he is.

"A crate would be cruel," Danny said to Sylvia while still holding Maurice. "You know, if you ever need a dog sitter, I love dogs, and your little guy seems to like me. I know you don't know me, but I'm very reliable. Danny Saunders. I live just up on Cranberry Street."

Danny Saunders, Danny Saunders, what a beautiful, beautiful name.

"Well, I don't know. I can't just let a stranger take Maurice."

"I understand. Well, I run by here every day. How about sometime you let me take him down to the dog run at the end of the block? You and your lady friend can stroll nearby. We won't be far."

"I don't know."

Maurice was surprised by Edgar's reticence. Was he concerned about his safety, or was he afraid that he would lose his proven decoy to ensnare women?

"Edgar, sweetie," Sylvia said, "the dog will be fine. This looks like a nice young man. We can go for a stroll tomorrow."

Edgar didn't know if he was coming or going. He was genuinely at a loss. He was very attracted to Sylvia, but for all his bluster, he was genuinely fond of Maurice and did not want any harm to come to him. "Maybe you could give me your number, Mr. Saunders, and we could set something up."

"I could take Maurice maybe for a trial outing. We could meet down at Brooklyn Bridge Park. It wouldn't be too far. You could keep an eye on us."

"You see, Edgar, it's all settled," Sylvia said. "I can meet you down at the park tomorrow at 3 p.m."

"It will be very hot," Edgar said, looking up at the sun.

"You can count on it," Sylvia added, licking her Botox lips.

"Then I will see you at 3 p.m. tomorrow," Edgar said.

"I'll meet you down there at 3, as well," Danny said, pointing to the park that was built on former warehouse piers below the Promenade. We can meet on Fulton's Landing.

I'll land anywhere you want. Danny Saunders, Danny Saunders, what a beautiful, beautiful name." Maurice kept repeating the words, a play on a lyric from *Funny Girl*, as Danny put him down and then began jogging slowly away. Danny turned around and waved one last time to Edgar, Sylvia, and Maurice.

"See you tomorrow, little guy."

Not if I see you first in my dreams tonight. Maurice was intoxicated. He followed Danny's frame until it disappeared into the dip in the sidewalk. He didn't notice Sylvia get up and give Edgar a kiss on his forehead. She went in the same direction as Danny. Man and dog sat there, tongues lapping at the air as the crowds went by. Murray walked past them about an hour later and, seeing them lost in lustful thoughts, made the universal mime gesture for self-gratification once again. Unfortunately, one of New York City's finest was walking past at the same time and thought the suggestion was directed at him. He gave Murray a citation for performing without a license.

3

Maurice could barely contain himself until the next day. He was waiting by the door for Edgar for nearly an hour. Edgar was equally eager. He performed intensive grooming rituals. He shaved, sprayed, and deodorized parts of his body with a vengeance. Edgar had never met someone in Sylvia's league. He grabbed his book bag and called to Maurice, who wagged his tail with delight. The two left the apartment at 2:40. It was a slow 20-minute walk to the park below the Promenade.

The pair walked down Columbia Heights. George waved as they went past him, but Edgar wasn't interested in conversation. Neither was Maurice, although he would have invested a minute in surveying Otto's attire. George was going for a tropical look—a white linen suit, an open cotton shirt, and a Panama hat. Otto's hat was far too large and almost consumed his head, so the hat appeared to be floating above the ground with a dog's body coming out the back.

But there was no time to offer Otto solace. He was going to meet Danny. Maurice ran hard and fast down Columbia Heights with Edgar wheezing at the leash. "Slow down, Maurice. I can't keep up." Edgar pulled at the leash; Maurice pushed onward. By the time they made it to the bottom of the little hill, both were panting.

"I hope you're happy. I have sweat stains under my pits."

You should have worn white cotton. Danny would have worn white cotton. If he wore a shirt at all. Danny Saunders, Danny Saunders, what a beautiful, beautiful name.

"I'm not sure where we are supposed to meet Sylvia."

"Hey there, little guy."

It's him! Maurice's tail moved into hyperdrive, and he bolted from Edgar into Danny's open arms. He took in Danny's scent and then looked up at the young tan face. Danny had brown eyes and some slight dark brown scruff. Maurice nestled into the face, licking with wild abandon. *Call me a ho, I don't care!*

"He's an affectionate dog."

"I've never seen him like this. There must be something about you that he's attracted to. Did you have bacon this morning?"

You think I can be bought with some bacon? How little you know me. I would turn vegetarian for Danny. I would eat tofu for you, Danny.

"Actually, I did. I know everyone is anti-meat. Vegetarians. Vegans. I say if God wanted us to be vegetarians, he wouldn't have made Peter Lugers."

I could just pee.

"Well, I will take Maurice for a walk around the park. Why don't I meet you back here in an hour?"

"Make it two."

"You're optimistic, aren't you?"

Edgar didn't have a chance to reply before Sylvia approached the two men and Maurice.

"There you are, Edgar. I was telling a friend of mine earlier today that you would probably be wearing a Hawaiian shirt, and you are. So satisfying to be right. Why don't we take a little stroll?" Sylvia took Edgar's left arm. "Let me take your bag? You don't mind, do you?"

"My bag is your bag."

With Sylvia on his left arm, Edgar was in ecstasy. The two walked toward the paths and small lawns of the pier to their left. Danny took Maurice's leash and said, "Let's go toward DUMBO, little guy. Do you like carousels?"

I will pee. I will pee right here and now. And if he starts singing "If I loved you," I may drop dead. Maurice's tail was wagging at warp speed.

"You look like you're trying to tell me something. But I will take that tail wag of yours as a yes. I love carousels. It's not very manly of me to admit it, but it comes from being in a college production of *Carousel*. I was Billy Bigelow. We have something in common: we've both been barkers."

If Edgar had said something so corny, Maurice would have grunted in mild disgust, but this wasn't Edgar, so he barked back at Danny.

"I think we understand each other, little guy. Off to the carousel."

The next two hours were a blur for Maurice. It was sensory overload for a love-starved, middle-aged Cocker Spaniel. Danny took him to the carousel near the water. He spoke to the operator of the ride and showed him something, perhaps flashed some cash, Maurice wasn't sure. Before Maurice could collect himself, Danny had lifted him up and the two were on a carousel horse going round and round. After they left the carousel, Danny walked Maurice over to a shaded grassy lawn. Danny gave Maurice some water, and they lay on the grass staring out at the East River.

When it was time to meet back with Edgar, Maurice had fallen fast asleep on Danny's chest. Danny scooped him up and walked back to Fulton's Landing. Edgar and Sylvia were just returning. Judging from Edgar's expression, it was a good afternoon for him as well.

"I will see you here in two days, same time," Sylvia said.

"That sounds great if Danny could take Maurice," Edgar said. "Did it all go well?"

Maurice was wagging his tail. Danny replied, "He's the perfect dog. I'd be happy to meet you—same place, same time, two days."

"Then it's all settled," Sylvia said firmly. "And Edgar, honey, can you stop at that juice place we went to earlier before we meet and pick me up a smoothie? Just tell them it's for me, and they will know what to make."

"Absolutely," Edgar said.

Mr. Tightwad must be getting a little something something. He never would volunteer to pay for another person's smoothie. Well, good for him. Maurice was surprised by his own generous thoughts toward Edgar. Was it loyalty or just the joy of Danny spreading sunshine all over the place? Maurice didn't know or care.

And so, it went on for weeks. June soon became July. Edgar would meet Sylvia like clockwork at exactly 3 p.m. at Fulton's Landing. He would stop at the smoothie store at 2:45 and ask for Sylvia's drink. The young woman behind the counter, her nametag said "Grace," would mix the concoction. Edgar wasn't sure what was in it, but it came out pink. Grace would put some extra napkins into Edgar's bag in case Sylvia needed a wipe after the smoothie. It all became an easy routine.

Maurice was patient with the smoothie. One, there was an attractive counterman, Benjamin, who always gave him a treat while Grace took care of Edgar. And two, Maurice was finally in a relationship. It had taken years—dog and human ones—for him to finally meet Mr. Right. So, while Maurice's tag said he belonged to Edgar, his heart belonged to Danny. The two would go to the carousel, walk around DUMBO or the Heights.

Sometimes, Danny would take him over the Brooklyn Bridge, which could have been dangerous with the bicyclists, rollerbladers, and tourists, but Danny would carry Maurice so he could see the view and be petted and admired by the passersby. On these excursions over the bridge, Danny would stop at one of the bridge's towers where there were lookout areas, put Maurice down with some water, take out binoculars from his backpack, and scan the Brooklyn side. It was a happy routine.

Maurice was excited about July 4. Sylvia had suggested to Edgar that they go to Coney Island and to the amusement park off the boardwalk. There was the annual hot dog eating contest and, later, fireworks. These were not as impressive as the East River fireworks, but this year, the big show had been moved further up the river and not visible from Brooklyn Heights. Danny had promised to take Maurice on the Cyclone, the legendary wooden roller coaster.

It would be a big day. They would take the N train out to Coney Island. Edgar picked up Sylvia's smoothie as usual. She insisted that she had to have it for the long subway ride.

Dogs, even ones as charming as Maurice, were supposed to be in carriers when on the subway. The rule was not heavily enforced but given the amount of people traveling to the beach and the probable state of intoxication among many, both Edgar and Danny agreed Maurice should go in a carrier for his own safety. Danny splurged on a new one as a gift. It was a Burberry knock-off. Maurice looked good in it.

The foursome got on the subway. Edgar and Sylvia and Danny and Maurice. Edgar didn't make much conversation, but he did occasionally wave his hand at Maurice. *He does seem to be making more of an effort. Maybe he's jealous of Danny?* Sylvia was working her smoothie and rummaged through Edgar's ubiquitous bag for a napkin. Danny sat there bronzed and fit with Maurice in his case on his lap. He slid the zipper at one side of the carrying case and put his hand inside to gently pet Maurice. They were one American family off to celebrate the Fourth of July.

The plan was to split up: Edgar and Sylvia to the main amusement area, Danny and Maurice to the Cyclone. They would meet up again where the hot-dog eating contest was being held.

When Danny and Edgar got to the rollercoaster, Danny again worked some magic. You can't carry a Cocker Spaniel onto a roller coaster in plain sight. Even in Brooklyn. Danny had it all arranged. He had a friend who was meeting him at the coaster. The man gave Danny a big hug. *Do I have competition?* Maurice had little time to be jealous. Danny took him out of the carrier and put his backpack down. He pulled out a light nylon zip jacket and pulled off his T-shirt. Danny held Maurice to his bare chest as his friend helped him into the jacket. It was big and bulky and, once zipped up, managed to conceal Maurice. Danny looked like he had a paunch, not a pooch.

And so, Maurice, with his face pressed against Danny's chest, got on his first rollercoaster. They were in a back car, which Danny thought was better for concealment. Once the coaster started, Danny unzipped the jacket enough for Maurice to get his head out to see what was up. As the coaster inched toward the first rise, Maurice wondered what all the fuss was about rollercoasters. And then the car, passing the crest, took off. Man and dog. Danny with one hand up and one hand on Maurice; Maurice with both ears up, feeling exhilarated by the rush of air, the speed, and the smell of Danny. *This must be what sex is like. If only I hadn't been fixed. Damn you, Edgar. Damn you!*

The ride lasted less than three minutes, but that didn't matter. Duration is not as important as being brought to climax. As a first-timer, Maurice was totally satisfied.

"That was fun, little guy," Danny said when he reunited with his friend. He put Maurice down, took the nylon jacket off, and pulled out a small towel from the backpack. He was soaked in sweat from the jacket and the heat of Maurice.

"Leave the shirt off," his friend said. "We're at the beach." His friend took off his shirt as well. Maurice was in a totally new situation. Two buff men were taking turns carrying the empty dog carrier, but Danny had control of Maurice's leash. Maurice should have been jealous of the new addition, but he was still high from the rollercoaster and the smell of Danny that lingered on his fur.

When they got closer to where the hot dog eating contest had been held earlier in the day, Maurice spotted Otto and then George. It made perfect sense that George would take his dachshund to a hot dog eating contest—the photo opportunities were many. He and Otto would end up on the news. They were in Uncle Sam-inspired garb. Red and white stripe pants, blue cutaway jackets, red bow ties, and white top hats with blue bands and white stars. Perhaps it was the spirit of the day, but Maurice thought they looked good.

George came over, recognizing Maurice and wanting to meet Danny and his friend. "Where's your daddy?" George asked Maurice. Danny looked at his friend, and without speaking it aloud, both recognized George's intent was "Who's your daddy?"

"Edgar and his friend Sylvia are meeting us in a few minutes," Danny said.

"Sylvia," George said, looking at his pants legs and wondering if there could be a replay of that fateful June day. That would be most unpleasant, what with the heat, the distance back home, and the fact that the Uncle Sam outfits were rented.

"You're mighty far from the Promenade, George," Edgar said as he approached the group.

"So are you," George replied. "I never thought you could go the distance."

"Me and Michael Bolton have had many careers," Edgar said.

That was actually funny, Maurice thought. *Things are looking up.*

"You remember Sylvia," Edgar continued. "We've been seeing a lot of each other."

"I've heard," George said. "You're quite the fixture at the smoothie shop. Just like clockwork. 2:45 p.m."

"I like being regular."

"Doesn't every man over fifty-five?"

"That could be us in like thirty years," Danny's friend said.

"I don't think so," Danny said. "I think they were like this when they were our age."

"Young man," George said to neither one in particular, "I'll have you know when I was in my early 30s, I was the toast of New York."

"And you know what toast is? Dry stale bread." Edgar replied.

Damn. The guy gets some regular sex, and he becomes Noel Coward. Maurice was impressed.

Edgar wasn't being witty. He heard that line in a movie the week before. He made a point of remembering it for the sole purpose of being able to repurpose it in an exchange with George.

"Do you want a piece of me?" George said.

Goodwill wouldn't want a piece of you, Maurice thought. He was surprised that he was starting to root for Edgar.

"I'll bean you," Edgar said.

"Does that mean you're going to pass wind?" George replied.

Edgar couldn't take it anymore. He knocked George's hat off his head. Ordinarily, that would not have been a big deal, but it was the Fourth of July, and George was dressed as Uncle Sam. A crowd quickly formed, yelling at Edgar for disrespecting Uncle Sam, a symbol of American pride. If only they knew that George was more Auntie Sam, a symbol of LGBTQ pride. The air was filled with the smell of sweaty, drunk men who had been eating hot dogs all day.

There was pushing and shoving. Edgar's bag got knocked to the ground and its contents spilled on the cement. Sylvia immediately crouched to scoop up the contents. That's when Danny's friend jumped in.

"Everybody, step back. Police." He pulled out a badge from his back pocket. Danny pulled out a badge, as well. Maurice had fantasized about Danny pulling something out from his pants, but never a badge. Within a matter of seconds, uniformed officers were everywhere. Maurice didn't know what to make of any of it.

It turned out that Danny was an undercover cop, and Sylvia and Grace at the smoothie shop were part of a drug operation. Sylvia had staked out the Promenade for weeks before deciding on Edgar. She needed someone who was so focused on getting laid that he would not be suspicious of a beautiful woman paying him attention. Edgar was the perfect stooge with his book bag and daily routine–she could wrap him around her little finger as easily as she could wrap her legs around him. Once she was sure Edgar was enamored, it was easy to get him to buy her a smoothie at the same place at the same time. Grace would put a packet of heroin wrapped in a wad of napkins in Edgar's bag when he would get Sylvia's drink. Sylvia would retrieve the heroin when she saw Edgar. Edgar was the perfect beard.

Danny and his partner had watched the scenario play out for weeks. They suspected Sylvia was running drugs, but they couldn't catch her until she hooked up with Edgar. Danny could have busted Sylvia weeks earlier, but he had grown attached to Maurice and didn't want the relationship to end.

The police arrested Sylvia and Edgar. Danny told George to take Maurice home with him until his shift was over. While George had issues with Edgar, he had a soft spot for Maurice. He saw a kindred spirit in the dog. Edgar agreed at once.

Epilogue

The ensuing trial was a tabloid sensation: "The Heights Connection." Sylvia and Grace made a deal with prosecutors in exchange for information on the head of the drug cartel, a slimy man known as "Pinky." He was apprehended at JFK, trying to flee to Colombia.

Sylvia and Grace went into the witness protection program and now sell high-end home cycling machines to rich couples in Winnetka, Illinois.

Murray gave up the mime routine and was elected to the New York City Council. George and Otto can still be found on the Promenade most good days. Last year, they were featured on *Morning New York* on Ann Miller's birthday.

Danny adopted Maurice. They first lived in an apartment on the Upper West Side, not far from Central Park. Every warm Sunday, Danny would take Maurice to the park where they would meet some of Danny's friends. Sometimes, they would bring a Frisbee or football. Sometimes, they would do nothing but stretch out in the sun, gossip, and munch on fruits and salads.

Maurice didn't think it could get better, but it did when Danny decided to move to Santa Monica, taking a job with the LAPD as a detective working in vice. Sometimes, Danny would take Maurice along when he was working a cruising area in Griffith Park. Maurice liked the adventure.

The Sunday routine was like the one in New York, except for the views of the ocean. Danny made friends easily, and he and his buddies would play volleyball on the beach until they were covered in sweat. Maurice would frolic among the men when they came back to where he was sitting under a large umbrella, but he only had eyes for Danny. Maurice would soon tire of the scene and curl up next to Danny's chest, close his eyes, and sleep soundly. He didn't recall his dreams. He didn't need to. His dreams and reality were now one.

And as for Edgar, time moved slowly. Even though he was a dupe in the scam, somebody had to go to jail and Edgar was charged as an accomplice and ended up serving six months in a minimum-security federal facility.

Edgar had a cellmate. His name was Maurice.

The Last Train

Architectural revisionists, of which there are many in New York City—they mainly live in their own ghetto called the Upper West Side—talk with great reverence of the original Pennsylvania Station, McKim, Mead & White's great temple to the gods of the Pennsylvania Railroad torn down in the early-1960s. More than fifty years have passed since its demolition, so odds are high that most of these people speaking of glory lost are not speaking from personal experience but from a smugness that rises like mist just north of 72nd Street and Central Park West.

These revisionists rarely take a train. Why should they? There are jitneys to the Hamptons, planes to ferries to the Vineyard, and if they do take an Acela from Manhattan to DC, there is the paean to the lost station, the Patrick Moynihan Train Hall, that face-planted inside the James Farley Post Office, also built by McKim, Mead & White.

This new train hall, an ersatz incarnation of the lost Pennsylvania Station, is west of the original station. So west that passengers inside Patrick Moynihan—which always sounded dirty to Brian—must walk almost two avenues east to find their trains once they descend from the train hall onto the track level.

Images replicating the elegance and scale of the original rail temple are displayed throughout what is now called Penn Station. The contrast between the former and the latter is jarring, as if a victim of a botched elective plastic surgery paraded about holding up an 8 x 10 glossy of how good he or she looked before deciding to self-mutilate.

The new attempts—from Moynihan to a large modern hallway that added height to the Long Island Railroad level—are more about political muscularity than architectural brilliance. And everything that has been remade bears the state's motto: "Excelsior," which Brian translated as "ever up yours."

A lifelong New Yorker, Brian vaguely knew the state's motto, which truly translates as, "ever upwards." But as a lifelong New Yorker, he also could smell the politics inside Penn Station. It was much like urine.

The excessive use of "Excelsior" was a remnant of a former governor who saw himself as a modern-day Moses, both Robert and the guy who ran afoul of Pharoah. This former governor was long rumored (although always denied) to have been involved in the creation of a campaign slogan for his father, who decades ago had run for governor against a popular New York City mayor. The slogan rhymed his father's surname with "homo," a pointed slur at the closeted mayor. The father won, and so did his son years later, who, in fairness, became a latter-day champion of LGBTQ rights.

But said son eventually fell from the more naturally burning sun like Icarus, and his rhyming political epithet ended with neither "homo" nor his surname, but with FOMO, fear of missing out on his father's legacy of brilliant statesman. Which he had.

So as Brian passed through Moynihan and saw "Excelsior" every which way, he muttered, "Ever up yours, Governor FOMO."

Brian was a boy when the original Pennsylvania Station started to come down. He remembered the row of columns on Seventh Avenue and the stone eagles perched atop the vast station inspired by the Roman Baths of Caracalla. Also, the glass panels that soared like real eagles in flight over the tracks that still took passengers on great adventures westward.

But mostly, Brian remembered the rows of coin-operated lockers for packages that sprawled across the Long Island Railroad level as the hookers did along 42nd Street in those days. And like the hookers, everything had been poorly tarted-up inside the station. The grandeur was hidden behind cheap mid-century upgrades, dirt, and the ubiquitous puddles of urine.

The protests that arose when demolition was imminent came too late. A temple to the Gilded Age was no match against a new temple for basketball, hockey, and ice shows that ironically was named after a long-ago demolished McKim, Mead & White building sited off Madison Square that lives in infamy as the place where Stanford White, of McKim,

Mead & White, was murdered by Harry Thaw, the husband of his mistress, Evelyn Nesbitt.

By the 1960s, the great rail station was doomed. And so, it came down. Piece by piece. Eagle by eagle. This great building, designed to survive for centuries, only lasted fifty-three years. The eagles did not land in the Sea of Tranquility but in the Meadowlands of New Jersey.

The current station was a study in contradictions. The Amtrak area had its own look. The Long Island Railroad had its own design, as did NJ Transit, the third railroad in the station. There were spaces where the various design aesthetics met like the old East and West Berlins—the Hilton Passageway was such a place. The title was another ironic nod to the past because there was no passageway to a Hilton—hotel or offspring.

There was once a connection to The Statler Hilton Hotel (which was built originally as the Pennsylvania Hotel by McKim, Mead & White, proving that New York eventually did to that once-esteemed architectural firm what Stanford White did to Evelyn Nesbitt). The passageway ran under Seventh Avenue and linked not only to the hotel but to Gimbel's subbasement level.

No more Hilton. No more Gimbel's. Although the full passageway exists. It is just sealed off like a tomb.

What is left is the station's back ally to the now non-existent passageway, a Cold War-era Checkpoint Charlie where the marble of NJ Transit meets urine-soaked cement flooring an arm's length width from the Long Island Railroad's concourses. Along these borders are the homeless, who are unable to find sanctuary on either side. In another bit of irony, a Lost-and-Found office is just paces from the ebbing tide of fetid humanity.

This part of the station fit Brian's mood. He had been uneasy ever since he picked up Davie's last novel. Published posthumously, the novel was atypical of Davie. His novels sold well but they never strayed far from a formula—clever in an Oscar Wilde kind of way. Which pretty much described Davie. This last one was sad and serious.

But it wasn't so much the novel that set Brian off, but his memory of how Davie had died, alone in bed. It was such a horrible way to die, to be found days later.

He had gone to the after-wake at The Crow, the West Village bar he knew was Davie's second home. Brian liked The Crow well enough, but it wasn't his second home. You needed a first home to have a second, and in all the ways that mattered, Brian did not have the former, so the latter was impossible.

Family eluded Brian. His parents were dead. He had a brother somewhere in the South, which meant Perth Amboy, New Jersey, to Brian, who barely traveled south of Canal Street. And as for a partner or husband, that train left Penn Station decades ago.

He had only one great love—an unrequited love at that—who died in 1994. August 4, 1994. Cal was one of the tens of thousands of gay men of Brian's generation who died of what Davie used to call the "disease that dare not speak its name." That was the case in the early 80s when gay men started dying of a mysterious, incurable disease. But by 1994, the plague had a name: AIDS.

Brian had made a panel for Cal after he died. Young gays today have little to no connection to the Names Project, more commonly known as the AIDS Quilt. The panels are not often assembled in great numbers anymore because gay men are no longer dying by the thousands. Young gays today have PrEP, which, to many, is a pass for having unsafe sex. With that and other effective medications, gay men in first-world America no longer die of AIDS in great numbers.

Being young is to be stupid and every generation needs to find its own way, so Brian did not judge the casual sex of the young. But this new generation didn't understand the high price paid for their sexual freedoms.

The Names Project was the grace—if there was such a thing as grace—that came from the devastation to the gay community in Brian's youth. The panels were something pure—an act of giving not just life back to the dead but restoring their humanity. No longer a grim statistic, but human. The personalities shouted out loud and proud from the homemade collages on pieces of canvas. The miracle of the whole thing was that it was not just the personality of the person on the panel that was shown; it was the personality or personalities of the people who, through an act of love, created the panel.

Brian was not artistic, but he did a good job with Cal's panel. He had reached out to other friends who knew Cal and together they laid out Cal's life, his short arc, on a 6' by 3' panel, the size of a grave. Brian had a copy made of his favorite photo of Cal for the panel. It was at a picnic in a park out on Long Island. Cal had been playing touch football with some of the other men. Brian didn't play. Brian watched; he took the pictures.

Cal was no bystander; he was all action. He posed with the football in one hand, his shirt off, which was normal whenever the temperature hit sixty. He looked happy, fit, and all of thirty-two, with no clue that in two years, his body would be ravaged by a disease without mercy.

There had been freedom in the air for gay men. They were coming out, maybe not by the tens of thousands, but the march forward was gaining members. And then came the disease. And if it wasn't death close to you, it was death near enough. Following you. Stalking you. Waiting for you not to be careful or no longer lucky. It was a numbers game. There are more than 48,000 panels in the AIDS Quilt.

Brian had seen Cal's panel on display only once and that was more than fifteen years ago. Somewhere, it was stored or hung—he didn't know where. All he knew was Cal, like the others who joined his panel, would speak to anyone who would listen. All they had to do was come.

Brian looked left and right down the Hilton Passageway. It was bleak. There were people moving to the subway at the far eastern end or taking right turns into the brighter corridors west that fed into the new grand hallway, not yet finished. They were all going somewhere through this passageway that literally led to a place that no longer existed.

If you looked hard enough, you could find small traces of the lost grandeur here and there—a brass banister, a piece of ironwork, a tiled arch near the No. 1 train entrance. But the station's demolition had been effective; nothing substantial was left of McKim, Mead & White's architectural masterpiece. To Brian, that was what AIDS did to Cal, to his college friends, to the men of his early days living in New York City when everything seemed so possible despite the urban decay of the 80s, the crime, crack, and gay bashing.

How many times had they all met in this station on their way to The Pines and Cherry Grove? There was no sign marking their journeys here.

They were not even the Statler Hilton memorialized in subway tile. They were not there. But they had been here.

He could see his lost collection of friends of different shapes and sizes off for a weekend of freedom from the city and conventional mores. He and Cal—they were always together, but not together in a sexual way— would have met earlier at his apartment and then taken the subway to Penn Station to meet the others. Then all of them would pile into a train to Suffolk County to catch a ride at the Sayville train station to the ferry to Fire Island.

By the time they got to the ferry, Cal would have stripped down to his short shorts and was flashing that smile. Cal was of the moment. Look where it got him, Brian thought. Look where it got all of them.

Brian walked aimlessly through the passageway and then through the Long Island Railroad concourse leading toward the construction of the new great hallway and found himself thinking of the short story "Araby" by James Joyce.

Araby is the name of a fanciful bazaar that a young boy is excited to visit, but when it comes to the big day, he is delayed and arrives when it is nearly closed. Yet there is enough there for the boy to see what he has missed, and he is old enough to understand the folly of his desires.

"Gazing up into the darkness I saw myself as a creature driven and derided by vanity; and my eyes burned with anguish and anger," Joyce wrote.

Brian felt a kindred spirit to that boy, walking past papered-up storefronts that still had no tenants and past painted plywood that suddenly gave way to an expanse of new construction that had no connection to anything around it, let alone to him and his memories of a fanciful time. Was this iteration of Penn Station a reminder of what had been and was being dissembled, or what was to come, or did it not really matter because Araby inside a municipal hall was always an illusion, a fake, a cheat?

In the end, if the illusion works, is that good enough? Brian's summer rides to Fire Island were journeys to Araby, a place not real, but fanciful and magical, where young men bound together by shared new freedoms became like characters in an old swashbuckling Technicolor film of the 40s. The place was an illusion; the young men were not.

But they were ghosts now.

Brian walked toward one of the new digital boards that displayed the train schedules. He looked at the familiar names. If you grew up on the Island and took the train into the city, you learned the stations on your branch line by heart. They rang out in the Penn Station over the public address system, and the not-so-huddled masses of suburbanites would scurry to Track 19 or 18, and then back to their little pieces of green—Rockville Centre, Baldwin, Freeport, Merrick, Bellmore, Wantagh, Seaford, Massapequa, Massapequa Park, Amityville, Copiague, Lindenhurst, and Babylon. That was his branch line.

No one lived there anymore.

He was tempted to hop on a train to Sayville and then a ferry to The Pines. But it was the wrong season. And he knew no one who still went there when it was the right season.

As much as The Crow was not family, maybe that was where he should go. It would be open and people he knew would be there. Sometimes you don't need family as much as you just need another person, Brian thought. He had to get out of Penn Station, as much as the boy in "Araby" had to leave a bazaar that was closing up all around him. Whatever Brian was searching for after reading Davie's last book as he walked with the ghosts of McKim, Mead & White was not to be found here.

He would go to The Crow. Brian followed the new grand hall to the subway and headed up the stairs to the No. 1 train, that would take him into the Village. The downtown platform was crowded by the stairs, so Brian headed toward the far end, where there were fewer people. No one was standing there. Brian gazed into the darkness and went back to Araby with Cal.

He looked up and saw someone approaching. It was Cal. His arms were outstretched to give him a huge bear hug, just as he used to, embarrassing Brian as he lifted him off his feet and swung him to the left and right. Brian had forgotten that part—the joy of being that close to Cal. His smell. His strong arms. Not the shell that became Cal at the end, but Cal in his youth when the Hilton Passageway actually led to a Hilton.

Gazing up into the darkness, Brian saw Cal walking toward him.

Cal was smiling. Brian closed his eyes waiting for the lift, for the rush of the warm summer's wind around his body as his big friend swung him to the right and the left, like a pendulum marking time.

Gazing up into the darkness, Brian saw Cal walking toward him.

Brian felt the lift, the wind around his body.

Gazing up into the darkness, Brian saw Cal walking toward him.

Brian could see Cal's face clearly. The deep brown eyes locked on his. Cal was smiling. Brian was smiling. Cal held him tightly. The pressure was strong, leaving Brian almost incapable of breathing.

Gazing up into the darkness, Brian saw Cal walking toward him.

Cal lifted him up. Brian was no longer on the ground. The wind and the rush were familiar. Cal looked down on Brian who was no longer young. Cal held his friend tightly, moved his head toward Brian's, and kissed him.

It happened quickly. A man came out of the shadows of the far end of the platform and shoved Brian onto the tracks just as the No. 1 train was pulling into the station.

Gazing up into the darkness, Brian saw Cal walking toward him. His eyes burned with joy and peace.

The Laird and Mildred Pierce

"Let's go through it again," John said as he put his tanned legs up on the coffee table. "You need to do it again."

"You're much nicer to me in the bar," Lee said, putting down his glass of water as he got up from his chair. He went over to his coffee table and started to move John's legs off the table. John's legs resisted.

"I'm much nicer to everyone in the bar," John said flashing a broad smile. "It's my job. But I don't usually socialize like this with anyone I meet there. I'm trying something new. You, mister, are an experiment." He added as he continued to resist Lee's efforts to move his legs off the table, "And you only got up so you could feel my strong, muscular thighs."

"You've been reading Barbara Cartland," Lee said with a slight smirk.

"Considering you are the one who immediately brought her up, the evidence would point to you and not me as the one with the romance novel addiction."

"I went to Princeton for English lit," Lee responded defensively. "A full ride."

"On NJ Transit about forty minutes from Manhattan."

"Very funny."

"Did I tell you I am on the cover of a romance novel?" John asked, stretching to fully extend his 6-foot, 3-inch frame. I was younger then, of course."

"I did not know that."

"Very few people know. Certainly, no one at The Crow knows. I don't need that circulating around my bar. So, you are sworn to secrecy."

"I will promise only if you show me the cover."

"Perhaps, someday. I look good, all ripped muscles exposed."

"I've seen them—as have all of gay New York—when you go rollerblading in Hudson River Park."

"But these ripped muscles were airbrushed. The sweat was artfully applied. And I am wearing a kilt. 'The Laird and the Lady,' that was what it was called. I don't remember the author. Long ago. But I do remember the photographer. Gino was his name. The artist who painted the covers worked from photos, so he arranged a photo shoot. Gino insisted I wear nothing under the kilt. I said it wouldn't show, and he said, 'I can change that. Give me about five minutes, but I need some water first.'"

"You are making this up," Lee said still hovering over John on the couch with his legs still firmly planted atop a stack of unread *New Yorkers*—as if there are any other kind in most New York apartments.

"Swear to God on a stack," John said, raising his right hand. "The book cover was for 'The Laird and the Lady,' but the photoshoot was for the Laird and the Queen."

"I hate that word—queen. It only is acceptable if we are talking about Freddie Mercury and/or Elizabeth II."

"Don't get all PC on me. It's only 1:30 in the afternoon. If 20-somethings can say 'queer,' I can say 'queen.' And Gino was. He definitely earned his title, let me tell you."

"This is all too cheesy."

"He had been eating burrata and tomatoes," John said with a smile. "That's why he needed the water," John added, laughing.

"You are making this up. None of this ever happened."

"You're just jealous of my many adventures."

"Not at all," Lee pouted. Grabbing John's legs, which were still outstretched on the coffee table, "Now please keep your strong, muscular calves off my furniture."

"Haters got to hate."

"From Barbara Cartland to Taylor Swift. The hits keep coming."

"They will be at the ballgame tonight, so you better buckle down, mister, if you don't want to look ridiculous."

"I was nervous already. You are not helping me."

"You'll be fine. Just go through it again and again. It will become intuitive."

"Intuitive?"

"I can take the train to Princeton, as well."

"I know you went to Dartmouth and Columbia. I can't imagine you like that."

"Like what?"

"All suited up in finance."

"You wouldn't see my legs, that's for sure."

"What a waste that would have been."

"Enough with the side chat, let's hear it or I will make you do pushups."

"Pushups?"

"Yes, and I don't mean putting on that bra you have in the back of your closet."

"I do not have a push-up bra in the back of my closet."

"I know you like the back of my hand or like you know the palm of your hand," John added making a self-gratification gesture. "You went as Mildred Pierce to a Halloween party last year at Ben's."

"How do you know that?"

"Pictures, mister. Ben showed me at the bar the next day."

"Nothing is private?"

"Not with me. You know that. I tell people all the time that it's like a confessional behind the bar. People tell me everything."

"Priests are supposed to keep it to themselves."

They exchanged looks and then roared with laughter.

"You looked good as Mildred, by the way," John said. "Some men can't get the eyebrows right. You make a good Joan Crawford. Maybe you should consider that as a career changer if tonight does not work out."

"Tonight will work out."

"Like it did for Tony, Maria, Bernardo, and Anita."

"Where does this come from? How can someone who looks like you be fluent in show tunes."

"It's not Mandarin. It's pretty easy. All I do is listen to the conversations coming from the other side of the bar. You should try it sometime."

"Me, behind a bar? I can't mix drinks."

"And neither could half the people I have hired to work at The Crow. It's mainly beer from a tap and vodkas with a splash of something. Gay men like their splash."

"Good information. But I am not going to be Mildred Pierce in another career. Tonight will be amazing."

"I'm just saying, if it isn't."

"You are not going to play this game with me. I am ready for tonight. I have been singing the National Anthem for years. I even know the other three verses."

"Well, that's helpful if anyone wants to hear the other three verses. Just make sure you get the first one right. Baseball fans are brutal when it comes to the anthem. You screw that up, you are toast."

"You are my friend, aren't you?"

"What day is it?"

"Not funny."

"Lee, by now you should understand our dynamic. I was put on Earth to keep you in touch with yourself, and looking at those callouses, you are doing a good job."

"They are from the gym."

"Don't make me laugh. The last time you were in a Jim, it was New Year's Eve 2022, and he was from Provincetown."

"He was not from Provincetown. He was from Providence."

"Close enough."

"Anyway, I go to the gym. Just not as much as you do."

"And if I didn't, you wouldn't be making excuses to touch my strong, muscular calves."

"Are we back to your calves?"

"Like an Italian is to veal scallopine."

"Oh, say can you see..."

"Now, you want to sing?"

"Anything to end this inane conversation."

"From the top and I know that is a new position for you."

"Are you going to shut up?"

"Oooh," John said dramatically. "That was very top of you. Bravo. Maybe you can get lucky tonight. Find yourself a sweaty baseball fan. Maybe one of those guys who paints his chest blue and has the hat with the beer cans and tubes?"

"That's not my type."

"I am your type," John said teasingly.

"You're everyone's type."

"Well, that is true."

"Modest to your core."

"If you had my strong, muscular calves, you wouldn't be modest."

"I have had it with your strong, muscular calves."

"If only that were true. Come over here."

Lee moved closer to John on the sofa, who grabbed him by the waist and planted a big, wet kiss on Lee's mouth.

"Where did that come from?" Lee said a little breathless.

"Do I need to explain everything? There are birds and bees, and some of the queen bees *are* queens, and their hives are like little discos with the queer bees dancing the day away. Where do you think honey comes from?"

"That's disgusting."

"I'll give you disgusting," John kissed Lee again. "I like you, Mildred."

"I like you too," Lee said, getting comfortable against John's body on the sofa. "I wasn't sure where this was leading—these past couple of weeks. Wasn't sure if you like me in this way or the Sally Field way."

"I really like Sally Field, but I don't want to kiss her on a couch."

"Good to know," Lee added, kissing John and moving his legs, so they touched John's on the coffee table.

"So now it's fine that your average-sized calves are on the furniture, but not my strong muscular calves?"

"My coffee table. My rules."

"Very top again. Should I be concerned?" he added with a boyish grin that defied his middle age.

"Not in this lifetime."

"Well, now that you have had a little sample, let's get back to work. This is the final game of the Gay Men of Chelsea Softball League's season. It's a great honor to be chosen to sing the National Anthem. You had to beat out a lot of queens."

"Again, that word."

"A lot of over-anxious sis-gender males who are attracted to other men."

"OK, queens was easier. But just between us. I was chosen fair and square. I sang it well. They liked my video, and then in person, I was on fire."

"I bet you were," John said, squeezing Lee's arms. "But go over it again."

"I will be fine. Here's the deal: if I sing it perfectly, you have to come into The Crow next Friday wearing a kilt and nothing underneath it."

"A wager? I am impressed by your competitive spirit. This bodes well, Miss Crawford." John kissed Lee again. "If you sing it perfectly, I'll wear the kilt. But if you do not, you come in next Friday as Mildred Pierce and you work behind the bar with me as a bar back."

"That doesn't seem a fair trade."

"Mildred Pierce slung chicken; you can serve drinks. Are you up to the challenge?" John kissed Lee again, this time with passion.

"You're playing me, aren't you?"

"Like a piano."

"You play piano?"

"Call me Billy Joel."

"OK, Billy, it's a bet. Let me get some more water. And don't get any ideas about your cheesy photoshoot. I'm thirsty. I always get thirsty when I have to sing later in the day. I drink gallons of water and tea."

"Doesn't that cause other problems?"

"I'm like a camel. I never have to go."

"At your age, you're less camel and more Dalai Lama, or perhaps I should say Dolly Levi Lama."

"That's the best joke you could come up with?"

"It's hard with you on top of me."

They both smiled knowingly. Lee got up, went to the kitchen, and poured a large glass of water, replacing the iced tea he had been drinking. "Do you want a glass?" Lee shouted from the kitchen.

"Not right now," John answered. "I am not a camel, and I have to head back to my apartment before the game tonight. I want to change."

Walking back from the kitchen, Lee asked, "Into shorter shorts?"

"Perhaps. Perhaps not. I am a man of many surprises. I will see you before the game. Stay hydrated."

"I will, but do you have to leave right away? I can run through the anthem again. All four verses."

"Four verses. Four verses," John repeated. "That will keep me here for what?"

"Hours and hours," Lee said. He then began to sing: "'Then conquer we must, when our cause it is just, And this be our motto—In God is our Trust; And the star-spangled banner in triumph shall wave, O'er the Land of the Free and the Home of the Brave.'

"That is the end of the fourth verse."

"You must take me through it, verse by verse," John said from the couch, signaling Lee to move closer.

"I will be happy to," Lee said, putting his glass down. "Oh, say can you see..."

"I can," John said and pulled Lee into him.

John left Lee's apartment after 4 p.m. Aside from Lee's many hydration breaks, it had been a romantic afternoon. Deciding to go all in with this new feeling, John had a plan; that is why he wanted to go back to his apartment before the game. He rummaged through his closet, found what he wanted, showered, and headed to the ballfield, turning heads as he went, particularly when he slightly mansplained on the subway. The strong muscular thighs always did that. When he arrived at the ballfield, Lee was already there holding a large water bottle.

"Oh my God," Lee said. "You're wearing a kilt. Damn."

"And there is nothing underneath in case that information is useful to you."

"But you didn't lose the bet."

"No, I won." John kissed Lee. "I thought you needed a big gesture for luck."

"I don't know what to say," Lee replied.

"Finally," John said and kissed Lee again. "Break somebody's leg."

"That's not the saying."

"It was in my neighborhood. Tony, Maria, Bernardo, and Anita played hard. I will be sitting over there. I will save you a space."

"Great. I should probably hit the bathroom quickly before the game starts."

"I don't think there is time. The players are assembling on the field. Hold it in. You're a camel."

John walked over to the bleachers and sat down in the front row. He knew most of the people from the bar and from around the city. It was a good group of people. Mostly gay men, but not all. There were some killer lesbian ball players from another team; a few trans-women had joined that team, as well. They all chided John for wearing the kilt and tried to look up it, but John was a little too fast for them. But he was enjoying being the butt of the joke for once. It felt somehow empowering to him as he watched his new boyfriend—two words he did not often put together—proceed to the microphone.

Lee was walking carefully, and John wondered if all that hydration had been a good idea—even camels have to go. But Lee was only singing one verse, and he knew all four verses perfectly. It would be fine, John thought. Lee proceeded to the microphone and John could tell he had the correct pitch to start.

Lee shuffled his feet slightly. The crowd went quiet, and he began:

"Oh, say can you pee by the dawn's early light…"

Not everyone in the crowd was sure Lee said "pee" instead of "see," but the damage was done. The rest of the anthem went flawlessly, and there was a good ovation. John looked over at Lee, who was dashing to a portable restroom. His face was crimson, part from embarrassment and partly because he needed to go urgently.

That night, John made Lee feel he was the king of the world. There was no mention of the gaffe. It was not the time or place. The following

Friday, the patrons at The Crow were surprised to see that none other than Mrs. Mildred Pierce was working as a barback.

Everyone said her eyebrows were amazing.

The Automat

Luke turned right at the fork. Muscle memory. He hadn't been here in more than a decade, but his arms remembered where to turn in a place where everything was designed to be the same. It wasn't really the same. Nothing is identical—even less so when effort has been made to achieve just that.

If there is a natural order, and Luke was not convinced there is, it is a natural disorder. Even here, where crosses were ubiquitous, no two were identical. Nature refused to submit to the stonemason's chisel. Once you looked, really looked, you could see this was no different than Levittown, a place created to be the same but failing in the end.

In the case of Levittown, it was a flawed compact that not only created identical houses but whitewashed them in codified racism. Nature could not leave that inequity in place, so white gave way to color, not easily, to be sure, but time wore away the whiteness, as it did the form and structure of the Cape Cods. There were a few holdouts that gave testament to the master's plan, but by and large, all that remained of the original scheme was the layout of the streets that made little sense to anyone.

Natural disorder.

It was the same here. The roads made little sense. They turned left or right or perhaps you went straight ahead. There was no scarecrow to offer directional assistance. You followed the road, as in life, as you saw it. Just as they had done, the thousands below slabs of granite that rose from the grass like flowers of the apocalypse.

"In Flanders field, the poppies blow between the crosses row on row," John McCrae wrote. Red poppies. Bursts of living color against wooden crosses. No poppies here, and flowers do not blow between the graves.

Here, the flowers, cut, already dying by degree after hot degree, are placed by visitors against the stones.

In spring and summer, the brilliant green grass provides the only contrast. In fall and winter, it is not quite a true brown against the stones; grass does not give up its life; it just lies in wait for Persephone's return. There is no return for those below the crosses.

Thousands of them. Fields of them. Neither an ocean that ebbs and flows, nor a garden where spring brings transformation. These fields of crosses jutting above the earth were something different, something that eluded the poetry of the Greeks.

Those poets had words and gods for what was below, but this human invention that surrounded Luke as he navigated the narrow roads in his rental car was beyond the Greek poets. It was so much less than that. It was just a real estate scheme conjured up who knows when by who knows who, but a real estate scheme, nonetheless.

Consider the proposition: Buy land for when you are no longer alive; a ridiculous construct, this real estate for the dead. A planned community like Levittown. Rows and rows of codified conformity enforced by compacts that determined the size of the cross, or if your cross could be substituted for a small—or not so small—marble Cape Cod devoid of plumbing and radiant heat.

Here, at St. Matthew's, the compact excluded Cape Cods. There were just crosses. The only buildings were for maintenance—grounds-keeping equipment and chapels. Both essential. People who planned ahead wanted their little plots to look better. It came down to the grass not just being greener next door; it cost more to cut.

It was a little ironic, the payments made for perpetual care at St. Matthew's, given that the historical Matthew had been all about money until conversion; he was a tax collector who walked away from his job to follow Jesus. Luke had joked to his 12th-grade religion teacher at St. Ignatius High School that Matthew left H&R Block to follow INRI. Brother Joseph was not amused.

Luke's experience at St. Ignatius was not devoid of its pleasures. It was there that Luke met John in his senior year, a towering presence at the high school, captain of the baseball team, muscular and with deep brown fur covering his torso. They shared an English class and PE. During gym, that brown fur, matted with sweat, would rise above the collar of his T-shirt. Luke tried not to stare for fear that his uncontrolled hormones would betray him and leave him humiliated in the locker room.

To Luke's surprise, one day late into the spring of his senior year, John cornered Luke after school behind the gym and kissed him full on the mouth.

Luke had never kissed anyone, let alone another boy. John had figured him out, but Luke had never imagined that someone like John could be gay, not back then. Homos and queers—the latter epithet in the 1970s had not metamorphosized into the politically correct cockroach it is today—were more like himself: bad at sports and usually undersized and/or overweight. At seventeen, Luke hit the trifecta. He didn't see himself as being sexually appealing, so the kiss took him by surprise.

There wasn't much more to that story, aside from Luke's awakening as a gay man. John would give him a knowing smile from time to time in the halls, but there was never another kiss. As time passed, Luke wondered if he had imagined it all. No one had been around to witness the event. But it had happened. It was real. It was the first taste Luke had of real passion, how it often makes little sense, and how the experience was the better for it.

As time passed, the kiss became a warm memory rather than a burning question. John got into Dartmouth on a sports scholarship and then to Columbia for his MBA. John was probably a titan of finance today.

Luke was surprised John came to mind as he continued to navigate the roads of St. Matthew's. He hadn't thought about John in years.

"There's the chapel," he said out loud in the car, squinting now that the car faced west and the July sun, at 1:30 p.m., was angled directly toward him.

The chapel meant he was getting close. The chapels, there were three in the cemetery, were not identical, aside from all being without architectural merit. It was as if the planners of St. Matthew's deliberately wanted to create buildings that could just as easily be turned into small bank branches—deposits only, no withdrawals.

There was a splash of colored glass—not really stained glass, colored glass—the required cross atop a roof pitched in multiple directions. It was either a nod to some trend when constructed or an attempt to point to heaven without knowing exactly where it was, just somewhere above.

The three Mike Brady-styled chapels ensured all would be well above. Not ground level above, but Above. Heaven.

Luke had dismissed the heaven of his childhood—the angels, the harps, the clouds, the flowing robes, and the sheer whiteness of it all. That was not heaven; that was a themed garden party in Locust Valley in the 1920s. To Luke, heaven was a place like the Horn & Hardart's of his youth.

Where else would cafeteria Catholics end up but the Automat, where they poured coffee from a dolphin spout or claimed a piece of pie from behind a little glass door?

That was heaven. Lemon meringue pie behind a little glass door in a wall of little glass doors with lemon meringue pies behind each one.

He must have been around six the first time he went to the Automat. He needed a boost to get to the pie, but his dad allowed him to put the coin in the slot, open the little glass door, and carefully take the pie out all by himself. Luke wouldn't put it on the tray with the other food. He held it tight in his own hands and brought it to their table.

It was another warm memory. That was heaven.

Luke caught the small smile on his face in the rearview mirror. It was still a vigorous face, if a little weather-worn with time, not unlike the granite around him. He fixed his eyes back on the narrow road. There was another turn coming up. His arms twitched, ready to move left soon. Turning right was not an option, so it would be a left down the seemingly identical roads.

He trusted his muscles and made the first left. The Automat laid flat on the horizon.

Luke did not have an actualized vision of hell as he did of heaven, only that hell was a place where accordion music played eternally.

As to his own ever-after, Luke planned to be cremated. He would be strewn at a place to be determined. He hadn't given it much thought, but as he saw the architecturally bereft chapel just behind him now, he was reminded he needed to figure that out. There was no one who would be lining up for his ashes, so he needed a plan. He wasn't sure what happened to uncollected ashes. The state needed to come up with some financial benefit for non-relations who took on that responsibility—perhaps an urn-ed tax credit, Luke thought, chuckling again to himself. Brother Joseph would have not been amused.

Luke's clock was ticking. It flashed in big numbers: 67. Maybe twenty years before it stopped? Maybe twenty months? Who really knew? Not the people who were no longer people below the crosses row on row.

This was why he never came out here—or at least one reason. You couldn't help but think of death in a cemetery. It was the general idea of the whole place. There are people who like going to cemeteries, he knew that. They picnicked on the grounds, attended late-night movies, or wandered among the hundreds of crosses imagining fanciful narratives for people who were never that remarkable in life. The fake narratives made the dead like so much boiled lobster on a plate; not of much interest until the addition of the secret sauce, and then like magic, they became something fancy, French or the incarnation of Colin Farrell.

Luke parked the car on the left side of the narrow roadway, just past the chapel. He took a breath, opened the door, and the intense July heat hit him hard. He had forgotten how hot it would be out here with little shade. There would be shade at their grave.

He would look for the tree. It was a big tree. When his parents bought the plot, they were excited about trees as if they were characters in *The Cherry Orchard*. All they could do was talk about that tree. It creeped Luke out at the time. Now, he chuckled at the memory.

He was so young back then. Early 20s. He knew little of life and nothing of death. By his 30s, that would change. Death became familiar. Not just his parents passing. That was to be expected. They were well into their 40s when he was born. It was his friends. It was casual acquaintances. It was everyone.

They didn't get buried. They were cremated. It was what was done because no one was comfortable with their remains, as if even dead they could spread the plague. Luke would never admit it out loud, but he had often thought during the pandemic that straight people who agonized over not having proper burials for their loved ones briefly experienced what gay men had for a full generation, his generation. He did not wish that on these grieving people, but he wondered why no one connected those dots. No one thought to talk with the survivors of that earlier plague about the lack of closure for their losses.

The men who died from AIDS were not buried in St. Matthew's. They were cremated and their ashes strewn somewhere or perhaps left in a box in the back of a closet, the latter a cruel joke on a gay trope. So, as much as Luke had experienced death and loss, cemeteries were not a familiar destination, although this one was familiar enough.

He had come here six or seven times since they both passed—once for each. They had not died together in a fictional embrace. He came back on the first anniversaries of their respective deaths—and then once or twice randomly, like today.

Random is an oversimplification. Nothing is random, just as nothing is identical.

Luke shut the car door. It was so hot. He loosened his tie. Why had he worn a tie? He unbuttoned the collar. It wouldn't be a long walk. He peered at the small marker close to the grass next to the car. The markers denoting the rows were barely visible. SS. They were in MM. No, not a very long walk. He began walking in the general direction of the chapel, going backward in the alphabet.

"I parked too far down," Luke said to the rows and rows of crosses, realizing even a relatively short distance was too long in this heat. He was sweating profusely. It was near 90 degrees. No shade. Luke took a moment to lean on a headstone at the end of row QQ. He was a little disoriented, almost as if he was going to pass out.

"Are you lost?" a voice shot out, startling Luke. He hadn't noticed the young man walking toward him.

"You startled me. I could have had a heart attack," Luke said.

"Well, if you're going to meet your maker, this is a pretty good place to do it," the young man said with a broad smile. He couldn't be more than twenty-five, with sandy hair partly hidden by a baseball cap, tall and broad-shouldered. He was wearing a forest green shirt and pants, a groundskeeper's uniform. The young man's shirt was splotched with sweat. Luke was attracted to him, which was disturbing. This wasn't high school gym class; he was an old man in a cemetery, and his parents were nearby.

"No, I'm not lost," Luke said, smiling at the young man. "I have a general idea of where I am and where I should be going."

"Is that an existential statement, or do you really know where you are? There's no shame in being lost."

"Excuse me...Matt, yes?" Luke saw the young man's first name sewn onto the pocket flap of his unbuttoned shirt, which revealed too much chest. "Are you a wandering philosopher?"

"All philosophers wander. Think of me not as a philosopher but as a good Samaritan. Have some water. It's crazy hot out. You must be dehydrated." Matt offered Luke water from the plastic bottle he was holding in his left hand. "Let me help you up."

Luke hadn't realized he was sitting on the grass. "When did I sit down?"

"Just before I approached you. It's the heat. Have some water. No need to be shy. I'm healthy. You need water."

Luke smiled and said, "I'm not shy." He took the proffered bottle and then a long swig. "Thank you. That feels good." As Luke began to stand up, Matt extended his right hand and helped him to his feet. Matt's hand was cold and wet from the water bottle; his grip was strong.

Luke still felt a little disoriented. "I guess the heat is more than I planned for."

"I can see that," Matt said. "You're dressed for church. Buttoned-down long-sleeve shirt, slacks, a tie! Who wears a tie?"

"I like ties."

"I like sweaters—in January."

"You have a point. I must look quite ridiculous."

"Not ridiculous. Helpless."

"I think I prefer ridiculous."

"Drink some more water. And no hat? I don't mean to insult you but men without much hair should wear hats. Skin cancer."

"You're not a philosopher, but the surgeon general?"

"I'm actually a seminarian—or I will be in September."

"The priesthood. I thought about that once."

"What happened?"

"I thought about it twice."

"Very funny, man."

"My name is Luke."

"Very funny, Luke. Good to meet you."

Luke felt the strong grip again. This time it was warm and wet with sweat. "You're a budding priest?"

"Like the flowers of spring," Matt added with a smile. "Although in this heat, I probably don't smell like a flower. Sorry about that."

"There are many things to apologize for in life. Smelling like a man who has been working hard is not one of them." As soon as he said that Luke wanted to take it back. It sounded like a cheesy pickup line, and the young man could almost be his grandson, and he was going to be a priest, no less.

"Glad you feel that way," Matt replied. "Some visitors get snooty when they encounter the grounds people. They expect us to be always fresh rather than occasionally ripe."

"You have a way with words. You sure you want to be a priest?"

"Shouldn't a priest have a way with words? We're supposed to console people, preach homilies, teach."

"You must be Episcopalian."

Matt laughed. "I take it you are a Catholic."

"I was raised Catholic. I grew out of it."

"No one grows out of being Catholic. It leaves a mark on you."

"I thought that was circumcision."

"We have that in common with Jews."

"Indeed," Luke said, now fixated on Matt's crotch. If Matt was an example of the body of Christ, Luke thought, it was no wonder that Jesus had so many followers.

This was not how a visit to the cemetery was supposed to go. "It's hard for me to imagine a young man wanting to be a Catholic priest anymore. There's so much bad history."

"I know, I know. But there's baggage in every profession. You name it, and there were bad people. If I said I wanted to coach football at Penn

State, would you frown? The priesthood is the same and I don't intend to be one of those priests, one of those men."

"If you don't mind my asking, what about the celibacy thing? No sex. Ever."

Matt laughed again. "Well, when you put it that way. Look, I intend to be a good person, a good priest. There's too much importance put on sex."

"It's important. Trust me."

"I know it is. Trust me, I know. Let that be on me. I believe I have a vocation. That's what seminary is all about, determining whether you do or you don't. Maybe it won't be for me, but I believe it will—it is."

"Good for you, then. I've known many priests in my life. I've known them."

"I catch your meaning," Matt said. "I think vows are like muscles." Matt flexed his right bicep.

"Very impressive, but what has that to do with celibacy?"

"Vows are like muscles. If you break a muscle down, it repairs itself and gets stronger. There is too much focus on never breaking a vow, which is not healthy, and not enough on how we can get stronger after each tear."

"You want to be a Jesuit, then?"

"You found me out," Matt added with a hearty laugh. "I'm not that smart. I want to be a diocesan priest in a middle-income parish somewhere on the Island. Regular people. Maybe coach a grade school ball team—not Penn State," Matt added with a chuckle. "Run Bingo on Friday nights. Baptisms, weddings, funerals," he said, pointing around the grounds. "It's all part of the process, you know. I kind of like working here. It grounds you—no pun intended. It reminds you of the journey we take and sometimes I get to meet interesting people like yourself."

"I'm not that interesting."

"It's like 112 degrees, and you're wearing a long-sleeve button-down shirt, a tie, nice slacks, and really nice shoes. No one dresses like that anymore. You're interesting. You have a back story."

"I see an orthopedist for that."

"So, are you a comedian? A writer?"

"I should tell you I am a visiting bishop here to check on you, but I am not. I'm nothing fancy. That's why I dress fancy."

"I will let that pass, Luke. You're not going to tell me what you do, then?"

"I don't think so," Luke said, looking at the rows of crosses. "We spend so much of our lives defining ourselves by our professions and where does it take us, but to a small plot of land with a granite marker. In a cemetery, everyone is the same."

Luke paused, looking at the Automat above the rows of stones. "I'll tell you something—I stood on Frank Sinatra."

"You stood on Sinatra?" Matt asked.

"I was visiting a friend in Palm Springs, and he took me to the cemetery where Sinatra is buried. Cemeteries are not my thing, but it was his thing, and he had the car so there we were on Sinatra's grave. Think about Sinatra's millions of fans over the decades who wanted to get close to him and here I was standing about six feet from him. It was a bit creepy."

"I don't think about the physical when I am here," Matt said. "Even though that is the whole point of burial. Who we are goes somewhere else."

"The Automat."

"Excuse me?"

"You're too young to know what the Automat was. Horn & Hardart's. You put a coin in a slot by a little glass door and pulled out a piece of pie. That's my idea of heaven."

"Pie behind a glass door?"

"The Automat is a happy memory. I was too young to see it as it was; I saw it the way it was to me. It's a much better way to view the world."

"I don't think of heaven as a place, more like a state of consciousness."

"Good pie is a state of consciousness."

"Descartes?"

"Martha Stewart."

"You see? You are fancy. You must be a writer."

"I could just be gay."

"No one is just gay like no one is just straight or trans or just anything. None of us are just anything. We are so much more. Look around you. These stones mark people who were not just a name on a stone. People are so much more than just something."

"Thomas Merton?"

"Matt Kellner. Me."

"Maybe you are right, Matt Kellner," adding the surname for effect. "But it doesn't matter in the end. We're all here in the end. Like Sinatra waiting for someone to stand on us." Luke paused again as he searched the sky for his lemon meringue. "Well, this is going in a sad direction."

"We are in a cemetery. It is a place many sad people come to find some release."

"I suppose they do," Luke said quietly, almost to himself. Matt looked at Luke as if he was waiting for Luke to say something more. Their eyes locked. After what seemed an eternity to Luke, it was Luke who spoke, "I am lost."

"I know," Matt said, moving closer. "I could see that when I walked up to you."

"Would you mind walking with me to their grave?" Luke asked. "You don't need to stay or anything. Just walk with me for a bit, OK?"

"Sure. Do you know the row?"

"MM. It's that way. They—Mom and Dad—are by a large tree somewhere over there." Luke pointed in the direction he thought the grave was located. "There's shade by that tree."

"Here," Matt said, taking off his baseball cap, his sandy hair almost black with sweat. "I know it's sweaty, but you can't be walking around here without a hat. I don't want you passing out. I'd have to carry you or dump you in open grave."

"What?"

"Just messing with you, Luke. I wouldn't dump you in an open grave. How would that look to the seminary? No, I'll keep an eye on you. Put the hat on."

Luke took the cap and put it on. It was warm, damp, and felt good. "Thanks. It adds to my look."

"It's definitely an improvement. Come on, let's get to the shade."

The two men walked slowly toward MM.

"It's that way," Luke said. "It's about even with the chapel. I can see the tree now."

They continued walking silently. Luke looked at the names and dates on the headstones: Simon Gradston, December 22, 1933—June 12, 1978, and Helen Gradston, February 4, 1938—May 10, 2020; James Connor, March 6, 1930—March 1, 2007, and Alice Connor, June 8, 1930—March 1, 2019; Michael O'Reilly, August 12, 1940—November 5, 2007; and Mary O'Reilly, February 27, 1941—November 5, 2019. The names spread out like entries in the Book of the Dead.

"They are all coupled," Luke said. "All coupled and this couple died on the same date, but twelve years apart."

"It must be hard to lose someone you've spent so much time with," Matt said.

"I think it's harder to have spent so much time without anyone," Luke replied.

"I'm sorry."

"Sorry for what?"

"Sorry, you don't see that you matter regardless of whether you are coupled to someone who is etched into the same piece of stone as you."

"Isn't that what we are supposed to do, couple?"

"With God, yes. With many of the people we encounter, yes, but not necessarily beyond that moment. With just one person? It is special, but it isn't essential."

"You're still young, and you're going to be a priest. You don't understand what it's like to be at the end of your journey alone."

"End of your journey? Do you want me to dump you into an open grave? Unless you do, you're not at the end of your journey."

"You know what I meant. I'm an old man."

"So, you're old…or at least older than I am. So what?" Matt added for emphasis. "Love—even big love—isn't bigger because it lasts longer. It's bigger because it just is. To put it in gay terms, Luke, size matters, longevity does not." As Matt continued, he became more passionate. "The last thing you should be doing is being envious of the dead because they are dead. Ended. Regardless of what comes next, their physical life is over. You've stood on Sinatra; you were not down there with him."

Luke didn't answer. He continued walking toward the tree looming ahead. Matt kept pace with Luke. Side by side, the two men walked down MM until Luke stopped and said, "They are there," pointing to the stone with the large surname—Brooks.

Below that were his parents' names and dates, but the elements had taken their toll on the north side of the stone, so his parents' dates of death were barely legible, and the carving of lilies near the top of the stone cross was slightly smoothed.

"The dates of their deaths are almost gone. Like they didn't die," Luke said, touching the stone. "I never did that before," he said to Matt. "I never touched the stone."

"How did it feel?" Matt asked, moving closer to Luke and then putting his hand on Luke's shoulder.

"Not like that," Luke said, responding to the touch. "Not warm. Not cold. Not anything."

"What did you expect? Some kind of magic?"

"Maybe I did. I don't know. It's strange seeing the stone so weathered and the grass so neat up against the stone. No sign of burial—like they are just the long dead—which they are. When I die, they end. No more of our family line."

"You think it works that way?" Matt asked. "It's bloodlines that keep us from dying? No, it can't be because there are people whose bloodlines connect to despicable human beings, and their offspring are not extensions of that evil any more than they can be extensions of someone else's goodness.

"What we do is what lives on. If they gave you something unique, they gave it to other people as well through their actions while alive. You had more exposure to it, so maybe you have a higher probability of passing it on, but it isn't about procreation in the physical sense. For a lapsed Catholic, you're too caught up in reproduction as being the end-of-it-all for human existence. I intend to be a priest. I'm not going to have children, and I don't think that means I somehow killed the Kellner family tree."

"Do you believe in fate?" Luke asked.

"Where did that come from?"

"Meeting you in a cemetery."

"Fate? I don't know. You looked kind of helpless and...a little bit like my type, so I walked over," Matt added with a slight smile. "And yes, I have a type regardless of the seminary. I don't think our meeting is fate. It's random within a certain given that if someone spends enough time in a Catholic cemetery, you will encounter a similar old soul."

"I don't believe in fate, either. But I don't know. You seem God-sent."

"That wouldn't be fate, as much as Divine intervention," Matt said like a Sunday school teacher. "And I don't think either of us rise to that level of God's attention. He, She, They," Matt gesticulated, "has bigger fish to fry. I'm just open to the experience in front of me, maybe more than others. That's my vocation, I believe. It's not fate. It's just fully opening yourself to what the other person is experiencing. It allows me to be present. People want to call that fate. I call that paying attention. You needed a shoulder. You need an embrace."

Matt put his arms around Luke and embraced him. The embrace was long and silent, other than the quiet sound of their breathing. Neither spoke. Finally, Matt moved slightly away, put his hands on Luke's cheeks, and kissed him.

"Peace of Christ," he said.

"That didn't feel like the peace of Christ," Luke responded. His eyes were watery. "I never had that happen during the peace of Christ in church."

"The peace of Christ isn't restricted to church or having an audience. It's not about show and tell—it's about give and receive. I wanted to give you that kiss, Luke. I wanted you to feel how much you matter to a stranger. Imagine how much you must matter to the people you know."

"You overestimate my potential."

"I don't think so. The whole point of having potential is to surprise yourself, let alone others. I don't underestimate your potential—maybe you do to yourself. Why did you come today?"

"I think I wanted closure."

"You had closure when they died. That's how it works."

"You know what I mean."

"I do. I do. People come here all the time looking for closure. I see that every day. None of them ask my opinion, but I would tell them what I am telling you now. Life is not about putting a button on something in the past—time does that. Life is about being in the present. The dead cannot tell us anything because they are dead. Move forward. If you want to come here and remember a special memory, that's all good. Memories are fantastic because they are not bound by the borders of reality. They flow where we want them to like your concept about heaven and the Automat. It's a warm memory. You don't need closure with the dead. You need new conversations with the living."

"I'm all talked out." Luke looked at his parents' gravesite. "I should have brought flowers. I didn't think of bringing flowers."

"They won't notice. The only people who notice the flowers are the other people walking through the alphabet of rows. Again, show and tell, not give and receive."

"Do you want to exchange numbers?" Luke blurted out. "That sounds cheesy, doesn't it?" He was already embarrassed by the question.

"No, it doesn't sound cheesy," Matt replied in a quiet, reassuring way. "Sure. But I can't promise we'll hook up. That's not where I am right now in life."

"I didn't mean it that way," Luke said. "Well, maybe I did. You're a good kisser."

"Thank you. If I ever become a cardinal, I will put that on my crest."

They both laughed and exchanged numbers. The moment was passing, and they both knew that.

"I will walk you back to your car. Can't have you passing out between QQ and RR."

They walked back to the end of the row and through the double alphabet until they reached Luke's rental.

"Can we hug again?" Luke asked.

"Absolutely."

They hugged, but there was no kiss. Luke went to return Matt's hat, but Matt stopped him. "It's a souvenir. Wear it well."

"Thank you," Luke said as he got into the car.

"And next time I see you here, you better be wearing it, or I will leave you for another groundskeeper to scoop up, and he won't be a good kisser."

"Understood."

Luke turned on the engine and then the AC, keeping the door open. "I need to let the car cool down."

"That will be in October."

They both laughed. Matt shut the door and, before Luke rolled up the window, said, "You are fancy." He stood back on the grass and waved as Luke pulled away.

Luke followed Matt in his rearview mirror until the road wound toward the left, and his muscles took over, navigating him toward the main gate. He wasn't sure what to make of the afternoon. He hadn't thought anything profound about his parents at their grave. He had been too busy focusing on Matt and fate and that kiss. That John kiss.

He wasn't sure what he would take away from today besides a baseball cap he would treasure. Maybe he would see Matt, but then maybe not. That isn't how things usually worked for him. And maybe, Luke thought, that was OK. It wasn't about the longevity of the love but the size of the love.

It was like John in high school and the one kiss. Another warm memory to hold close when it was no longer July.

When he reached the gate, Luke turned right onto the side road to get back to the main road that would take him north toward the expressway. When he reached the turn, his arms moved the wheel south, not north. As the car seemingly guided itself, Luke began to realize where he was heading, where muscle memory—no, warm memory, was taking him.

He drove for another twenty minutes, and then the scenery became familiar. It was his hometown. He didn't need his arms to direct him now. His brain was fully engaged while his heart pumped faster past remnants of his childhood. Many of the stores were gone. But he was as sure of his destination as he had been sure about the tree at St. Matthew's. Some things stay because they are well-rooted.

He saw the sign on the side of the building. It was still there. He pulled into the parking lot and bounded up the concrete steps with more energy than he had had in months. The cool air inside felt good, but it was not the air conditioning that buoyed his spirits. He saw it in the case near the door.

He took a seat at the counter. The waitress, not more than seventeen, came up to him and asked, "Do you want to see a menu?"

"No," Luke said. "I don't need to see a menu. I would like a slice of lemon meringue pie."

Mr. Picky Comes to Town

Julius Caesar on the down low
By Harry Douville
Herald-Sun Theatre Critic

Julius Caesar is the luckiest person in the William Gillette Theater; he dies before intermission. For the rest of us—audience, cast, stagehands, vendors, ushers, and the vermin scurrying in the basement— director Dimitri Sasoon's $45 million Miami-themed interpretation of *Julius Caesar*, which he now calls *Julio*, is a tragedy of epic proportions. Where Caesar is repeatedly stabbed and mercifully dies quickly, we, the unlucky, must endure three hours of pulsating, ear-splitting nonsense.

The curtain goes up not on a Roman street, but on an oceanfront drive in South Beach, Florida. Marc Antony should enter dressed for a celebration, but Mr. Sasoon has Antony enter in a Speedo. And unless Jerry Mills, the well-chiseled film actor cast as Antony, was in a state of extreme happiness solely for entering on cue, said brief garment was given an added enhancement that would be best described as measure for measure. It was the only uplifting aspect of Mr. Mills' performance.

Best known for popular flicks known as "bromances," Mills is an interesting choice if one could or should think of *Julius Caesar* as a bromance, a buddy movie for the Tudor court. But you need more than abs for Shakespeare; you need acting chops. Alas, poor Mills is toothless.

Mr. Mills looks good, and that may be all Mr. Sasoon was going for in this homoerotic, semi-clad production that will be remembered for its excessive use of stage blood, cross-dressing, and body oil. Cassius is literally slick, slathered like meat on a spit. It is a testament to the proverbial sticking place that the well-lubricated George Taddings, a talented stage actor who riveted audiences last season as Richard III, did not slide off the stage. One wished he had, not for the injury, but for the easy exit. Ah, to die! Perhaps to sleep!

Mr. Sasoon's Rome is one endless circuit party. Great monologues are framed by blaring salsa music. Antony delivers "Friends, Romans and countrymen" as a bloodied, naked Caesar lies atop a tanning bed as a Cuban-infused song plays in the background. Caesar died not for grabbing too much power but for living *La Vida Loca*.

The heart of *Julius Caesar* is Brutus. Orson Welles made history in the part. Larry Silver made history last night as well, as the first cross-dressing Brutus. To show his conflict between preserving the Republic and his love for Caesar, he was alternately clad in female and male garb. In fact, all the senators are dressed in drag when they assassinate Caesar; Mr. Sasoon's bizarre metaphor is that the female side is evil, and the male is honest and good. By play's end, Brutus is again honest, good, and stripped down to the barest essentials.

Audiences should be warned that when the "ladies" of the Senate stab Caesar, stage blood spurts all over the place—on the actors, on the stage, and on the unfortunate inhabitants of the first three rows of the orchestra. Behold a tableau of blood-soaked drag queens. Is this supposed to be Shakespeare or backstage before an open audition for *La Cage aux Folles*?

In Act II, Brutus delivers this line to Ligarus, "A piece of work that will make sick men whole." Ligarus replies, "But are not some whole that we must make sick." Clearly, that must have been Mr. Sasoon's mantra.

If *Julius Caesar* is an indictment on the pursuit of power, its corruption, and the lies that men tell themselves to justify heinous acts, *Julio*, while not a literal assassination of a ruler, is an attack on the brilliance of Shakespeare's words and stagecraft. I am not a purest when it comes to Shakespeare or the works of other great playwrights, but the director's vision cannot overshadow the source material. And if the director is led not by vision, but ego, if he is shaped by the worst pop influences of the moment and not driven by a passion to make words most glorious resonate with new influences, he is bound to fail. And fail, Mr. Sasoon, has done.

Never has there been a tale of such woe than that of Dimitri Sasoon's production of *Julio*.

◆ ◆ ◆

Harry Douville left his apartment at 9 a.m. He picked up his morning paper at the front desk in his lobby. "You crucified Dimitri Sasoon," Marco, the doorman, said, holding up Harry's review that was on the front page of the Arts section of *The Herald-Sun*.

"It's the season for it, you know. Easter is in four weeks," Harry said with a smile as he stuck his newspaper into his new leather Mark Cross case. Harry told his friends he bought the Mark Cross case because it made him feel like a black Grace Kelly in *Rear Window*.

"You should be careful writing stuff like that. What if Sasoon gets angry and threatens you?"

"Dimitri Sasoon is a short, squat man of fifty-five. He once got wedged between a table and a banquette at Balthazar. They had to bring in the Jaws of Life. In the end, a sommelier pulled him out like a dry cork from a bottle of not-so-nouveau Beaujolais. I am not intimidated by cork unless it's used as a wall covering—that does scare the shit out of me."

"You're not a nice man," Marco said jokingly.

"You have no idea," Harry replied as he left the lobby.

◆ ◆ ◆

The Herald-Sun was the third-largest circulation newspaper in New York City. What it lacked in circulation, it had in cachet. It was a newspaper populated by personalities as large as the city it served. And unlike *The Journal* and *The Times*, it had no pretensions of being global or national. But if it happened in the four boroughs—*The Herald-Sun*'s publisher, Addison Greystone III, refused to accept that Staten Island was not part of New Jersey—it happened on the pages of *The Herald-Sun*.

In this competitive city filled with competitive journalists trying to make their respective marks, Harry Douville was a star. As the principal theater critic for *The Herald-Sun*, he could affect the success of a struggling show. In an age when revivals trumped new plays, and Hollywood names trumped established stage talent, some shows were review resistant. For example, there is a musical based on a comic book hero that has been running for seven years on Broadway without ever officially having a first night.

"America would never have been stuck in Afghanistan if only this musical's director had traded Broadway for the Pentagon." Harry had written when said musical celebrated its third year in previews.

"A military quagmire exists for lack of an exit strategy, but this director brings a different skill set: no entering strategy."

Harry Douville was more than a single character; he was the whole goddamn keyboard. Tall and lithe, his light chocolate complexion and tightly cropped hair set him apart from his peers, who were yellowing with age. The vast majority of New York critics were dipped in sepia. Harry was as gay as the next theater critic—and it is as hard to find a straight theater critic in Manhattan as it is to find a taxi in the Bronx— but Harry was not bitchy for the sake of a good *bon mot*. His prose was something to savor, a good wine with notes of cherry, cocoa, and maybe a little something unexpected and sweet.

His theater reviews were perceptive but rarely positive, earning him his nickname, which appeared above his handsome face on the sides of city buses: "Mr. Picky."

Harry walked through the Features department to his desk, which was near a window, a coveted position. His cubicle was immaculate. Everything had a place: press kits, Playbills, volumes of play anthologies. Posited atop the corner of his cubicle was a bust of Arthur Miller. A bust of Miller was, in itself, not common. It wasn't like a Shakespeare bust, but this Miller had an Ann Miller wig, a big, lacquered black number that could take out somebody's eye. It was a gift from an Ivy League theatrical society who knew of Harry's love of both Millers. The wig was their way of acknowledging that while adding a bit of whimsy. It was Harry's favorite possession at work.

He booted up his computer, hung up his coat, and went into his editor's office to steal a cup of coffee.

"I came for some coffee. Are you growing the beans in here as well? It's like a hothouse," Harry said, walking with his mug to the small coffee maker on a file cabinet. It was the only surface not covered by plants.

Features editor Steve Mulrooney loved gardening, but he and his wife lived in a rent-controlled apartment without a terrace and with little light. They dreamed of a home in Montclair, NJ, a place not really like heaven but more like the Upper Westside if the strollers were replaced with SUVs with child seats.

In the absence of a garden or home in Montclair, Steve had turned his office into a conservatory. The room was always hot and moist from the three humidifiers. There were small plants on the windowsills and large potted plants on the floors, but mostly, there were roses, roses of every kind and description, which meant nothing to Harry. He had an aversion to any living thing whose principal function was to facilitate romance.

"It must be 100 degrees in here," Harry said sipping his coffee near the open door. "I'm *schvitzing*."

"You can't be *schvitzing*. You're a Black Baptist from Virginia. You don't *schvitz*, you sweat."

"I spent two years dating Sol Goldstein after graduate school. And then there was Bernie and then David. I have had more Jews inside me than Zabars."

"Too much information," Steve wearily said as he misted an American Beauty. This was the normal morning banter between Harry and him. "And none of what you say is true. You make up your personal life because you have no personal life."

"If you stab me, will I not bleed?" Harry replied in mock offense. "I have friends."

"People you have to tip are not your friends."

"I am loved by the masses," Harry replied. "Loved." Harry was in a very good mood.

"You know," Steve began in a tone that indicated a change of direction; the editor could prune a conversation like a prize rose. "You were a little too pleased with yourself when you wrote the *Julio* review. If I hadn't taken a day off, this copy would not have passed through." He picked up the Arts section, put on his glasses, and read: "'And unless Jerry Mills, the well-chiseled film actor cast as Antony, was in a state of extreme happiness solely for entering on cue, said brief garment was given an added enhancement that would be best described as measure for measure.' Really, Harry? Isn't that just a little beneath you? And that's a rhetorical question, so no smart-ass response. You know, I won a Pulitzer for investigative reporting when I was thirty-three. Look what you have brought me to."

"Play the violin somewhere else. My string section is full. You've been telling me that sob story for four years. You wanted to make a switch to Features because you wanted quiet."

"Yes, I did. But I got you."

"You know I'm the best theater critic in New York."

"I saw it on a bus." Steve began pruning again. "About this review," he said, getting back to his original subject, "my phone has been ringing all morning. Sasoon is beside himself."

"He's morbidly obese. He's beside himself every day."

"That's not funny. Body shaming is not acceptable. I sent you to a class about this. And more to my point, Sasoon said he's going to get every Broadway producer to pull their ads from *The Herald-Sun*. Do you know how that will sit on the 10th floor? Corporate is beside themselves."

"Maybe their other half can get together with Sasoon's and all of them can have a four-way. A quadruple?"

"That doesn't even make sense."

"Neither does this conversation. Who cares if they try to pull their ads? They need us. They won't pull the ads. Anyway, it's not my job to care about the ads. And the controversy will get us attention. I bet I'll be on CNN."

"Ah, true love requited at last," Steve said, turning his attention to another rose plant. "You're speaking at the theater league luncheon today, aren't you? It's your last public duty for this newspaper before going on sabbatical. I don't know why anyone would take four weeks off in March and go upstate."

"The North Mountain Lodge is more than a century old, been completely restored, has a three-star kitchen, and I can work on my new book undisturbed. If I went some place in season, I would never write. Too many people would recognize me and buy me cocktails. And it's impolite to say no to a free cocktail. A gay man can never refuse something with a compound name comprised of the two most important body parts. Cocktail is like 'jug-handle' to a straight man, although that is a noun and a verb. But you get my point."

"Hardly ever," Steve said as he cut some more blooms and put them into a small vase. "Well, you must deal with your adoring public this afternoon. The league luncheon is in the rotunda of the Spencer Building, yes?"

"Have I ever told you about my cousin Rotunda?"

"Every day for four years. She doesn't exist."

"She's a big woman, Rotunda. Big, black woman," Harry said imitating his formidable first cousin.

"She doesn't exist. Your cousin, Rotunda, does not exist. It's an invention just like your other cousins, Beaujolais, Frappe, and that infamous slut, Demi-Glace."

"Lordie, you cut me to the quick, Steve. Not to mention the relative. Demi-Glace is no slut—she's just friendly. I don't have to stand here and have my relations insulted. I must go. I must *go*," Harry added for dramatic effect.

"Yes, you must, Harry," Steve said from behind a large fern he was trimming. "You have a luncheon. Entertain the theater ladies. Try not to offend anyone. You just have to kick off the event. Think of yourself as a literary aperitif."

"You know I had a cousin, Aperitif, but she now identifies as a man, so we call her Aperol."

"Go!"

◆ ◆ ◆

The Spencer Building is a great example of Beaux-Arts architecture, and its soaring rotunda is often rented out for catered events. The Empire Theater League was as old as The Spencer. A remnant of a more elegant time when people dressed for the theater and the only "f" word heard on Broadway was Fontanne.

The League held two luncheons each season, one in the fall and one in the early spring. Theater luminaries, rising stars, and chorus boys with connections mingled with old and new money over a five-course meal. Harry was asked to open the program, give a few amusing remarks, and then introduce the cast of the new musical version of *Gilligan's Island*. Harry had reviewed the show in February and wrote, "A three-hour cruise that ended in being shipwrecked on an uncharted island was a more pleasurable experience than this two-hour journey with Gilligan, Skipper, and all the rest."

It was going to be a bumpy afternoon.

Harry breezed into the rotunda. He was in his element. These were his people, theater people. They lived and breathed the same Henry Higgins' oxygen as he did. Dressed in head-to-toe Prada, he looked more like a well-tailored man of a "certain age" in a print ad than a theater critic. Harry looked good. And he knew it.

Chesney Latrice greeted him as he entered. She was the *grande dame* of the League, a big fan of both Harry and the stirred gin martini. Harry adored her.

"Ah, there he *eees*," she said in an affected accent. Harry was not sure where Chesney picked up her accent. It was not French, Italian, or European. It sounded more Bombay, as in Sapphire. "My dear, Pick*eee*. You were very bad today. I love *eet*. That little toad of a man has ruined the stage. He deserved what you wrote. I saw his *Hedda Gabler* last year. What a disaster, my dear Pick*eee*. What did you write?"

"Hedda Lettuce would have been better in the lead. And she would have. Hedda Lettuce is creative, original, and fun."

"Yes, yes, you mean, sex*eee* man. I love *eet*. Well, you know he is coming, that toad, that pig, that Sasoon. He bought a table. I must confess, I hate him, but I love his mon*eee*. Be prepared my precious Pick*eee*. Gird your loins."

"I always have protection, my dear Ms. Latrice."

"You wicked, wicked man. Ah, look, there she *eees*," Chesney said as she turned her attention away from Harry and toward another arriving guest. After she was gone, Harry was left with the faintest scent of Channel No. 5 mixed with gin. It reminded him of his mother.

As he turned toward the dais, the rotunda went silent. He pivoted and saw Dimitri Sasoon by the entrance with members of the cast of *Julio*. If looks could kill, Harry would have been a dead man. The maligned director, with a twenty-something boy on each arm, strutted toward Harry. "I spit on your Prada, you pathetic newspaper hack," Sasoon said as he spit on the floor.

"Better Prada than *schmatta*," Harry said, ignoring the spittle that just missed his right shoe. "What were you wearing the last time I saw you in Balthazar? I think it was a banquette. I must say, not everyone can wear vinyl like you."

"You think you are so smart? I make more money than you. *Julio* will run for months because of you and your smug, snide, stupid remarks."

"Congratulations. But it doesn't change the fact that your production of *Julius Caesar* is an abomination. It lacks taste, coherency, and vision. It is not my concern if people want to pay for garbage, but in my opinion, *Julio* should be put inside a brown paper bag, dropped on your doorstep and set on fire. It's crap. And that is what one does with crap."

"Crap? You say crap?"

"I say crap."

"You will rue the day that you said 'crap' to me. I will cut you like so many pieces of bacon. And I know how to cut up bacon."

"I quake in fear, not of you and your bacon-cutting skills, you untalented little man, but of what next you will put on the stage. Have you no respect for Shakespeare, for his transcendent use of the English language? How can you defile him to satiate a poorly conceived homoerotic fantasy? You spit on my Prada? I won't waste my spit on you. You're as worthless as a Manhattan made with bourbon. Good day, sir."

Harry turned on his heels and walked to his seat at the dais, leaving Dimitri Sasoon speechless. Sasoon made a loud "hrummp" and grabbed his two "twinks" by their arms and went to his table. The luncheon attendees who heard the conversation spread it to those who had not. Before Chesney Latrice introduced Harry fifteen minutes later, the exchange between Mr. Picky and Sasoon had been tweeted throughout the theater community.

Chesney went to the microphone to begin the program. "My *deeers*, welcome to the Empire Theater League's Spring Luncheon. As you see outside, the snow is melting; spring is almost here. And what a winter we have had. So many shows. So many adventures in the dark, as I like to say. And we have a special treat today. New York's own Mr. Pick*eee*, Harry Douville, who has had his share of adventures in the dark this season as well. I have asked him to talk about his job and what it is like to see theater day in and out. I give you Harry Douville, our very own Mr. Pick*eee*."

Harry was king of the world. The audience applauded, minus a table to his far right. Sasoon was seated with the *Julio* cast near a wall of the rotunda, his back to a faux marble column. He went to spit on the floor in protest, but one of Sasoon's "twinks" brushed his hand along Sasoon's thigh, causing Sasoon's head to jerk up as he spat, sending the nasty projectile into the face of George Washington, no relation to the Founding Father, but a two-time Tony-winning actor, seated at the next table. The audience gasped and tweeted simultaneously: "Demitri Sasoon spits on George Washington."

Washington was both a big and an unhappy man, a bad combination, like scotch and vermouth. Washington rose like a cresting wave about to capsize Dimitri Sasoon as if he were the SS Poseidon.

"Do you have a problem?" Washington said, moving toward Sasoon.

"No, I was spitting at that hack up there?"

"Really? He is not sitting in my direction. Are you saying I look like Harry Douville because we are both black? Do all black men look the same to you?"

Harry said nothing at the microphone. He, like everyone else, was transfixed by the unfolding drama. It was getting him a little sexually excited, too. Impending physical violence did that to Harry.

"I love black men," Sasoon fumbled. "In fact, I have had many black men."

"Do you think I'm gay, then? Do you think I'm attracted to you?"

"No, I didn't say you were gay."

"I'm not gay. You know I'm not gay. There's nothing wrong with being gay, but I'm not gay. So why are you calling me gay?"

Everyone in New York knew George Washington was gay, but no one would publicly say it. But they might, and in fact did, tweet it: "George Washington is gay." Unknown to the luncheon attendees, not only was the theater community now buzzing across New York, but the Daughters of the American Revolution were apoplectic in all thirteen of the original colonies.

"I didn't call you gay," Sasoon said nervously. He was trying to pull his chair as close to the table as possible for protection. He might have to hide under it.

"I, for one, want to hear what Mr. Douville has to say. There are not enough honest voices writing about the theater. There is too much trash on Broadway. And you are the trash king of the Great White Way."

"I don't want a problem," Sasoon said meekly. He was fearful he might soil himself at any moment.

"You are crap," George Washington boomed across the rotunda. "Crap" echoed everywhere. "You spit on me! You spit on George Washington! And now you cower like a weasel. Be a man or forever be a pile of defecation." While the conversation was riveting, it was a real buzz kill on the *pate de foie gras*. "You should leave. I insist you leave."

Sasoon turned to Harry, who had yet to say anything. "You win this round, Douville, but I will win the war. I may leave this luncheon, but I will triumph. You wait and see. *Julio* lives. Long live *Julio*!"

"Are you leaving?" George Washington said. "Or will I have to escort you out?"

"I'm going," Sasoon said, but as he attempted to rise from his seat, he could not. He had wedged himself under the table so that his girth was caught between the tabletop and the faux marble column behind him. He struggled to free himself as his two boy toys attempted to push him from below. There were all sorts of groans and sighs from the table as the three men labored.

Harry, who had been standing silent at the microphone, said, "Someone call 911. I think we need the Jaws of Life."

The room erupted in applause. Harry was king of the world.

◆ ◆ ◆

Three hours later, Harry was back in Steve's office. Mulrooney was buried in a Ficus. He looked up and said to Harry, "George Washington is gay."

"No wonder he slept around so much. You know that might explain why he lost all his teeth."

"Stop right there. There are some things that are sacred. He was the father of our country, not its queen."

"That's funny, Steve."

Mulrooney ignored Harry. "I heard all about what happened at the luncheon, as has most of New York. Your review is the most read, e-mailed, and shared story on our website. I don't know how you do it."

"I'm the best, that's how."

"The problem is you keep telling me and everyone else that. A little humility goes a long way."

"I'll remind myself of that when I'm driving upstate tomorrow morning. You won't see me for four weeks. You'll miss me."

"We'll always have Paris," Steve said, sniffing a rose. "I don't know how the theater will survive without you."

"I don't either," Harry said almost seriously. "But nothing is opening for four weeks. It will be quiet in town."

"Yes, it will. Whenever you are not here, Harry, it is quiet."

"I'm wounded."

"Save the theatrics for the moose and antelopes upstate. I don't know how you will manage away from Manhattan."

"The North Mountain Lodge is an oasis of civilization in the nether reaches of New York. They still dress for dinner."

"Then pack your evening pumps. You really are something else."

"I am Mr. Picky."

"I know. I know. I read the busses. Let me get back to my Ficus."

"Did I ever tell you about my cousin Ficus?"

"Go!"

◆ ◆ ◆

Harry spent a few hours at his desk, sending out e-mails and setting his review schedule for mid-April. The following month would be busy with openings. Harry took a cab from *The Herald-Sun* to The Pierre, where he would have a martini in the lounge. He loved The Pierre. It was old New York without feeling old. His maternal grandmother lived there, but she was away visiting other grandchildren across the South. The headwaiter, Jerry, knew Harry and brought over his martini just as he liked it—Grey Goose very cold, straight up, and no fruit of any kind.

An attractive bearded man in his mid-fifties was seated at a table across from Harry. They made eye contact. The man was appealing and interested, but Harry was not up for it. Perhaps not the right phrase, because Harry could be up for an attractive man around his own age even if he wasn't particularly in the mood, but he was tired and had a long drive ahead tomorrow. There would always be attractive men at The Pierre and Harry always waited for the other man to make the first move, forcing that man to expose his interest first. Harry raised his martini glass and smiled at the bearded man. Harry finished his drink and left without turning back.

The next morning, the sun was shining brightly. It was near 50 degrees, very warm for March in New York. Harry crossed the lobby of his apartment building, wheeling his suitcase.

Marco saluted him: "George Washington is gay."

"I didn't write that."

"It's all over the Internet. There's a YouTube video of Dimitri Sasoon being pulled from his table. It's hilarious."

"He should have worn Lycra, I'm just saying. He should have worn Lycra."

"Are you going away for business, Mr. Douville?"

"Sort of business, sort of pleasure. I need some time away to finish my new book. It's about my life as a theater critic. The working title is *Picky on the Aisle.*"

"Enjoy yourself."

"I will. I'm writing about me," Harry said with a smile as he walked out of his building. There were barely any traces of snow on the sidewalk. And Harry could have sworn he heard birds singing as he walked the three blocks to his garage, where he picked up his car.

He put the suitcase in the trunk and eased his tall frame behind the wheel. He adjusted the mirror, turned on the radio, popped in a CD, and pulled out of the garage, heading north. The traffic report said there was little outbound traffic. It was a perfect morning as Harry turned his back on his beloved Manhattan.

Inside his BMW, he felt as if he were still at home. Renee Fleming was singing Richard Strauss as the tall buildings of the city twinkled in the sunshine in the rearview mirror. Ahead lay a break at a luxury mountain retreat where he would be feted as befitted "Mr. Picky." Life was more than good; it was the way it was supposed to be.

Nothing could go wrong. It was a perfect day. Harry glanced at the clock on the car's console to check the time and noticed the date. It was the 15th, the Ides of March.

II

Harry had been driving for more than two hours when he saw the sign for Greens. It was a large, wooden billboard, faded like the hotel it heralded as being a mere two miles ahead.

Dozens of similar weather-worn billboards still dotted the secondary roads off the thruway leading drivers to some long-forgotten Manderlay—post-Mrs. Danvers' redo. The Catskills was once the premiere destination for middle-income and working-class families from

New York. It's where Baby came to learn how to dirty dance while her sister did the hula in a musical revue rated P, for parve. This was where bad jokes came to die, and on a cold winter's night, some say you could still hear the sound of an accordion wafting through brisket-scented mountain air.

Grossingers, The Concord, The Granite, The Pines, The Nevele, Browns, and, of course, Greens. These resorts were little sovereign city-states like the Vatican, except they had pools, tennis courts, and banned shellfish. That was long ago. The Catskills had been dying for decades up through the 80s, and then the hotels finally gave up the ghost. Now, two decades into the 21st century, there was no pulse.

Casinos were supposed to change everything. Casinos might bring one or two hotels back to life in a new form, but there would never be dozens of fabled resorts across the Catskills ever again. In their heyday, these hotels, with their state-of-the-art theaters, launched the careers of many an entertainer, as well as cushioned the fall of stars dropping from orbit. The history tugged Harry out of his driving lethargy. He wanted to see the inside of one of these places before they were all gone. Maybe there would be a column in it or an anecdote for his book. It would only be a slight detour into a small town where he could find out if Greens was still open at all or if there was a caretaker on the grounds who would give him a look inside.

The sign for the Greens' exit beckoned ahead like a mermaid on a rock. Harry took the exit. There were no cars on this secondary road. About two miles along, he saw a chamber of commerce sign: Welcome to Hemlock. Founded 1827. "We tan your hides."

That certainly got Harry's attention. While his leather fascination trended toward Prada, there were a few secret fetishes he would rarely admit to and as he pondered one of them after reading the sign, he realized he was getting an erection.

He saw a main street up ahead. On his left were Vandergelder's General Store, a hair salon, a wig store, a butcher shop, and a diner. On his right were a post office, another hair salon, a storefront church, an old movie theater, and a sprawling Victorian house that had been converted into a bed and breakfast. The street ended at a traffic circle. Inside the circle stood a flagpole and a statue of a man holding up a belt. The man was Henry Whitmore, the founder of New York Tannery, once a leading producer of leather for belts, wallets, and shoes in this region. The hotel resorts killed the tannery businesses because of the attendant smells. Now, the hotels were gone as well, leaving the people of towns like Hemlock with nothing but the lingering chemical damage of tanneries and thousands of brined briskets.

Behind the small traffic circle was a federal-style municipal building. There was no one walking on the sidewalks. Cars were parked diagonally on both sides of Main Street. Harry looked for another Greens' sign at the traffic circle. But there was none. The circle fed into another road that was at a right angle to Main Street. Should he go left? Right? Some people choose to go both ways, he thought. There was never a singing and dancing scarecrow when you needed one.

What Harry also needed was a restroom. He parked in front of the diner. It looked right out of the 50's. Lots of chrome. Big plate glass windows. He could see inside a row of booths lined up against the windows. There was a long counter across from the booths. He walked inside.

"A customer," a slim young man said. "Welcome. Would you like a booth or do you want to sit at the counter?"

"A booth," Harry said. "But where is your restroom?"

"Just past the counter. Make a left at the picture of Carol Channing. You can't miss it. I will set you up at the booth at the far end."

"Thanks," Harry replied. The young man twirled around and headed toward the counter. Harry chuckled to himself and walked toward the restroom, checking out the other diners as he went. Two men in the front booth were buried in their menus, another set of men sat two booths down, and three other diners were loudly talking to the cook in the open kitchen behind the counter.

Along the walls were pictures of Broadway leading ladies—Ethel Merman, Mary Martin, Barbara Cook, Angela Lansbury, Patti LuPone, Bernadette Peters—it was a shrine to the women of Broadway.

Harry saw Carol Channing and went left. Bea Arthur stared at him over the urinal.

When he walked back into the main sitting area, he noticed the customers were all looking at him. Harry checked his shoes and fly. All were in order. Yet, he was aware he was under scrutiny.

"What are you talking about?" a very large woman of color said as she came from the kitchen. "Who did you say was here?" She saw Harry and pointed. "It's you! The evil one. Harry Douville. Why are you here? You want to close this place, too?"

"I don't know what you're talking about," Harry said nervously. The woman reminded him of a bigger, younger version of his maternal grandmother.

"This is my diner. I call it Divas. It is dedicated to the women of the theater, the women of the theater who thrived despite people like you who closed theaters like Rudy Giuliani off his meds."

"What are you talking about? I don't know you."

"Shawna Capers."

"Sorry."

"I was in the 2002 revival of *Hello Dolly*!"

"I remember you now," Harry said. "You were terrible as Dolly."

"You wrote the leading lady is so bad, the show should be renamed *Goodbye Dolly!* and the cast would be better served if they skipped the Harmonia Gardens for dinner and left the theater to go directly to Joe Allen, where a poster of this flop would already have been hung on a wall in the restaurant before the second act curtain."

"You were bad. You were very bad."

"I was poorly directed."

"To an acting career, I would say."

"You can't come into my diner and disrespect me. Leave."

Other diners stood up and shouted, "Leave. Leave. No Picky. No Picky."

"I played Lancelot in *Camelot*," one diner said. "You wrote you wished I could have blended into the scenery so a stagehand would have removed me like a tree."

Another man spoke, "I was Biff in *Death of a Salesman* and you wrote that while a resemblance to Willie is not a bad idea in casting Willy Loman's son, Biff is supposed to be his son, not his older brother."

Another man: "You closed my show."

"Mine as well," from yet another.

"You said if the Marconigram on the Titanic tapped like me, no rescue ship would have ever come," a lanky 30-year-old said.

"What is this place?" Harry asked. "The Island of Misfit Actors?"

"You're in Hemlock, Mr. Picky. This used to be a great town that supported the trade up at Greens. Lots of actors and stagehands worked here during the summers. Now, it's a sanctuary for actors who had their careers destroyed by you."

"You're kidding?" Harry responded.

"Do we look like we're kidding?" Shawna Capers said. "As Dolly Levi says, 'Wave your little hand and whisper so long dearie.' Get out of my diner."

Harry realized he needed to go. He was sweating, which was uncharacteristic. He walked briskly out of the diner and got into his car. The diner patrons followed him outside. He could see people coming out of the stores and shops. He backed out too quickly and his car careened into the flagpole in the circle. The pole snapped and landed between the legs of the statue of Henry Whitmore.

Two policemen came running out of the municipal building, guns raised. As Harry was being led into the municipal building, one of the cops said, "I played Herod in *Jesus Christ Superstar* and you wrote they crucified the wrong man."

"You were fabulous, Bernard," the other cop said.

Harry winced.

After spending two hours in a holding room where he was forced to listen to the original cast albums of a musical version of *Gone with the Wind* and a Spanish-language production of *Annie*, Harry was delighted to be brought into a small office.

A short, squat man with a shock of black hair and long sideburns sat behind a desk. He looked like a compressed Elvis. Harry tried to think if he had ever slammed him in a review.

"So, the famous Harry Douville has come to Hemlock," the demi-Elvis said. "I'm Sheriff Franklin Shepard."

"Like in the musical *Merry We Roll Along*?"

"I hate musicals."

"I thought everyone here was an actor."

"Hemlock was a great place until they started coming. First one, then another, then the next thing you knew, everywhere you turned was an Equity-carrying, down-on-his-or-her-luck actor. You used to be able to walk across the town and say good morning. Now, people are tapping, kicking, and singing. Everything is a friggin' production number. It makes me want to vomit. What's even worse, they recruited my daughter. Yes, siree. My little girl, Julia. I don't care whether you're gay, straight, black, white, brown—you can get it on with a flock of sheep—I say live and let live, but I draw the line at musical comedy. Musical comedy, it's an oxymoron, Mr. Douville. There's nothing funny about musicals. People singing and dancing—it's just not natural. I wanted to build a wall to keep them out, but you know what the townspeople said after they finished singing and dancing the first production number from *The Music Man* at the town meeting when I suggested building a wall? They said it would be like a fourth wall and they would break it. I don't even know what that meant aside from that it was pointless to build a wall. Untalented actors are like cockroaches; they just keep coming and coming. Roaches."

"Have you thought about becoming a theatre critic?" Harry said, both horrified and impressed.

"Here's the deal, Mr. Douville," Sheriff Shepard continued as he tapped his short, hairy fingers on the desk. "We can play a legal dance here. You can get a lawyer. You can plead not guilty to the willful destruction of public property—an act witnessed by many, I might add—but I will make sure you are denied bail because you're a flight risk, impound your car, and call the New York City papers and make you the laughingstock of Manhattan or we can do each other a favor."

"A favor, Sheriff Shepard?"

"My daughter loves reading you. She thinks you're a god. And she wants to be in the theater."

"I can't give her a good review."

"Did I ask you to?" the sheriff snapped. "She has a degree in theater. Her mother insisted that I let her go to Syracuse and she got a useless degree in theater, but so far, no jobs. So, she is back home with me and her mother. Every day she is at that goddamn piano singing about 'My White Knight.' It's like chalk on a board."

"She can't sing?"

"She can sing. But it's those damn show songs. Whatever happened to rock and roll? Whatever happened to Janis Joplin?"

"Drugs."

"It was a rhetorical question, Douville. Here's the thing. Each year, these no-talent people of Hemlock stage a musical, thinking people will come and see the natural beauty of Hemlock and someone will invest in Greens and restore the property. And each year, they put on the worst, goddamned show ever. Did I tell you I hate musicals?"

"Yes, you did. How do I fit in?"

"I want you to direct their show."

"I can't direct."

"They can't act, sing or dance. It's a perfect match."

"You know, that's almost a line from *Fiddler on the Roof*."

"You're testing my patience, Mr. Douville. I hate musicals. I hate that musical the most. They did it here last year. Tevye was a gay little person named Karl from Ohio."

"That *is* a song, 'Summer in Ohio,' by Jason Robert Brown—doing summer stock 'with a gay midget named Karl playing Tevye and Porgy.'"

"Do you want me to reinstate the death penalty? Enough with the showtunes. If you direct the show, the charges are dropped. If you don't, I will see that you are stuck in a cell for the next four weeks."

"I don't think I like this. What's the show?"

"*The Sound of Music*."

"I hate *The Sound of Music*."

"Flattery, Mr. Douville, won't work with me."

"No, I really hate it. I love Rodgers and Hammerstein, just not that show."

"The show is scheduled to open April 12. Four weeks. We'll put you up in town."

"Four weeks in a cell or four weeks directing *The Sound of Music*. It doesn't sound like there's much of a difference. I was supposed to be spending the next month at the North Mountain Lodge."

"We'll put you up here. There's a nice bed and breakfast in town. You won't mind the showtunes."

"Everyone hates me here."

"Everyone hates you everywhere."

"Well, that *is* true."

"They hate you because you destroyed their lives. Here's your chance to make it up to them. Make them better. Just one more thing."

"What now?"

"You have to cast my daughter as the lead."

"As Maria?"

"Maria. Gladys. Pippi Longstocking. I don't care as long as she's the lead. Give them a show. Make my daughter happy. Then you can be on your way."

"You're not giving me much of a choice."

"You're not in Manhattan, Douville. This is the real world. I'm in charge here. Welcome to Hemlock."

◆ ◆ ◆

Harry weighed his options. He could call someone in New York to try to extricate himself from the clutches of Hemlock, but he also knew that it would become a gossip item. Dimitri Sasoon was looking to get even. He said as much. All the nasty, untalented townspeople would have a field day making a mockery of him, Harry Douville. More than anything, Harry cared for his reputation for being smarter than everyone else in the room.

When Sheriff Shepard said the musical was to be staged in the old theater of Greens, Harry began thinking there was a way to make limoncello out of this lemon. He had wanted to scout around Greens. If he spent four weeks in its theater, roaming the grounds, maybe he could get a book out of that—the lost theaters of the Catskills from Mr. Picky's perspective. Maybe something good could come of this, he thought. He told the sheriff he would give it a try, but since the sheriff didn't completely trust Harry, his BMW was impounded. His luggage was taken to the Rodgers and Hart Bed and Breakfast across the square. Everything in Hemlock had a showtune name.

It was an attractive Victorian structure with a wide wraparound porch. Toward the front, there was a dining room, a large sitting room with a grand piano, and a sweeping staircase to the bedrooms on the two upper floors. Harry was to be given the front room on the third floor. It was called the Tower Room because it had windows in the turret.

Harry was greeted by the manager, Leon Prince. Leon was, of course, an actor. Not as old as everyone in town, about forty-five, Harry guessed. He had a short career as a male ingenue, but his hair had an even shorter lifespan. He had gone mostly bald at twenty-six and bought himself a hairpiece he called Mortimer, or Morty. Leon was in pretty good shape, and he wasn't as hostile as the people in the diner. Apparently, Harry had closed the last Broadway show Leon had been cast in, but his part was too small to be of notice. Leon told Harry that the show *Clean Cole*, a story about strip mining in rural Kentucky interspersed with Cole Porter tunes, was indeed an abomination, and he held no grudge against the theater critic. In fact, coming to Hemlock was the best thing that he could have done.

Leon liked running a B&B, and he had persuaded Phillipe, an old friend living in LA, to come join him. He would be arriving later in the spring.

"You'll like Hemlock, Mr. Douville," Leon said. "It's very pretty here. And friendly."

"I wasn't feeling any love this afternoon. And please call me Harry."

"They will come around, Harry. They are all excited about you directing the musical. Despite what they say, they all respect you. They know they are terrible. They just didn't like that you wrote that. They will come around. You just have to make nice with Shawna Capers. If she accepts you, you're in."

"I don't think that will happen, Leon."

"The theater is a place of magic."

"If Doug Henning comes back into fashion, I'm all set," Harry said sarcastically.

"Did anyone ever tell you you're a negative personality?"

"Everyone on the west side of Manhattan."

"Harry Douville, I heard you were in town," a man said, coming down the stairs carrying a dachshund.

"George Montross," Harry said, "what are you doing in Hemlock?" Harry knew George Montross, a theater set designer of limited abilities, for many years. Harry found himself conflicted by George's work. There was always a small element of a good idea, but somehow it never worked.

"I should not be nice to you, after all you have said about my work, but we are to be collaborators."

"How is that?"

"I am doing the sets for *The Sound of Music.*"

"In God's name, why?" Harry asked.

"Leon is my nephew. Don't give me that look, Harry. He really is my nephew. My sister's son. I gave him the down payment for this place. I figured it might be a good retirement place for me and Otto." George pointed to his dachshund. What was also notable was that they were identically dressed. Head to toe to paw in Burberry.

"I can see you here, George," Harry said.

"Don't be catty with me, Harry. I'm not as foolish as people think." George added with emphasis.

"Understood," Harry said. For the first time, he respected George. He liked the pushback. It didn't happen often. "You have ideas for the set?"

"Not really. Do you want to go over to the theater and see the space? Auditions are scheduled for tomorrow."

"Lead on, George."

George, Otto, and Harry climbed into Leon's Mini Cooper. They drove about a quarter mile before reaching the entrance to Greens. It was startling. The sign was too big for the site. Faded. Scary. Enticing. As the car bumped along the pitted drive, Harry's heart started pumping. He didn't quite know why. It was a long time since he felt human.

The main building, designed in a faux Tudor style, was in fair shape. The brick needed repointing, but vandals had not stripped the place of its last piece of dignity. The theater was a separate building connected by an open-air passageway to the building's northside. To the west of the building was what was left of the pool and tennis courts. The theater loomed like an unburnt Thornfield Hall.

"Let's turn on the juice," Leon said as he unpadlocked the stage door. Inside, Harry could smell the age—musty, stale, but rich in history and promise. Harry, usually meticulous, ran his hand along the dusty call board near the door. He was smiling.

"You look strange," Leon said to Harry.

"He looks happy," George said. "Otto agrees." Otto's tail was wagging.

"Don't be ridiculous," Harry said, trying to contain his glee at walking inside a piece of history. "I'm never happy unless I'm having a martini at The Pierre." No one believed him.

Harry walked onto the stage. Leon lit the ghost light first and then went to get the house lights. It was not a glorious space. It was part barn and part Vegas. It was garish in its day, in deep greens with white flourishes. The seats were faded now. The walls showed some water damage and the large lighting fixture—a collection of glass globes assembled in some formation that was high-style in 1964 suburbia—was covered in dust. But the bones were good. The stage was large and fanned out from the proscenium arch. Harry could see there was a section of flooring that could be removed to reveal the orchestra pit.

He walked out into the house and looked at the stage, pulling his phone from his pocket. He started making notes. "How are you with ramps, George?"

"Better than with stairs. My knees are going."

"Any other time, I would crack a joke at your expense, but not now," Harry said animatedly. "I'm thinking a framework of a set. Ramps— semi-circular ramps on either side that go up to a second level and then upstage on that level small similar ramps to a third level and again to a fourth. All the ramps wrap around a central mountain. I want that the focal point—one big Alp that is in the middle of all the action."

"I like that, Harry. I can do that."

"Great, George. Is there any place to get a martini in this town?"

"I make a great martini," Leon said.

"Maybe this won't be so bad," Harry said.

◆ ◆ ◆

Harry tried to remember his optimism when auditions started. The townspeople came out in force, including the diners from Divas. The pianist was the music teacher at the neighboring high school. He would recruit adult musicians who had retired to Hemlock for the orchestra.

Harry needed to find a lot of women to play nuns. Not surprisingly, there were not a lot of women living in Hemlock. That led Harry to add a question to the audition sheet, "Are you comfortable playing a woman on stage?" Not only did every man reply that he could play a woman, but one response read, "Praise Jesus, yes!"

"I would like to audition for the Reverend Mother," Shawna Capers said. She was challenging Harry not to cast her. She was dressed as Pam Grier in *Foxy Brown*. Shawna was a big woman, and she was flaunting it. Harry and George sat eight rows back from the stage and watched Shawna turn "Climb Every Mountain" into a sexually suggestive song. While the moves and interpretation were downright scary, her voice was strong. She had the top notes, and she was a real woman. Harry cast her.

The awkward greeter at the diner who directed Harry to the restroom was cast as Rolf. The few women were all cast as featured nuns. That left Harry still without von Trapp children, a Captain von Trapp, and the Baroness, and he still had not heard the sheriff's daughter Julia read or sing.

When she arrived, Harry was delighted. Julia was beautiful, could sing, read well, and looked the part. But he still was missing most of his principals. "This isn't good," Harry said to George. "I still don't have a Captain, children, or the Baroness."

"Try Leon, he didn't audition," George said. "Have him read for the Captain. He just lacks confidence."

"Leon, could you read with Julia?" Harry said, walking over to Leon, who was standing near the stage. "I just want to see how it looks." Harry was open to any idea. Leon was the right age.

"You want me to read?" Leon asked. "I don't act anymore."

"That hasn't stopped anyone in New York. No worries, just read," Harry said.

Leon was nervous. He looked the part, but he was not stern or commanding. Harry cast him anyway. He would find a way to bring out his confidence. He was, after all, Mr. Picky.

"I think I may have to cast a man as the Baroness," Harry said.

"You have men playing nuns...why not the Baroness?"

"Men as nuns are not screaming drag. The audience might not even notice. But I would need a man who could be a woman."

"You know how many times I heard that?" George said with a mischievous smile. Harry's opinion of George was rising by the minute, and although, he would never admit it, Harry thought Otto was adorable. Today, he and George were in Prada. "The dachshund wears Prada," Harry said to George when he saw them come down for breakfast earlier that morning.

"Why don't we call it a day?" Leon said from the stage. "You've cast almost the entire town. There's barely anyone left. Except Sheriff Shepard."

"Well, he won't try out. I think I may be on shaky ground casting his wife as the housekeeper, but she seemed pleased,' Harry said. "She wasn't bad. I can see where Julia got her talent. When do we see the children, Leon?"

"There are two elementary schools nearby and one high school. I set up auditions in the high school tomorrow at 4 p.m. You only need seven."

"Like the Seven Samurai," George said, remembering one from his youth who was impressive with and without his blade. "I will start on the set. I will order some lumber. I'm thinking of using plaster of Paris over metal mesh to make your Alp. I'm going to see if I can recruit some high school kids from a shop class to help build the set."

The three men and dachshund went back to the B&B. Leon had a new guest checking in before dinner. His name was Gene and was from New York. He was in his mid-forties and slightly built. If he had been Asian and about twenty years younger, he would have been George's usual type. As it was, Gene was an amiable guest. He also was starstruck that he was staying in the same place as Mr. Picky.

"I can't believe it's you," Gene said. "When I tell my friends at The Crow that I met you they won't believe me. Actually, most of them won't really care. There aren't lots of showtune guys at The Crow, but it's my place."

"I've been to The Crow," George said. "Years ago. Nice dive bar. Big hunky guy behind the bar."

"John. He's the owner."

"Nice man. Not my type, but a nice piece of Kobe."

"Never been," Harry said. "Where is it?"

"Buried in the West Village."

"Let that not be on my tombstone."

"They won't bury you, Harry. They will cremate you, hopefully after you're dead."

"I didn't know you had this bitchy side, George. I really like it."

"I don't know you," Gene said to George, "but I like you too." Gene smiled at George.

Harry started formulating a plan. "Do you sing, Gene?"

"Not much. I always wanted to sing, but I have a high voice and it's not very pretty."

Harry went over to the grand piano by the bay window in the main sitting room. His maternal grandmother had forced him to take lessons, and he was rather good. "Let's try something, OK?"

"OK," Gene said nervously. "What do you have in mind?"

"What's your favorite musical?"

"It's silly."

"There are silly actors. There are silly plays. There are no silly favorite musicals."

"*Damn Yankees*. I love Gwen Verdon. I used to sing 'Whatever Lola Wants' in my bedroom when I was a kid. My dad walked in once when I was imitating Gwen Verdon from the film. It was more embarrassing than if I had been jerking off. It was then that he knew I was gay and a disappointment."

"OK, Gene. There are no silly favorite musicals. But those were downright silly asinine things to put in the same sentence," Harry said, sounding more like a father than his usual autocratic self. "Being gay is not a disappointment; it's an enhancement. It makes us a little smarter, a little edgier, a little more interesting because that's how we do more than survive in a straight man's world. I think of being gay as having an 8-inch dick."

"You have an 8-inch dick?" Gene asked, taking Harry literally.

"If you do, they should call you Mr. Dicky, not Mr. Picky," George added.

"I was trying to give a pep talk here," Harry added, just a little bit annoyed. "Leon, do you have a tablet I can call up the music for 'Whatever Lola Wants?'"

"I can do one better," Leon said. "I have vocal scores to everything. In this town, vocal scores are like baseball cards." Leon pulled *Damn Yankees* from a shelf.

"Gene, I want you to sing this song like you're sixteen in your bedroom, your father never walked in, and I want you to be Gwen Verdon. Can you be Gwen Verdon?"

"I will try."

Harry began to play and little by little, Gene shed his inhibitions and was Gwen Verdon in body, but with a lighter voice. Harry took it further. Can you read music?"

"Not really. But I can pick up tunes quickly."

"Great." Harry played one of the Baroness' songs. "Now I want to hear you sing it in falsetto, but I don't want you to sing like a drag queen doing falsetto. Don't force it. Think Julie Andrews."

"Can I be Barbara Cook?" Gene asked.

"Gene, you can be anyone you want as long as she's a soprano," Harry said.

Gene started singing, and in falsetto, his voice had more heft. Vocally, he was perfect.

"Gene, can you be a woman?" Harry asked.

Gene blushed, embarrassed and excited. He was a 45-year-old man in search of an adventure, and he was finding one in Hemlock, New York.

Leon took the initiative. "Gene, let's get you settled. Let's have a nice dinner and some cocktails, and then after dinner, let me take you upstairs and do a little costume magic. I have a nice collection of costumes and makeup and let's see what we come up with. It will be fun. Like Halloween."

"OK," Gene said, trying to hide his growing excitement.

After dinner, Leon took Gene upstairs while Harry and George had a cognac. Otto munched a biscuit at George's feet. Leon came down first, stood at the bottom of the stairs, and looked up with a grand sweeping hand gesture, "I give you the Baroness."

Gene, holding the railing for dear life, came slowly down the stairs. He looked like a dead ringer for Eleonor Parker in the film version of *The Sound of Music*.

"How do you feel, Gene?" Harry asked.

"Like a woman," he replied. "Like a real woman."

Harry and George high-fived. Otto barked. All Harry needed was his von Trapp children. The next day went equally well. Children and teens came out of the woodwork when they heard Harry Douville was involved in Hemlock's spring musical. By cocktail time, *The Sound of Music* was cast.

The next seven days were more of a struggle. Harry had never directed a show, so he needed time to devise blocking. His set idea of ramps and platforms would not materialize for another week, so he had to have mostly bad actors grasp movements on levels not yet built.

The first read-through was tense. The townsfolk burned by Mr. Picky were initially resistant to his direction, and Harry, not known for being patient, had to keep his quips to himself because Sheriff Shepard's daughter and wife were in the cast. He had to be on his best behavior.

Shawna Capers wasn't trying to be funny when she auditioned like Foxy Brown; that was her one note—a sexy, black woman from the 70s. Leon was timid. Gene was self-conscious. Only Julia was solid from the start.

Harry was not going to accept defeat. The more he delved into the project, the more he began to understand what the people he had spent a lifetime picking apart actually did. As a theater critic, he saw the final product—good or bad. But he had never spent quality time in the creative process that takes a cast from its first read-through to its opening, and sometimes if Harry hated the show, to its closing on that same opening night.

The more Harry worked with the untalented actors, the more he realized they were more than untalented actors—they were people with dreams, and there is no such thing as an untalented dream. Harry had never been hampered by having dreams bigger than his abilities. He became exactly who he had intended to be—he was Mr. Picky, feared and revered. But Harry also began to realize he didn't have what these untalented actors had, which was a community.

He wanted to tell them in his best Mr. Picky voice that he had saved them by destroying their pathetic careers—he wanted to say it that way. But Harry did not say it that way. Or in another way. While he tried to make them actors, they, in turn, were making Harry a person rather than a personality.

Week two, the set arrived, and so did the return of Mr. Picky.

"It's a penis, George! It's a tall, thin, fucking penis!" Harry had his first look at the set. The ramps and platforms were as Harry envisioned, but instead of an Alp in the center, there was a tall, narrow plaster of Paris penis.

"I don't think it looks like a penis," George said defensively.

"Really?" Harry said sarcastically. "Maybe you need to take a look at a penis. Someone show George a penis."

It was fortuitous that no children were present when nearly thirty men did just that.

"It was rhetorical," Harry said. "Wow," he added when he noticed the size of the third nun from the left's penis. "I don't want a penis. I want an Alp," Harry continued to rant to George. "I can't have the von Trapp children singing 'My Favorite Things' around a penis. We'll be arrested."

"I'm using high school shop kids," George explained, "I said I wanted a towering mountain."

"Find some straight high school shop kids," Harry said as he stormed out of the theater.

By week three, Harry had started having lunch at Divas. Shawna Capers and Harry mended their fences when he applauded her after she sang "Climb Every Mountain" in character, not as Foxy Brown.

It wasn't that Shawna was all that good, but she was no longer all that bad. Harry had begun to realize that many directors had to make the best of the cast they had, not the ones they wished they had. The von Trapp children had learned their lines and were staying as focused as little children can stay focused. The male nuns had proved more challenging.

One of them, Harvey, the less-than-boffo Biff in *Death of a Salesman*, had proven to be a prankster. He liked cracking up other actors during rehearsals. Harry had little patience for such nonsense in Manhattan, but in Hemlock, he had to roll with the vagaries of the personalities. He knew he was being tested by the cast, and the more he could withstand, the more he could push the cast.

At the beginning of the third week, George unveiled the new Alp. It was no longer a penis.

"You gave me a giant breast," Harry exclaimed. "It's a breast."

"You wanted wider. I gave you wider. You wanted straight high school shop class kids. I found straight shop class kids."

"I don't want a breast."

"It's not a breast. It has snow on the top."

"That's not snow on top—it's a titty. It's a nipple. A nipple! There are no nipples on Alps."

"You're projecting that nipple. There's no nipple."

"George, it's a wide, round breast with a nipple. It needs to be taller, green in the middle, grey with white snow on the top. It's supposed to be part of the Alps. A mountain with no nipple. I can't have little kids walking around a large breast. This is *The Sound of Music* for Christ's sake!"

"I am doing my best, Harry. I'm not working with an experienced crew. I told them to build me something that you could imagine climbing on top of. You wanted me to find straight 17-year-old boys in shop class."

"I don't care how you do it, George. Tell them whatever you have to tell them. I want an Alp, not a breast or a penis. A mountain. The song says to climb every mountain, ford every stream. Oscar Hammerstein did not write about genitalia."

George decided to bring both the gay and straight shop kids together and see if, collectively, they could make one mountain. Meanwhile, Harry continued to work the cast. The rest of the set was in good shape; it was just the mountain in the middle that was wrong.

Harry found himself increasingly pleased by the experience. It was nothing like anything he had done before. He could still be smart and snarky when he wanted, but he found himself surprised by how much he enjoyed not being either for a short while. The little children in the cast had no clue who he was. Their parents knew of him, but the kids had never heard of Mr. Picky and when someone called him that, one of the youngest children in the cast thought that meant that he picked his nose. Harry in New York would have chopped such an offender into tiny pieces, but in Hemlock, NY, inside the theater of Greens, Harry just fell down laughing.

He laughed uncontrollably so that everyone around him started laughing because he was laughing, and when Harry thought he regained his composure, he started laughing again. He would never think of Mr. Picky quite the same way.

Aside from the mountain, the show was in good shape by the final dress rehearsal. The new mountain was shaped out in mesh and covered in plaster of Paris. George promised his crew would work through the night and the next morning to get everything poured and painted.

Harry had turned his lemon into limoncello.

III

Harry woke up early. He was nervous about how the show would play out. He looked out his window and saw his BMW parked out front. Sheriff Shepard was no longer concerned that he would skip town, so his car had been released from impound. Harry realized that tomorrow he could drive back to Manhattan, back to his former life. He longed for The Pierre, but as he surveyed the center of Hemlock from his bedroom window, he felt a tinge of regret.

He looked down the street and saw George walking Otto. His heart skipped a beat. He rushed downstairs still in his robe.

"George, why are you wearing that wig?" Harry asked.

"It's her birthday. April 12. Ann Miller's birthday. Every April 12, I put on this wig and tap shoes. So does Otto. Otto was wearing an identical large brunette wig. Normally, George would have put specially made tap shoes on Otto's paws, but the streets of Hemlock were not like the Brooklyn Heights' Promenade that George and Otto lived near. He would save the taps for later.

"I love Ann Miller," Harry said. "I have an Ann Miller wig on a bust of Arthur Miller at my desk at work. I didn't know you liked Ann Miller."

"She was a goddess, Harry. Mocked in her later years, but a great dancer and a glorious symbol of the old studio system."

"I don't know what to say, George. She's my guilty pleasure. I didn't know anyone felt that way about her except me."

"You're not going to get all emotional on me, are you, Harry?"

"No," Harry said, checking himself. "It must be all this fresh air screwing up my brain. But this being Ann Miller's birthday is a sign. It's going to go well. Yes."

"I agree," George said.

Harry had asked the cast to assemble in costume at 7 p.m. for cast photos. They had the day free until then. George spent the afternoon with Gene—they had become a couple.

As rehearsals had progressed, Gene gained confidence as a man by playing the Baroness. He told George about his fantasy of meeting Gwen Verdon, which could no longer happen since she was dead. George told Gene that he had met Verdon several times and showed him pictures of the two of them at a restaurant.

Gene was more than impressed. He had spent so many years at The Crow picking at crumbs that he didn't know what it felt like to be sitting at the main table. Almost no one at The Crow even knew what he did. He was an adjunct university history teacher with the winter/spring semester off. He had been worried about losing the income this year, when he didn't pick up some classes, but it turned out well.

George was just the kind of man Gene wanted. Flamboyant, eccentric, boring, and predictable. George was at first distant, but as Gene incorporated the Baroness into his off-stage persona, George began seeing a man closer to his age who had the sexiness of a 25-year-old Asian chorus boy and the maturity of a man who understands good first acts are easy; it's the second act that makes the show.

George wanted a good second act. He wanted more than spending his free time sitting along the Brooklyn Heights Promenade with Otto, looking for adventure to come to them.

Gene had called John, the bartender at The Crow, to tell him that he was playing the Baroness in *The Sound of Music*. Gene didn't have many close friends; his life played out at The Crow. John didn't deliberately tell anyone about Gene's call, but as it would happen, Dimitri Sasoon was slumming with Todd Pinner, the set designer who created the ill-conceived South Beach look for *Julio*. It was Pinner who heard John mention Harry Douville's name and the town of Hemlock.

Pinner knew some former actors who had moved to Hemlock after their careers were ruined by Harry. Once Pinner had a piece of damaging information on someone, he ran with it. His Hemlock friends explained Harry was directing a production of *The Sound of Music* and that George Montross was designing the sets. For Pinner, this was too perfect. He detested George almost as much as he detested Otto, who had peed on him when Pinner said Otto and George looked ridiculous in matching outfits.

After Pinner told Sasoon about the show, Sasoon called two other major print theater critics and a local news show with a theater critic. They would all take a road trip to Hemlock and embarrass Mr. Picky.

Harry was blissfully unaware of this plan at 7 p.m. when he was ready to face his cast before the photographer took some shots on the stage and they readied for the performance. Harvey, the prankster nun, came up with the idea of all the male nuns putting on fake ink mustaches for the photo. He thought it would be hilarious to have all the male nuns look like Hitler. Harry chuckled when he saw the nuns, allowed them to take a photo that way, and then told them to take them off. They couldn't. Harvey had applied a super glue to the mustaches instead of a spirit gum. The mustaches wouldn't move.

Harry went online looking for a solution, but there was none that would work with so little time. All the male nuns looked like they were aping Hitler. This was not a good sign. If that wasn't bad enough, George's crew was still applying the last touches of paint on the wet plaster Alp. But Harry had to admit the Alp finally looked good. It was massive.

Harry and George got their next whiff of impending doom when John and Ben, the resident jokester of The Crow, showed up backstage looking for Gene. They said Gene had called them, and they wanted to show their support. Harry and George wondered if anyone else in New York knew about the show. George went to look for Gene, and Harry went to check the front of the house.

Leon, who was still nervous about playing the Captain walked past John and Ben. "You OK, handsome?" Ben asked. "He was partly playing with Leon and also slightly attracted to him. Leon looked good in his costume.

"Nervous," Leon replied. "I never played a romantic lead role. I never had to kiss a woman on stage or off."

"Neither have I," Ben said.

"Sorry, guys," John said. "My lips have been everywhere."

"Well, here's a good luck kiss just to make sure your lips are doing the right thing," Ben said and grabbed Leon by his ass, moved in close, and kissed him hard.

Leon was speechless.

"You OK?" Ben asked. "I didn't mean to offend you."

Leon remained speechless. He wasn't offended in the least. He smiled broadly as his posture changed. His chest expanded and he stood at his full height. Leon looked every bit the Captain von Trapp. As Mel Brooks might have put it, apparently the best way to become a von Trapp is to get von shtupped.

"Break a leg," John said.

"Yeah, same from me," Ben added. "What's your name?"

"Leon, but you can call me Captain." Leon turned and walked back toward the dressing rooms. His stride was longer. Two of the nuns noticed the change.

"What got into him?" he asked his brother sister.

"I don't know, but if it's the tall guy in the T-shirt, I'm amazed he's walking at all."

Harry didn't notice that Gene was chatting with John and Ben when he came backstage. Gene kept repeating the same word, "Sasoon. Sasoon. Sasoon."

George came over to him. "I just saw it on my phone. Dimitri Sasoon heard about the show, and he has brought New York critics and a camera crew."

"I will be the laughingstock of New York," Harry said. "I have Hitler male nuns, a male Baroness, and a Reverend Mother who still looks like Foxy Brown. What else could go wrong?"

There was a rumbling, then a crashing sound, followed by a splat. The much plastered and painted Alp had just fallen into itself. It was 7:58. No time to adjust. The curtain would go up. Harry went out into the now-darkened house and stood in the back to survey the damage.

The lights went up. Maria entered to applause. But instead of a long narrow penis, or a wide breast with a nipple, or the majestic Alp that Harry had envisioned, there was a splayed mass of paint and plaster that looked like only one thing—in the middle of Harry's Austria set, there was a massive vagina. The ramps led to the vagina. The platform surrounded the vagina. Harry stood there in the dark aghast, mouthing, "vagina, vagina, vagina."

And so, the show progressed. The male Hitler nuns. Foxy Mother Brown. A pitch-perfect Gene as the Baroness, but Harry doubted the illusion worked. The children were fine but thrown by the vagina. They weren't sure whether to enter it or skirt it. The same was true for Foxy Mother Brown and Maria during "Climb Every Mountain." The plaster had spread onto the platform where their scene was staged, so they were playing the scene just downstage of the vagina. "So long farewell" was sung around the vagina, and the final scene had the von Trapp Family Singers not leaving Austria over a mountain but into a vagina.

The audience appeared to like it, but these were people used to Hemlock productions. There were two top New York theater critics in the audience, plus a TV crew who swooped in at the final curtain to get a shot of the cast standing in front of the vagina.

Dimitri Sasoon saw Harry. "What a tragedy, Mr. Picky. The toast of New York dies in Hemlock. Just like Euripides."

"It was Socrates who drank the hemlock, you little toad," Harry said. He could at least still sound like Mr. Picky. "I'm surprised they let you out of New York. I'll be even more surprised if they let you back in," Harry added.

"Don't be high and mighty with me. In about two hours when those two colleagues of yours file their reviews and that TV crew edits its footage, you'll be history."

Todd Pinner, who was standing with Sasoon, added, "And this will kill Montross' pathetic career. Where is he? That set was a mess."

George walked over to the men. Otto followed. They were still in Ann Miller outfits.

"Who are you supposed to be?" Pinner asked. "Lainie Kazan?"

"Ann Miller," George replied with more dignity than his outfit would suggest. "It's her birthday."

"You look more like Arthur Miller. And who likes Ann Miller?"

"She was a great actress," Harry said.

"I spit on Ann Miller," Pinner spat in George's general direction.

Otto did not take insults lightly. Otto tapped—George added the specially made dog tap shoes once they got inside the theatre—over to Pinner, raised his leg (and Otto had a good extension for a dachshund), and peed on Pinner's shoes.

"Your dog just pissed on me."

"He's a dog," George said. "You spit at me. What's your excuse?"

"I won't take this. You will be destroyed by midnight. You and your wig-wearing, tap-dancing dog." Pinner exited. Dimitri Sasoon turned toward Harry, "I'm going to enjoy tonight for the rest of my life. April 12th—the day I took down Mr. Picky."

Dimitri Sasoon left the theater. Harry and George stared at one another.

If nothing else, they had become friends. Other cast members gathered around the two men. Harry should have been upset. He knew the reviews would make him into a joke, but he looked at his absurd cast—the Hitler nuns, Foxy Brown, Gene, Leon, and the talented Julia— and he saw friends. He was taken aback by the flood of emotions. In this sad little town, in this once great Catskill resort, he found a family.

"Let's get good and drunk," Harry said. They did.

At 12:30 a.m., the first review in *The Times* was posted online:

Sound of Music reborn for 21st century
By Michael Hartnett
The Times

There's an adage that those that can, do. And those that can't, write. Inside the catty world of theater, it's been said that those who can't do either become critics.

Many a disgruntled actor would happily raise a glass of *schadenfreude* if Harry Douville's—my colleague at *The Herald-Sun*—first foray into directing was a disaster. They will be disappointed. Put down the *schadenfreude* and raise the champagne flute. What Douville has done to *The Sound of Music* is a brilliant allegory on Nazi Germany and modern America.

The show is staged around a giant vagina—yes, a vagina. But this vagina does not offer monologues but instead gives birth to the good and bad in our society. When Maria enters, she is surrounded by it, by her fear of being sexual. The children dance around because it shows the fertility of Captain von Trapp. Seven children! But its brilliance is during the climactic scene where the Reverend Mother tells Maria she must face her feelings for the Captain. They sing outside the vagina. At the song's conclusion, the Reverend Mother enters it, returning to the womb as the great Earth Mother she is. It is sheer brilliance.

The cast is spot on, from newcomer Julia Shepard's glorious soprano to the hard-edge Reverend Mother portrayed by Shawna Capers, not seen in New York for many a year. Douville has shown the dichotomy of the Catholic Church by casting a feisty, worldly woman of color as the leader of a group of cloistered nuns. Capers' strong performance as a woman of color shows us the power of the Church. But by having most of his nuns don Hitler mustaches,

Douville is raising questions about whether the nuns and the Church were too close to the Nazis. And that the Hitler nuns are played by men, Douville is showing the conflict between Hitler's Fatherland and Austria's Motherland. Again, this is brilliance.

Gene Cassava as the Baroness was another stroke of genius. He is both beautiful and commanding as the ice princess. When played by a woman, the Baroness often comes across as rich and spoiled, but Cassava shows she is playing a part she was born to play. She is trapped in a role. He brings a level of poignancy to what is often a throwaway part.

While I could write more about this great production, I must close by saying George Montross should get a Tony—if there were one for really off-off-Broadway— for set design. His is a vagina for the ages. Someone should bring this production to Broadway. Perhaps to the William Gillette Theater, where that abomination *Julio* will certainly have closed, soon leaving a vacant house on the Great White Way.

Until then, at least in Hemlock, NY, the hills are alive with the sounds of music and the thrill of great theater. Harry Douville's production is revelatory. All hail, Mr. Picky!

The review in *The NY Tribune* and on NYC 8, the 24-hour cable network, were equally glowing. Not only was the show a hit, but *The Times'* reviewer had taken a jab at Dimitri Sasoon.

Despite the revelry of the previous night, Harry was sitting in the dining room of the Rodgers and Hart Bed and Breakfast at 8 a.m. He had to make his own coffee; no one was awake. He was reading *The Washington Post* online when George entered.

"What are you reading?" he asked, looking for the coffee pot.

"*The Post. The Washington Post,*" he added so there was no confusion. "There's coffee in the kitchen. I had to make it. Leon isn't up yet."

"He was up all night," George said. "Isn't that right, Otto?"

Harry peered over the screen and saw Otto wagging his tail. He looked different. It took Harry a moment to realize Otto was not in any matching outfit. Otto was naked and George was still in his bathrobe. "You're letting Otto let it all hang out this morning."

"He's among family," George said, heading into the kitchen.

"Indeed," Harry said, petting Otto's exposed belly. "You had a big day yesterday, too. You peed on Todd Pinner. You're alright in my book, Otto."

Otto barked approval. He liked being naked.

"Please, please, my head," Leon said, coming down the stairs in just his boxers. Harry had never looked at Leon barely clad. He had a good body—his chest was broader than Harry would have surmised from his usual posture, and there was a light trail of hair that traveled down his chest to his lower abdomen. He looked sexy.

"Do you have any coffee, babe?" a male voice said, also coming down the stairs. It was Ben from last night. He clearly had spent the night with Leon. He was in briefs.

"Am I the only one who dressed for breakfast?" Harry asked, amused by all this semi-nudity.

"This is what it's like living with men, Harry," George said, coming out of the kitchen with a coffee. "Didn't you ever have a roommate in college?"

"No. I didn't like people much. And sex was sex. There wasn't a group."

"Pity," Ben said, grabbing Leon's ass. "I need coffee."

"In the kitchen," Harry said, going back to his computer screen.

"You're very nonplussed," George said, sitting down at the table with his coffee. Thankfully, Harry noticed, George's bathrobe was closed. "We're a hit, Harry."

"George, you know this kind of thing doesn't last. Even if the whole show's success wasn't predicated on a series of mistakes, it doesn't last. I write review after review, shows open and close, but none of this lasts. The accolades, the pans—it's all fleeting.

"That's why this is important," Leon said.

"Male nudity?" Harry asked in his Mr. Picky voice.

"Family, Harry. That's what theater is all about—family. Instant family when you're in a show. Lasting family when you're not. Either way, it gets you through the horrible slings and arrows of Harry Douville's reviews."

Harry didn't respond. He pretended to read the article on the latest crisis in the White House, but he knew Leon was right. He knew he enjoyed every minute he had spent in Hemlock and that he would miss these men.

"Where's Miss Thing?" Harry asked still trying to sound unaffected by emotion. "Where's the Baroness?"

"Vienna," Gene said coming down the stairs. Like Leon and Ben, he was not dressed, but wearing very tight briefs. He also was wearing George's Ann Miller wig.

"Do not ask," George said to Harry before he could open his mouth with a comment. "Give me a kiss," George said to Gene.

"Have you brushed?" Gene said as he glided across the dining room toward his new boyfriend. "And I wasn't talking about his teeth," Gene said coyly to the room as he ran his hands across George's abundant chest hair.

"This is getting way too adult for me," Harry said, closing his laptop. "It seems everyone paired up but me. I'm going over to Divas for breakfast since I don't think I'm going to get any food here before I drive back to New York. I can give you a ride, George?"

"No, thanks, Harry. Gene and I are going to stay through the week and come down for Easter. The three of us are going to do the Easter Parade, me, Gene and Otto."

"Of course you are," Harry said.

"Ben and I are going to join them," Leon added with his hand on Ben's lower back. "Want to come, Harry?"

Harry normally would have said, "I would rather swallow cracked glass," but instead replied, "Maybe." He walked outside the large Victorian house. His BMW was parked in front. On the windshield was a piece of paper:

Dear Harry:

Thank you. Three agents have already called my daughter Julia, talking about representation. You gave her a good start, and she is leaving for New York tomorrow. And I heard there's an investor interested in restoring Greens.

Come back to Hemlock. We'll take care of you.

Sincerely,
Sheriff Franklin Shepard Inc.

P.S. I got the "Merrily We Roll Along" joke. My daughter has played that CD for years. I just didn't want to give you the satisfaction of knowing what your joke was about!

Harry smiled. He wondered if the sheriff really hated show tunes or if it had been an elaborate con to force him to launch his daughter's stage career. It didn't matter now. Harry strolled over to Divas. He walked inside.

It looked much as it had four weeks earlier. Ethel, Patti, and Carol were all on the walls. But the people inside were no longer hostile strangers. The awkward greeter had been turned into the 17-going-on-18-Rolf, the suitor who woos a von Trapp and then betrays the entire family. There were the nuns, the assorted Nazis, other characters, stagehands and crew. And then there was Shawna Capers, Mother Foxy Brown herself.

"Give me some sugar," she said to Harry as she hugged him and squeezed his ass. Harry hadn't been felt up in years and never by a real woman. "You got a nice ass, Mr. Picky."

The diners let out a cheer.

"Last night was amazing," she continued. "My old agent called. He thinks he can relaunch my career."

"You're coming back to New York?" Harry asked.

"I told him no. This is where I belong. Last night was wonderful. I will always have that memory."

"We'll always have Paris," Harry interrupted.

"Exactly, girlfriend. This is where I belong. This is home. This is my family."

"I keep hearing that this morning," Harry said. "I always thought family was overrated."

"It is by people who don't have one. You're always welcome here. I've named a sandwich after you."

"I'm afraid to ask what's in a Mr. Picky."

"It's called the Douville, so there. You're not Mr. Picky here. You never were. The Douville is really a Monte Cristo or a *Croque-monsieur*. I may use the French explanation on the menu because it's fancy, and you are fancy."

"You want to make me cry," Harry said with a smile.

"I don't reach for the stars, honey. A smile is good enough for me."

They embraced. Harry made the rounds of the diner, shaking hands, and hugging. It was emotional, not as emotional as the final goodbye at the bed and breakfast would be later, but Harry knew he would see those men in New York soon enough. He would see them all again, Harry realized—that's what having a family is all about.

Harry got in his BMW and headed toward the thruway. Renee Fleming was still in the CD player. Harry switched to Sirius and searched. He found the channel. Janis Joplin was singing "Me and Bobby McGee."

"This is for you, Sheriff Franklin Shepard Inc. This is for you."

IV

"What happened to the North Mountain Lodge," Steve Mulrooney asked behind a rose.

"Did you miss me?" Harry said, sitting down in the editor's office between two rose plants.

"It was very quiet until last night. You were busy on your sabbatical. Are you going to direct now?"

"My phone was ringing all the way back to the city. Offers to do plays. Even to transfer my vagina concept to film. I told them all no. I like writing. That's who I am."

"You're Mr. Picky, Harry."

"Yes, that's part of who I am, Steve. But I want to be Harry more of the time. I like Harry."

"You're going human on me," Steve said. "I can't have you human. I can't have you life-sized."

"What am I, Alan Swann?"

"I don't understand."

"You fed me a line from *My Favorite Year*."

"You see, you're Mr. Picky. Always a theater line. I need you nasty, Harry. Nasty sells newspapers, gets clicks online."

"I can tap into that. I just want a little more. Was thinking about writing a book."

"Wasn't that the reason for your trip?"

"This would be a different book. It wouldn't be about me but about this town in upstate New York where a group of actors who could never find life in the theater found life in the real world.

"You want to kill me, Harry? That's what this is about? I don't want happy. 'Mr. Picky goes to town and loses his mind.'"

"You know, I like part of that title. I may use it," Harry said, standing up. "Don't worry, I can get mean for the next Dimitri Sasoon production. I heard he was being driven back to New York when he read the online reviews of my show. He was sitting in the passenger seat of an SUV and was so upset by the good reviews that he slammed the dashboard so hard with his laptop, it engaged the airbag. They needed to get the Jaws of Life."

"That's my Harry. Think mean. Now go. You're bad for my flowers. You suck out all the oxygen in the room."

Harry left Steve to his plants and headed up to The Pierre. He wanted a proper martini. Jerry greeted him at the entrance of the lounge like a returning hero. He could hear the buzz in the room—vagina, vagina, vagina—it was electric. Harry smiled his Mr. Picky smile.

He sat back in a chair, stretching his long legs. It felt good to be back in the city. He looked across the room and saw the handsome bearded man he almost flirted with a month earlier. Harry signaled to Jerry. "Bring my martini over there," he said pointing to where the man was sitting. "I'm going in."

Harry stood up and, with a big smile and extending his right hand, walked over to the man who was nursing a Manhattan. "May I join you? My name's Harry Douville."

Searching for Clooney

"I'm getting another beer. Do you want one?" Jay asked.

"I'm the designated driver, remember?" Kyle said. "I already had two. That's my limit for the evening."

"I forgot," Jay said with a smiling pout that would have worked so much better on Kyle if Jay was twenty-five years younger, hairy, and blond. How many times had this same scenario played out over the past twenty-eight years, Kyle thought as he watched his slightly younger friend navigate the bar like a politician working a rope line.

Jay had a way of saying hello, putting his large right hand on a man's shoulder and moving slightly into the unsuspecting face so the guy had no choice but to stare into Jay's hazel eyes. Usually, Jay moved on quickly as he worked his way to an open spot to order a drink, but when the eyes locked on something irresistible, he lingered, standing close to the guy but not too close. It was instinctive with Jay, yet Kyle liked to imagine that Jay, when 20 and illegally getting into bars, learned his technique from some older man who had a ruler and measured out the exact distance like snooty butlers did with glasses and cutlery in the dining rooms of grand English houses on British television.

Kyle wanted to be in an Edwardian drama, while Jay was perfectly content being in some guy named Ed from Woodland Hills. They had worked together decades earlier—Kyle was older and more experienced at work. Jay was younger and more experienced at play. Their friendship made little sense because their interests were not similar most of the time. Yet somehow, they had become brothers, listening to each other's failures and successes in life and love.

At present, both were unattached. For Kyle, that was not unusual, but Jay always had a relationship going or as Kyle would say, "a relationship going badly." For a man who wanted to play the field, Jay had a way of getting entangled in impossible situations. He would hook up with a slightly younger man who screamed trouble, but Jay wouldn't hear it. A man's penis can do many things; listening is not one of them. After some weeks of fun, Jay would be ready to move on, but the other guy would have already moved in.

It was a pattern that would repeat like a pastoral scene on toile wallpaper, over and over again. Jay was currently between bad choices. The last guy, Phillipe, wouldn't move out, so Jay did. And it was Jay's house. Phillipe was planning to move to New York in another month. Most of Jay's exes had to get far away from Los Angeles. Phillipe was moving to a small town in the Catskills where Leon, a friend of his, lived. Phillipe and Leon were unsuccessful actors, and Leon had said this little town was just like heaven with a little theater scene; when you walked down the street, you felt you had firm support. When Jay told that to Kyle, who had spent his childhood lip-synching to Angela Lansbury singing from *Mame*, such a small town sounded like perfection. Jay, whose sensitivity came from a bottle of Boy Butter, responded it sounded like a jockstrap.

Tonight, the unlikely duo was on the town—if that's what a bar crawl through West Hollywood was for gay men nearing sixty. Older single gay men have two options: embrace being a Daddy to some youngster who probably will leave you when he realizes your sexy, silver chest hair runs all the way up to your nostrils and ears, or look for a man your own age. The latter requires an admission of whatever that age is, and when it comes to age, gay men can only subtract, not add.

Jay enjoyed being a Daddy, but he did not want to end up with a young man as a life partner. Yet, he continued to pursue the younger men who stroked—among other things—his ego. Kyle would point out the flaw in Jay's pattern. That was followed by Jay pointing out how Kyle continued to drool over inappropriate men, as well.

So, this evening was another night for the two myopic homosexuals to prowl. They started at Backlot, a retro bar on the eastern end of Santa Monica Boulevard in West Hollywood. Backlot was a nod to old Hollywood, and it got a mix of older men, and younger men attracted to older men. There were some men in the middle, but not many. It was a highly polished space—everything was reflective, the black faux marble floor, the walls with too many long, vertical mirrors, the sides of the ebony piano in the front room, and the shiny bald domes of the men who lined the banquettes staring at the asses of the younger men who got their drinks in the circular second bar in the back room.

The music was live in the front—a pianist playing show tunes, some energetic Broadway queens belting out songs from *Gypsy* ("for me, for me, for me!"), a varying cast of lawyers, bankers, and agents in suits mingling with more casually clad, usually younger men. In the old days, Backlot had been a bar called Bugsy, after the gangster Bugsy Siegal. But the place was poorly managed and over time, Bugsy stood for insect and rodent infestation. The owners of Backlot had the place gutted. No one mourned.

Kyle had moved from the back room where he had been talking with Jay to the front of the bar. He liked the piano area in small doses. The crowd was still small at this hour—just past 9 p.m. Jay could still manage to stay out late, but Kyle would start shutting down by midnight. The pianist was playing songs from *Follies*. Kyle decided to break his vow and ordered a white wine—three drinks would not be a game-ender for driving home hours from now. And he would drink it slowly because he really didn't like white wine, but red in a bar full of drunks was a cry for a dry cleaner.

There was a handsome man on the other side of the piano, younger than Kyle, but not by much. Kyle guessed early fifties, with a broad smile that matched the shoulders. He was wearing a blue dress shirt that opened down two buttons, in shape but not slim, which appealed to Kyle because you can't trust a man in his fifties who looks like he lives at the gym. The man was having a good time, and Kyle could see light sweat marks on the shirt. Their eyes met, and the man smiled and raised his martini glass. Kyle raised his glass and smiled back.

He was inclined to move when he felt a large hand on his shoulder. It was Jay. He was drinking a beer.

"So, Kyle, see anyone you like?"

"Well, actually, yes. Other side of the piano."

"The guy in the black T-shirt with the arms?"

"No, two over. The guy with the martini and the brain."

"He's not bad. Let's go over there."

"I don't know."

"Of course you do. You're getting hard already."

Kyle, who knew he was not, still looked down.

"Made you look," Jay said before taking a swig on the beer. "We're gonna get laid. I can feel it."

"It's probably some guy's hand on your ass."

"It's got to start somewhere, Kyle. Loosen up." Jay unbuttoned Kyle's second shirt button. "Show the kitty," he said playfully, pulling at Kyle's chest hair. "Come on, or I undo another button."

Kyle followed Jay around the piano, and they stood behind the guy with the martini, while Jay checked out the guy in the black T-shirt's ass.

"It's a nice crowd tonight?" Jay said to no one in particular. It was his way of seeing who would turn around. All three men in front of them did—Kyle's guy with the shoulders, Jay's guy with the arms and ass, and the man in between the two. Jay extended his hand to the arms and ass. "I'm Jay and this is my friend, Kyle."

"Good to meet you both. I'm Charlie. I saw you both across the bar, checking me out."

"Only one of us was checking you out," Jay said.

"I hope it was your friend," Charlie said, much to Jay and Kyle's surprise. Charlie extended his hand to Kyle. "You looked like you knew your way around a showtune."

Kyle was taken aback. Charlie was drop-dead hot. "I like *Follies*," Kyle said. "It's one of my favorite shows. I saw the original in New York years ago."

"So did I," said the broad smile and shoulders. "Didn't mean to butt in."

"I like butts," Jay said trying to regain his game. "Butt right in."

"I'm Stephen, like in Sondheim," smile and shoulders said, extending his hand to Kyle first, then to Charlie, and then to Jay. "I saw you across the bar. I wanted to come over when you were mouthing the lyrics to 'God-why-don't-you-love-me-oh-you-do-I'll-see-you-later Blues.'"

"What's that?" Jay asked.

"The story of your life," Kyle said with surprising glee. He had never found himself the center of attention between two attractive men. "It's a song from *Follies* about a man who, when he gets the woman he wants, wants the woman he just rejected."

"It's a great song," Charlie added. "I played young Ben in summer stock last year."

"I can see that," Stephen said. "And I could see Kyle as older Ben," Stephen put his hand on Kyle's left shoulder.

"I agree," Charlie said, putting his hand on Kyle's right shoulder.

"I'm feeling left out, here," Jay managed with a forced grin.

"My name is Barry," the man seated between Charlie and Stephen said. If Stephen was smile and shoulders and Charlie was arms and ass, Barry was neck and ears. He didn't have the former and the latter reminded Jay of a head of cauliflower. He was between Jay's and Kyle's ages. "I'm not a big fan of show tunes. I only come here because there's a good happy hour. Did anyone ever tell you that you look like George Clooney?"

Kyle almost spit out his wine. Jay was a handsome man, but George Clooney? For starters, Jay had red hair—not so much ginger, as really red. Like firetrucks with Dalmatians red. Like jungle red nail polish red. He was tall, about 6'2", always with some reddish-brown stubble, and because he was usually animated, many a man said Jay reminded them of a hot Muppet. George Clooney was a stretch. Barry clearly wanted a piece of Jay. And you're not going to get laid if you ask someone if they know Kermit the Frog.

"I don't think I look like Clooney," Jay said. "But thank you. Clooney's a fine-looking man."

"You're fine yourself," Barry said putting his small hand on Jay's left bicep. Barry could not reach Jay's shoulder without standing on a box. "Let me buy you a drink."

"I don't know. I have to be careful driving."

"No, you don't, Jay," Kyle said. "Remember, I'm the designated driver tonight. Drink. Drink."

Jay shot Kyle a look. This was new territory for them both.

"What are you drinking?" Barry asked.

"Vodka. Definitely vodka."

Kyle, Stephen, and Charlie grouped together against the piano. They were singing from *Company*. Kyle was in the middle.

Jay was trying to shake off Barry, who had attached himself to Jay like a dog humping a leg. Jay was trying to be polite, but Barry couldn't take a hint.

"I can just see you in *Gladiator*," Barry said.

"That was Russell Crowe," Jay said.

"That could have been you, as well," Barry said squeezing Jay's bicep again. He really couldn't reach any higher. "*Ocean's Eleven*, that was him."

"That was him," Jay said throwing back the vodka.

"That was you," Kyle said pulling himself away from Stephen and Charlie. Kyle was thoroughly enjoying the moment.

"We really should get going," Jay said realizing that departing the bar was his only way out. "Kyle, we really need to meet up with our friends Robby and Jim."

Jay used the safe words, "Robby and Jim," the two most stay-at-home gay men they knew. Nothing would get Robby out of the house this late at night unless it was half off everything at Ralph's supermarket. When either Jay or Kyle brought up "Robby and Jim" when they were out in a bar, that meant it was time to leave quickly. There was no negotiation.

Stephen and Charlie both put napkins with their phone numbers into Kyle's pockets, which was very old-school in a smartphone world. Kyle loved it, and he did not want to leave, but this is what friends do for friends, and he could see Barry with no neck and a piece of crudité on the side of his head was going to be a problem for Jay. Stephen gave Kyle a kiss on the mouth and put his fingers on Kyle's chest as he said goodbye. Charlie gave Kyle a strong hug, almost lifting him off the ground and kissed him behind his ear.

Barry made a move toward Jay, but Jay shifted to the right and Barry ended up in the arms of someone who was singing "The Best of Times is Now" from *La Cage Aux Folles*. Jay and Kyle left the Backlot and started walking west on Santa Monica Boulevard.

"You owe me," Kyle said. "Pulling that Robby and Jim thing on me. I could have gotten laid—twice."

"You got numbers. Call them later. I couldn't shake Barry."

"It's your own fault, Mr. Clooney. Or should I call you The Cloonster?"

"You know I can hurt you."

"And I can call back to Barry."

"Let's go to The Prancing Pony. I like to watch those cowboy bartenders dance on the bar."

"It's because of the chaps."

"It's because of the chaps and no jeans."

"You're a real pig, Jay."

"I'm George Fucking Clooney."

"Yeah, right."

The two men walked ten minutes further west and went inside the ersatz western bar. There was loud country music coming from a jukebox. The floors were wide wooden planks, the tables were made of old kegs, and the bar had been meticulously scratched, etched, and distressed to look authentically old. Like many of the younger men in The Prancing Pony, it didn't quite come off as intended. The bar looked staged. That didn't really matter. The closest that the men gawking at the chorus boy bartenders in chaps had ever come to experiencing the Old West was Frontierland at Disney. And given the number of large, hairy men that hibernated in the back room every Tuesday night, a few animatronic bears with guitars would hardly have been out of place. This was not a Tuesday; the bear count was low.

"I need a drink," Jay said.

"Take it slow. You usually just do beers. You had two vodkas with Barry. George Clooney is into moderation."

"I need a vodka shot and then a beer. What do you want?"

"Stephen and Charlie."

"I'll get you a bottled water. Fizz or flat?"

"Definitely fizz. I'll get a table over there by the mirrors so you can see the men in chaps two ways." Kyle walked over to the right wall; the bar took up the entire length of the left side. The barmen were starting their routine. "This would be so much more believable if the guy on the far right didn't look like someone I saw in a production of *Hairspray*," Kyle said out loud, not paying attention if anyone was listening.

"You did. He used to date my roommate. My name is Sean. The dancer's name is Cyan."

"You mean like the color?"

"Yes."

"Jesus!"

"That's my roommate's name."

"Really?"

"No, I'm kidding. My roommate's name is...look, I don't want to talk about my roommate to a cute guy like you. Is that your boyfriend over there? The big guy with the orange hair."

"No," Kyle said. "He's not my boyfriend. We're good friends. Definitely not my boyfriend." Kyle felt he had entered a parallel universe where he was attractive and Jay was not. He liked this new place. "I'm Kyle."

They shook hands. Sean was Kyle's fantasy blond man. It was a little intimidating. "Is this your normal hang-out place?" Kyle asked.

"I don't go out much. I'm auditioning all the time. Actor, singer and OK dancer. Didn't get a part I was hoping for, so I thought I would wallow in my sorrows and a vodka cranberry. What about you? This doesn't look like your kind of place."

"How can you tell?"

"A vibe. The fact that you came over here instead of sitting at the bar where you can see the guys' asses up close was a clue."

"I'm more curious whether the chaps chafe with all that high-stepping movement."

"We could conduct a study. I'll take the guys on the left, you the ones on the right, and then we can compare notes. Or we could just sit here and talk. Did I tell you that you are very cute?"

"Here's your fizz," Jay said as he handed Kyle his sparkling water. "I'm Jay," he added, extending his large hand to Sean.

"I'm Sean." The two big men shook hands, trying to outdo the other one in strength. It was a draw. "I've been talking with your friend," Sean added.

"So I saw," Jay replied. "I don't think Kyle has ever been this social. He's very popular tonight."

"I expect he's popular all the time. Here's to new friendships." Sean raised his glass to Kyle's bottle of sparkling water.

"It would be more official if I had a real drink, but I'm the driver tonight."

"So that means you guys are traveling together?" Sean asked, the disappointment clear in his tone.

"That's the plan," Jay said, sounding more and more like Kyle than himself. Jay was beginning to wonder if his deodorant had failed and was going to sniff at one of his armpits when a small hand squeezed his left bicep.

"There you are," Barry said. "We all met a little while ago at Backlot. Doesn't he look just like George Clooney?"

"You're kidding?" Sean asked.

"He's not," Kyle responded. "I'm beginning to see the resemblance, just like Clooney in *Gladiator*."

"Exactly," Barry said.

"But Clooney wasn't in *Gladiator*, it was Russell..."

Kyle stopped Sean midsentence. "We know."

Jay looked like a big, caged animal. Barry was not letting go of his prey. Kyle turned to Sean and asked, "You want to see if Cyan is black and blue from the chaps?"

"I'm your man."

"I have no idea what you two are talking about," Jay said to Kyle and Sean as they headed to the bar.

"Let them be," Barry said. "We can talk a little more with an emphasis on the little more."

Jay downed his vodka. "I need another drink."

"I'll join you." Barry squeezed Jay's other bicep.

Kyle and Sean hit it off. They were talking and joking, while Jay couldn't break free of the humping dog on his leg. "We have to go now," Jay said to Kyle.

Jay had walked over to where Kyle and Sean were standing, just below Cyan. Barry was still attached to his left bicep. Jay was like a wolf with a foot caught in a trap. Barry trailed him across the bar. Kyle and Sean were looking up at Cyan, who was kicking up a storm in his boots and chaps on the bar. "Those chaps must get pretty funky by the end of the evening," Kyle said.

"You have no idea," Cyan shouted as he kicked higher.

Jay would normally be entertained, but Barry's hold on his bicep was beginning to bruise him. "We have to go, Kyle," Jay said again. "We just missed Robby and Jim and they're expecting us. Kyle, we have to leave—now."

"Are you sure?" Kyle said. "I think Robby and Jim might come back here." Kyle was enjoying the moment.

"Here's my number," Sean said. "Maybe we can get together sometime?"

Kyle took the napkin with the phone number—again, another old-school gesture—and put it in his left pants' pocket where Charlie's phone number was already stashed. Sean leaned into Kyle and kissed him. "I enjoyed meeting you."

"I did, as well," Kyle said before Jay practically lifted him out of the bar.

"This is insane. All these hot guys want you and I'm stuck with this no-neck with ears the size of Pomona."

"Now, now, Cloonster. This is not very becoming. You are the epitome of cool on camera. I'm really disappointed in you."

"This isn't funny."

"It's fucking hilarious. This is what I have gone through for years."

"You have never had Quasimodo humping your leg."

"True enough. Any way Quasimodo rang bells. You gotta ring them bells, you gotta ring them bells."

"That's a show tune, isn't it?"

"It's a Liza song."

"Whatever happened to talking sports?"

"Whatever happened to Baby Jane?"

"Don't change the subject. I hate when you get clever."

"I can't help that I am naturally adorable tonight."

"Keep this up and I will kill you like in *Gladiator*."

"That wasn't you. You're 'Oceans Eleven through Twenty.' You do suave."

"Suave my ass."

"I think Barry would like to do that. Ouch!" Jay gave Kyle's ass a friendly but firm swat.

"Come on, let's go to The Harness," Jay said.

"The Harness? You have to be kidding me? I don't do The Harness."

"You don't have to wear one. You'll be fine. This isn't a code night. You can get in like that."

"You just want to take off your shirt."

"I want to show off the merchandise."

"That's so 80s. No one is into brick-and-mortar anymore. It's all online."

"You can't touch online," Jay said as they approached The Harness. The entrance was on the side of the building facing a small parking lot. Men were gathered outside smoking and cruising. Kyle felt out of place. Jay had his shirt off before they made it through the door.

The Harness was dark. The tile ceiling had been painted black. The bar was black. The cement floor was painted black. Dim red lights illuminated the path to the men's room which was notorious for its trough inside and the phalanx of men who groped whoever passed by. The bar was not long. It was stocked with beer, scotch, whisky and tequila. That was it. Jay dragged Kyle to the bar.

"We can call a ride-share. Your car is in an all-night lot. I'll pay. You're doing shots and you're taking that shirt off. Let's have two beers and two shots of Jack Daniels."

"I don't want to take off my shirt," Kyle said right before a man crashed into him and spilled a beer all over his shirt.

"Now, you have no choice," Jay said, smiling.

"Man, I'm so sorry. I slipped on something on the floor. I don't even want to know what it was. You're soaked." Kyle wanted to be upset, but the shirtless man was very attractive. Dark. Muscled. "Let me dry you off." Before Kyle could object, the man had Kyle's shirt off and was drying his chest with his T-shirt that had been tucked in at his waistband.

"I'm Kyle," was all Kyle could manage.

"Craig."

"I'm Jay."

Craig didn't notice Jay. In a dark bar filled with big, muscled men, Kyle stood out. He wasn't out of shape, but he was not tall or sculpted. Because he didn't look like he belonged, he was a magnet, while Jay was just like everybody else.

"Let me buy you a drink," Craig said.

"I haven't even done this shot and beer."

"Do the shot and I'll buy you the next round and one for your friend...?"

"Clooney," Kyle said. He was a little buzzed. "Clooney."

"Like Rosemary?"

"Fuck!" Jay said. "Even here? Rosemary Clooney? Really?"

"What's with your friend?" Craig asked. "Doesn't he like Rosemary Clooney?"

"It's a long story. It had something to do with jerking off to 'White Christmas.'"

Jay was about to say something profane out of frustration when he felt a small hand on his shoulder. He turned around. It was Barry. A wooden crate was on the floor, and Barry was standing on it.

"My man, Clooney," Barry said. "This is my lucky night. I keep running into you."

"Did you put a microchip under my skin?" Jay asked rhetorically. "I feel like I'm being tracked like a lost dog."

"You're a mastiff," Barry said, putting his hands on Jay's bare chest. "I've thought about doing this all night. Such a strong chest."

Jay was wincing. He couldn't escape Barry. He downed the shot Craig had bought for him.

"I've only been in here once before," Kyle said to Craig. "This isn't my scene."

"I get that. But everyone needs more than vanilla and pure white. There's a lot of flavors and color."

"There's Cyan," Kyle said.

"I don't follow," Craig responded, perplexed by the specific color reference.

"No need to," Kyle said as he pulled Craig forward and kissed him on the mouth, moving his tongue inside. Anywhere else, Kyle would have been embarrassed, but not at The Harness. It was the booze, the night of flirtations, and now a dark, shirtless muscle man standing too close. They started to make out. Meanwhile, Jay was kicking back shots and trying to ditch Barry who would not take a hint.

"We're going to have to go," Jay said to Kyle. "Robby and Jim are waiting for us at Moonstone in Los Felix."

Kyle was trying not to pay attention to Jay, and he was doing a good job of it. He and Craig were kissing and touching, but Jay would not be ignored. He had not only pulled out Robby and Jim, but he also added Moonstone. That was the panic place. The place you sent people to that you never went to. It was the final ditch effort. Kyle didn't want to leave; he had had a good time. Craig wrote down his phone number on Kyle's arm. There was something sexy about having a man write a phone number on your arm. His shirt was still wet, but Kyle put it back on. He left it untucked and barely buttoned.

Jay told Barry to meet them at Moonstone. Jay knew that was not honest, but he could not shake Barry. It was either that or he would have to have sex with Barry. When Barry got to Moonstone two hours later, there was no sign of Jay or Kyle. But there was a guy who really looked a lot like George Clooney. Barry and the faux Clooney are now living together in Palm Springs.

Kyle followed up with all the men he met that night. Sean became a close friend. He introduced Charlie and Craig one night at The Prancing Pony. They dated for a while but split after they couldn't agree on who was the definitive Mama Rose in *Gypsy*. Stephen was the keeper. He and Kyle knew the answer was Angela Lansbury.

Jay's mojo returned the very next night when he went out without Kyle. A cute twink came up to him and said, "You look like the guy in *Gladiator*. Who's that actor?"

Jay responded, "George Clooney."

Our Lady of Mocambo

The Mocambo was the perfect Los Angeles creation: authentically fake. Its name came from a fabled West Hollywood nightclub of the 1950s. In keeping with the Latin American theme of the forgotten club, the developers of this open-air shopping mall created an ersatz tropical paradise with animatronic jungle birds, thick foliage, and a grotto. At the entrance to the grotto, past the palm fronds, visitors were greeted by an animatronic parrot, Sade, who beckoned all to proceed to the waterfall beyond, where until sunset, the music pumped faster than 30-year-old men at Equinox.

Adjacent to the grotto was a small restaurant with an upscale bar. During the day, The Mocambo was crawling with tourists from parts east of Los Angeles willing to plunk down credit cards or flash smartphone pay apps to purchase items from the very same stores that lined almost every mall in America. But at night, the bar at The Macambo Grill became the cruisiest place for LA gay men in late middle age. It was a respite from the bars on Santa Monica Blvd. further north, quieter than The Backlot, where the piano attracted show tune divas, and several steps up from The Prancing Pony.

The Mocambo Grill was classy; there were crisp, white cloths on every table. And the handsome Latino waiters, when they subtly grabbed your crotch as they placed a linen napkin on your lap, gave you a big toothy smile as they leaned in close to your face so you could smell their cologne, Babaloo, a Mocambo signature fragrance available for purchase at Desi, a boutique adjacent to the restaurant.

Elliot and Gil were visiting from New York. They had known each other for many years, both regulars at The Crow in the West Village, but it wasn't until this past New Year's Eve that they realized each had a good friend living in Los Angeles. They decided to split the cost of a four-star hotel by planning a joint vacation.

Gil had been a cop and had become increasingly active in an NYC LGBTQ police meetup group over the last ten years. He was like a dad to a young gay cop, Danny, who had moved West the previous year. He knew Danny could show him a great time. There was something about having a handsome young man near you that raised the cachet of any late middle-aged man.

Gil had kept himself in great shape. He had massive arms that he liked to show off in tight T-shirts. John, who owned The Crow and had a fine physique himself, used to say Gil paid someone to sew his shirts on his body because they hugged his torso like a drunken date at 3 a.m. Great body or not, Gil was sixty-two, and at sixty-two, his dating options were diminishing.

Elliot had worked in marketing for an ad agency. He was not by nature a wallflower, but he tended to fade in the background because he was attracted to flashier friends. Harris, his old drinking buddy who was now on the wagon and moved West ages ago, always had the spotlight. That was certainly true when Elliot and Harris met.

Harris was doing voiceover work for Elliot's agency's big client, a purveyor of high-end single malt scotch. The men became fast friends and even faster drinking buddies. They varied their journeys depending on their mood—sometimes dive bars, sometimes the elegant bars in New York's old grand hotels, sometimes the sidewalk near a notorious place shut down by police in Midtown East. Those were the salad days. As Davie, a now-deceased friend, used to say, "When you're young, you're living your salad days. When you reach fifty as an unattached gay man, all you have are crouton nights. Everything has gone small and stale."

For all the years Gil and Elliot had known each other, they were getting acquainted for the first time on this trip because they were out of their element—The Crow. They could not retreat into familiar patterns because, here in LA, nothing was familiar. And The Mocambo Grill was nothing like The Crow, the perfect dive bar. At The Mocambo Grill, the bartenders were all young and lithe. Elliot and Gil appreciated the eye candy, but both men were looking for beef.

Elliot was sipping a gin martini, and Gil was working a whisky neat.

"I don't think I ever saw you drink a martini," Gil said, sipping his whisky.

"No one drinks gin martinis at The Crow," Elliot answered as he swirled the olives along the side of his glass.

"Sure they do. I've seen guys with martinis. Cosmos, too."

"Those aren't martinis. Vodka martinis in places like The Crow are just cold vodka in a glass that was swirled in vermouth and then tossed out. A gin martini, my friend, is a relationship between the gin and the vermouth. The gin is dominant."

"So the gin is a top?" Gil asked, amused.

"If you want to be crude, yes. The vermouth, which is present in a smaller quantity, is the submissive. The two combine—twirled and swirled in an ice bath until they become one. It's very physical."

"I can see that," Gil nodded. "I guess a proper vodka martini could be called 'Fifty Shades of Grey Goose.'"

"You should tell that to John back at The Crow," Elliot replied biting one of the olives. "That would be a great name for a dirty vodka martini."

"But you said The Crow isn't the bar for martinis."

"Things can change, Gil. Things can change," he added for emphasis looking at this old friend he hardly knew. "Anyway, you never talk to the guys with martini glasses."

"Sometimes I do," Gil replied. "It depends on what I'm hungry for," he added with a grin. "Every now and then, a good twink hits the spot."

"Don't give me that. You don't go for twinks. You want a guy drinking a beer who looks like you. I've seen you work that bar. Even in winter, you peel off a sweater to show off your guns and strut like the cock of the roost."

"I like that image, Elliot. Cock of the roost," Gil repeated as he kicked back his drink. "Anyway, I was a cop. I have a license to carry."

"Yeah, well, most guns don't have tattoos," Elliot said, pointing to the inked compass on Gil's left bicep. "What's that about?"

"I needed direction. I got it before Google Maps."

"You got it before Google. That's an AOL dial-up tattoo. We're old, Gil. Look at that bartender. I bet somewhere in my apartment I have an expired pack of Trojans older than him."

"You know that is sad, Elliot. Really sad," Gil added for emphasis as he drained the last drop of whisky from his glass. "Let's get one more round."

"Why not? We're not driving, and Harris is always late," Elliot added, finishing his martini.

"So is Danny. He never can leave that damn dog of his. It's not natural. Maurice."

"Maurice?"

"His dog is named Maurice."

"That is so gay."

"I think the dog is gay."

"He has a gay dog? Do you have proof?"

"It's just a feeling," Gil said as he signaled to the bartender, pointing to their two empty glasses and making a thumbs-up sign, the international signal for refills. "Every time that dog hears a show tune, his tail starts swishing."

"Swishing? That's so politically incorrect, Gil."

"We're talking about a dog, Elliot. A damn dog. A Judy-Garland-loving dog."

"Enough about this very gay dog," Elliot said to Gil. "That is *so much more* gay." Elliot pointed to two men younger than them who had just walked in. Their colognes proceeded them by thirty seconds. The taller one was extremely handsome, and he knew it. He was wearing an untucked patterned dress shirt populated with pineapples that showed off his tanned, hairy chest. His companion, slighter, shorter, and trim, was in khakis and a white polo. They both had a studied look as if they cut out pictures from men's fashion magazines and went to stores to copy the image and then bought the exact same merchandise. That, of course, was ridiculous; they used their smartphones and shopped online.

"I told Ken he really needs to pick up the pace," the taller man said to his friend as they sat down on the two stools to Elliot's right.

"You don't call him Ken," the shorter guy said as they walked to the bar.

"Not to his face, Sumner."

"No, you do other things to his face, Hatton."

"Jealous, aren't we, my little short man."

"I'm not jealous. I'm not short. And you know I'm in a relationship."

"The only long-term relationship you have ever known was your right hand with your penis."

"Very funny, Hatton. This from a man who finds a squeeze in the bushes."

"I don't do that—much," Hatton added, knowing he frequented the cruising area in the park often. "I like being anonymous. It's very sexy."

"And very dangerous."

"Yeah? Well, so is this. No one cares, Sumner. This is the 21st century. This is LA. We can do what we want with who we want. And I'm too protected. No one's going to mess with me."

"You're playing with fire, Hatton."

"Just like Moses, Sumner."

The two New Yorkers were entertained by the LA men's banter.

"Let's have two shaken dirty vodka martinis," Hatton said to Sumner, signaling to the bartender. The bartender came over and shook their hands, "Gentlemen, good to see you. Let me guess, two shaken dirty Grey Goose martinis." Elliot shot Gil a look, wanting to interrupt with the cocktail name. Gil frowned. The bartender continued, "And I believe Hatton likes his the dirtier, the better."

"Honey, you can add some of your own sweat," Hatton said, making a gross gesture.

The bartender was nonplussed. This was a job. He responded with a smile as authentic as The Macambo, "I'll rub the olives under my arms."

"He's hot for me," Hatton said to Sumner as the bartender walked down the bar to get chilled martini glasses.

"In your dreams."

"Every night."

The waiter returned with the glasses first and then came back with two chrome shakers and poured the cocktails. "This one is the dirtier one, Hatton," he added, winking as he touched the edge of his underarm. As the bartender turned around, his face said, "If I only can sell my screenplay and be free of these assholes."

Gil read faces. He had been a good cop. He caught the bartender's eye and said, "I think we'll have a third round, and here, this is for you. You're earning it." Gil moved a twenty across the bar.

"Thank you," the bartender said. "I'm Claudio. Are you guys visiting?"

"Are we that obvious?" Elliot asked.

"You're new. That's the tell. The regulars here are a small group. I know them all. And since there are two of you, the odds that you live here and neither of you have been here before is unlikely."

"You should have been a detective," Gil said. "I'm Gil."

"And you are a cop," Claudio said.

"Was a cop. Very good, though. What was the tell?"

"If a gay bartender can't spot a cop, he's as useless as a vagina at The Harness. The next round is on me."

"Duckie, I told you never say that when I am near. I take that as a direct challenge." Harris had arrived. "The only thing that is holding me back is I don't drink alcohol," he said to Claudio who smiled that fake smile.

"Harris, you always know how to make an entrance," Elliot said, hugging his friend. "Great to see you. I don't think you met Gil when you were in New York last. There were so many guys at Davie's after-glow if that's what a post-memorial bar crawl is."

Gil stood up and shook Harris' hand. "Great to finally meet you."

"Duckie, what big hands you have," Harris said with a twinkle in his eye that was made more mischievous by the sound of his Scottish accent.

"The better to grip with," Gil said, feeling playful and experiencing the effects of two whiskies, no dinner, and jet lag.

"Duckie, what big arms you have."

"The better to flex with." Gil was enjoying himself.

"Duckie, what massive pecs you have."

"The better to bounce with."

"Duckie, what a big..."

"Hold it right there, Red Riding Hood," Elliot interrupted. "Let's leave the tour before we go too south."

"Duckie, you're no fun," Harris responded. "You know, Gil, Elliot was never any fun, but I used to be too drunk to notice that."

"I think you have been busted," Gil said to Elliot, who was patiently smiling.

"Now, now, duckie," Harris began looking at Elliot, "as they say, 'I love you like my luggage.' Tumi or not Tumi, that is the question."

"I have the answer," Elliot said as he put his hand on Harris' shoulder. "Dinner. Let's get dinner."

"Good idea," Gil chimed in. "Danny will be here soon. You'll like him, Harris. He's handsome and young."

"That may be, duckie. But I want to sit next to you," Harris said, grabbing Gil's left arm. "I'll just follow your compass to the table."

"Oh, dear," Elliot said. "This will be a bumpy night. Claudio, can we get a table?"

"Certainly. Just walk toward the back. I'll make sure they treat you well."

"I want Juan Carlos," Harris said, referring to his favorite waiter. "Juan Carlos does wonderful things with a napkin."

"I have no idea what you are talking about," Elliot said grabbing his fresh martini and handing Gil his third whisky.

"You will, duckie. You will."

◆ ◆ ◆

Gil woke up at 5:30 the next morning, his body still on New York time. Despite the copious amounts of whisky that he had the previous night with Elliot, Harris, and Danny, who arrived, as predicted late, Gil was wide awake. Elliot was passed out in the bed across from his.

It was Sunday and Gil wanted to get in a workout in the hotel gym before going to Mass. He knew Elliot would not approve of either activity. Elliot was not into religion or any kind of exercise that required him to sweat without the promise of sex. Perhaps that was an oversimplification by Gil of Elliot's philosophy on religion and exercise, but Gil didn't get why other men didn't find satisfaction in working out. As to the Mass part, well, that Gil understood. Even he couldn't rationally explain why he still went to Mass despite the homophobic hypocrisy of the Catholic Church.

He was raised Catholic, and so many of the men he knew on the job had been Catholic. And when push came to shove when they buried brothers and sisters lost in the line of duty, he found comfort in the rituals, liturgy, and pageantry. It made no sense, but Gil, at age sixty-two, knew very little in life made sense. You have to roll with life like a coaster going up and down and trust the car never leaves the rails. And never close your eyes because no one has enough time to miss out on any opportunity that passes by in a flash.

After an hour in the hotel gym, which he had all to himself, Gil went back up to the room where Elliot was still out like a light. Gil showered, shaved, and put on a collared short-sleeve cotton shirt and a pair of khakis and grabbed his brown loafers. He had oatmeal in the hotel restaurant and then called a ride-share car to get to church. He had inquired at the front desk and Our Lady of Consolation was the closest.

It was an 8:30 Mass, and he was early. The church was a sprawling Spanish affair—the kind of structure that went up in Los Angeles in the 20s and 30s. It had lots of terra cotta tile on the roof, a white stucco exterior, and a wood-beam ceiling inside.

He took a seat toward the front, defying his Catholic upbringing which had informed him to sit as far back as possible. Gil's dad took that to the extreme and stayed inside the green Chevy Impala in the parking lot, which annoyed his mother to no end. As Gil sat down near the center aisle, a woman passed him coming from the sacristy behind the altar and headed toward the back of the church. She was in her early fifties, Gil surmised. He was a good judge of ages.

The woman was too old for her outfit—a short floral dress that was a little too tight and a little low in the bosom. She was trying to pass for late-30s, Gil surmised, but it didn't work. Her blond hair was long. Gil wasn't sure if the length or color were authentic. What made her truly memorable was the smell of gin that followed her like a rain cloud waiting to burst. Gil had known his share of alcoholics as a cop and a gay man. This woman was tanked at 8:10 a.m.

He watched her walk to the back of the church and up to the choir loft where she spoke with the organist, who Gil could see backed away slightly when she started speaking, apparently reacting to the gin. Gil could hear her arguing with the organist, whose name was apparently Robby, that he always played too fast. Robby said he played the notes as written, and if she sang what was written, it would all come out the way it should.

Robby played the responsorial psalm for the Mass, and the woman began to sing. "The Lord is my shepherd; I will follow where he leads." was the response the congregation would sing in between verses. The woman's soprano was neither good nor bad. Her voice was like a grilled cheese at a diner at 2 a.m.—it got the job done. The two musicians ran through the other songs for the Mass, and then she came back down into the main church. Robby began playing a prelude.

The woman walked past Gil once again, incensing him with juniper, coriander, and some unidentifiable citrus. She went to the lectern, shuffled through the music, took her purse, and returned to the sacristy. The church filled up.

At 8:30, she walked back to the lectern. From Gil's vantage point, she looked less steady. A bell sounded, and the organ played the entrance hymn. Everyone stood up as the celebrant walked up the aisle with the lector and two teenage altar servers. When Gil looked at the priest, he guffawed and had to mask it as a very loud sneeze. "Allergies," he said to the woman to his left. It wasn't allergies; the priest was Sumner from the bar last night. There was no mistaking that one half of the flaming duo at The Macambo Grill was a Catholic priest. Probably his friend was too, Gil thought. Sumner caught Gil's eye and smiled.

Gil looked at the church bulletin he had picked up when he entered. Our Lady of Consolation: the Rev. Sumner Reynolds, pastor. The cantors were listed as well: Paul Kennelworth and Gina Maria Playa del Rey. Clearly, this was not Paul. Gil wondered if Gina Maria drank because of her name or was her name what happens after too many Gordons, Hendricks, and Tanqueray.

Father Sumner began mass. After the first reading, Gina Maria stood up and went to the lectern. Robby began to play. She sang the response first alone. "The Lord is my shepherd; I will follow where he leads."

As the cantor, Gina Maria was supposed to signal to the congregation to sing along by raising one hand, but instead, she raised both, signaling them to stand. The congregation stood. She started singing again and realized no one was supposed to be standing, so she signaled for them to sit. The congregation sat. She sang the second verse and signaled for the congregation to stand when they sang the responsorial. And so, it went for five more verses. Every time the responsorial psalm was sung, she had the congregation stand and then sit. There were old people clutching their walkers.

Robby stopped playing.

The lector, who was supposed to do the second reading, went to the opposite lectern and signaled for the congregation to sit. Normally, he was low-key, but he said sternly, "Sit down as I read from the First Letter of Paul to the Corinthians."

The congregation looked to Gina Maria for guidance. Stand? Sit? She signaled for them to sit as she giggled. After the second reading, Robby played the gospel acclamation. The congregation was not so quick to rise this time. They had been fooled before. Sumner said loudly, "Rise. Everybody rise. Rise. Rise. Rise. Rise. Rise."

Even Gil, who was not a big show-tune guy, realized Sumner was falling into a song from *Company*, "The Ladies Who Lunch."

Gina Maria sang the "Alleluia." By now, the gin was really kicking in and her "l's became "w's. She was Elmer Fudd in a skirt. Whatever fun Sumner Reynolds had the previous evening at The Mocambo Grill or elsewhere afterward was no longer remembered. He realized this Mass was going to be a test of wills between him and Gina Maria.

The Gospel reading was the parable about the prodigal son. Sumner had preached it many times, so despite being annoyed with Gina Maria, he was confident he could get through the homily without skipping a beat.

He was halfway through, talking about when the prodigal realizes he has squandered his opportunities and should return home to his father's house and beg to be treated just as a worker, when Sumner quoted directly from Scripture: "His son said to him, 'Father, I have sinned against heaven and against you. I no longer deserve to be called your son.'" Sumner paused for effect. "So what does the father do?" Sumner continued. "What does he say to his son?"

It was a rhetorical question to the congregation, but Gina Maria took it literally. She rose, quickly walked to the microphone at her lectern and sang, "Young man, there's no need to feel down. He said, young man, pick yourself off the ground. He said, young man, 'cause you're in a new town, there's no need to be unhappy." She raised up one hand, encouraging the congregation to sing with her, and continued, "Young man, there's a place you can go. He said, young man, when you're short on your dough, you can stay there, and I'm sure you will find many ways to have a good time." Now she raised both arms, signaling to stand and sing.

The congregation had no clue what to do next. They sat there silent.

Gil wanted to jump up and sing, "It's fun to stay at the YMCA!" But instead, he not-so-quietly chuckled at the absurdity of what was happening. A drunk off-her-ass cantor had upstaged this silly queen of a priest.

Sumner tried to get Gina Maria to stop, but "YMCA," once started, had to run its course. Gina Maria was doing the choreography, working up a sweat that sent a cloud of juniper, coriander, and a still undefined citrus across the sanctuary of Our Lady of Consolation.

Finally, after the last "YMCA," Sumner said loudly into the microphone clipped to his vestments, "Let us pray."

Realizing he was not even halfway through the service, Sumner made a cutting motion across his throat to Robby up in the choir loft, which Robby assumed meant one of two things: Slit Gina Maria's throat or stop playing for the rest of the service.

Sumner whispered to the lector, who then walked over to Gina Maria. He tried to escort her from the church, but she started to protest. "I'm not finished. We still have to do the Electric Slide." She signaled to the congregation to stand. They did. Catholics are notoriously compliant.

"Sit down, please," Sumner said, annoyed. "There is no Electric Slide in the Catholic liturgy. Our cantor is unwell. A reaction to medication."

"Beefeaters," Gil muttered just loud enough for the man in the row in front of him to chuckle.

The two altar servers went over to where the lector and Gina Maria were standing. They each took hold of one of Gina Maria's sweaty arms. "I'm not finished," she said as they walked her off. "Young man, put your pride on the shelf. Young man, you're the size of an elf," she directed at the teen to her left, who was trying not to breathe in the gin. Sumner waited until the altar servers had Gina Maria in the sacristy before he continued the Mass.

Try as he might, Sumner could not focus. He was a little hungover from the previous night, and Gina Maria threw him completely. He moved quickly through the rest of the Mass since there was no longer any singing. When he got to the consecration, he raised the host high, but instead of saying, "Behold, the Lamb of God," he proclaimed loudly over his microphone, "Behold, the Leg of Lamb!" And then, after a slight pause during which Sumner realized what he had just said, "Shit!"

◆ ◆ ◆

When Gil told Elliot about morning Mass, he regretted sleeping until 10 a.m. Elliot was still in bed, propped up with his laptop.

"Don't you use Grindr on your phone?" Gil asked jokingly.

"Yeah, the only thing I can successfully grind at my age is coffee. I don't even know which way you swipe. Left? Right?"

"Right, if you're interested. Dating apps aren't for us unless we want to hook up with a 22-year-old looking for a Daddy. I don't want that."

"You're a dad to Danny."

"Big distinction, sleepy man. I'm a dad, not a Daddy. There's nothing sexual between me and Danny. Funny, when I think about it, there never was anything sexual. He's this big-hearted younger man who needed an avatar."

"Fancy word," Elliot said, putting down his readers. "You surprise me, Gil."

"That's because we don't know each other, really. You were a lot of fun last night. You should drink gin martinis more often. I saw a whole new side of you."

"You saw my butt when I changed."

"Hate to tell you this, but that butt isn't new. What do you want to do today?"

"I want to go to the Griffith Observatory. I have this thing for those sky shows. I loved them as a kid at the Hayden Planetarium. It sounds geeky, I know."

"I used to go with my dad whenever he would take me. I loved that. It was all about space exploration. I'm in."

"Great. Let me get this old butt out of bed, and then we can get some lunch. I was thinking of renting a car. You can't navigate around here without a car."

"You're willing to drive in LA?"

"Yes, I am. I thought about renting a convertible so I could feel the wind blowing through my hair."

"Are you going to hold your toupee with one hand?" Gil asked as he sat down on the opposite bed facing Elliot.

"This is real," Elliot said, tugging at his still full head of hair. "All of this is real," he added, patting his slight paunch."

"Let me have a piece of that," Gil added playfully as he lightly smacked Elliot's bare stomach and pulled back the sheets. "If that's real as well, I'm impressed," Gil said, looking at the aroused bulge in Elliot's shorts.

"It's real."

"I think I require proof."

◆ ◆ ◆

"You guys look like you got some sun today," Claudio said as Gil and Elliot sat down at the bar of The Mocambo Grill after having dinner with Danny and his latest boyfriend. "You're both glowing."

"We were up at the Griffith Observatory," Elliot answered. "It was a very nice day," he added, looking at Gil.

"It was indeed," Gil replied, looking at Elliot. Their dynamic had changed.

Claudio looked at the two men. "Somebody has had sex."

"Maybe," Gil grinned.

"Gin martini and a whiskey neat?" Claudio asked, remembering their drinks from the previous night.

"Make that two gin martinis," Gil said. "I'm kind of curious what you put in your mouth," he added giving Elliot a devilish pinch on his right thigh.

"It's kind of late for that question, isn't it?" Elliot responded.

"Do we need a room?" Claudio asked.

"We're fine, Claudio," Elliot answered as his hand grabbed hold of Gil's fingers on his thigh. "It's all good."

Claudio returned with the two drinks.

"Where's the shakers?" Gil asked.

"Where they belong. Over there," Claudio said, pointing to the middle of his station behind the bar. "You're not supposed to shake a gin martini, although some fools insist you do. You shake cocktails with citrus, like lemon."

"That's it," Gil interrupted. "Lemon. It was lemon."

"What was lemon?" Elliot asked.

"The citrus I couldn't identify with the juniper and coriander coming out of Gina Maria Playa del Rey."

"She's a bitch," the three men heard from up the bar. It was Sumner, deep in a vodka martini. "She made a fool of me this morning."

"You're a fool all the time," Hatton said, returning to his seat next to Sumner. "I just checked with the kitchen. They have a great rack of lamb tonight. Or maybe lamb chops?"

"I need another drink," Sumner mumbled.

"Yes, you do, lambakins," Hatton said in a tone that was more nasty than friendly.

Elliot leaned into Gil and said, "I don't like him. He's not a good friend to that other guy. There's a line between ribbing and stabbing. And he's stabbing."

"It will come back to him," Gil said. "Guys like that are so cocky that they always trip themselves up. Let's get some air. Want to stroll?"

"All right," Elliot said as he took Gil's hand. He paid Claudio for the untouched cocktails. This was new and familiar. Elliot had spent hours and hours talking to Gil at The Crow, but talking and touching are two completely different things.

The two old friends walked toward the grotto. As they approached the entrance, they encountered Sade, the animatronic parrot, for the first time. "Welcome to the grotto. Welcome to the grotto. Aaaawk! You look fabulous. You look fabulous. Aaaawk!"

Those were Sade's opening lines. There were several speech programs designed for Sade, and they varied depending on the time of day and season. If there was a special event, a program could be custom-designed for a hefty fee. For example, when a reality show staged a bachelorette party at the grotto, Sade said, "How big is it? How big is it? Aaaawk! You're a slut. You're a slut. Aaaawk! The maid of honor slept with the groom. The maid of honor slept with the groom. Aaaawk!"

The generic program stuck to greetings and pleasantries. "You look fabulous. You look fabulous. My name is Sade. My name is Sade."

There were Internet rumors that Sade was the brainchild of an artificial intelligence software company with ties to the Department of Justice. She recorded everything that was said in the grotto and could trace it back to anyone's cellphone if they had their Bluetooth on and from there, Sade could identify the phone number and the identity of that person. It was probably not true. Probably not true. Probably not true. Aaaawk.

Gil and Elliot moved into the grotto toward the waterfall. Sinatra was playing on the sound system. The loud music of the day gave way to romance at night. There were couples seated on benches. It was nearing 9 p.m. and the stores were closing. It was remarkably intimate.

"You look fabulous, Aaaawk," Elliot said to Gil.

"So do you," Gil replied as he pulled Elliot close. They kissed. Tentatively at first and then with more passion.

"What is happening?" Elliot asked. "After all these years, what's happening?"

"Does it matter? Maybe we have to be in a completely fake place to see what is really true. I don't know why I never saw you clearly until now. You're kind of sexy."

"Kind of sexy. I was hoping more."

"You'll get more. You'll get a lot more."

"My reflexes want to make a joke, but my mouth just wants to kiss you."

"Follow the mouth. Reflexes are overrated."

The two men kissed again and held hands, looking at the grotto and the waterfall.

"It needs something," Elliot said. "Like a statue or a Madonna."

"Maybe Gina Maria Playa del Rey can pose for one. Or better yet, sing here in the pool as she walked around like the actress in *La Dolce Vita*."

"You've seen *La Dolce Vita*?"

"Yes, I'm not a Neanderthal. I watch foreign films. Or at least I saw some with Danny. He loves all that stuff, and some of it is really good."

"Indeed."

They kissed again. "What happens now?" Elliot asked.

"After we get back to the hotel, and we have amazing sex?"

"Yeah, but we don't have to hurry through the amazing sex to get there but yeah."

"We go back to New York where we have friends, except now we also have family there—us."

"You're going to make me cry."

"Yes, but that goes back to when we had the amazing sex." Gil added jokingly, but he changed his tone immediately, "You're right. This place needs a Madonna, something that shows it's special. Almost blessed. Our Lady of Mocambo. That would be a good LA virgin."

"There are no good LA virgins."

"Certainly not us," Gil added. They kissed again. Gil took Elliot's hand. They started walking back toward the restaurant. "I want to tell Danny about us, although I think he sensed something had changed since last night."

"When I tell Harris, he's going to be crestfallen."

"No, he's not, Elliot. I'm not his type. Whatever Harris says he wants, he really wants someone softer than me. He's a gentle soul trapped in an overamplified personality waiting for permission to be gentle." The two men looked at each other, stopping at the entrance to The Mocambo Grill. Elliot was standing on Gil's left. "You asked me about the tattoo yesterday, Elliot. It does have meaning. Look."

Elliot looked at the compass on Gil's left bicep. The compass had been tattooed on Gil's arm at a slight angle, so that "North" pointed not straight up but closer to the 10 o'clock position on a watch. "I don't understand," Elliot said.

"It points to you, Elliot. When I got the tattoo, I was young and romantic. I had this fantasy that when I finally met the man I wanted to have at my side, I would be able to show everyone that that man was my North Star. The needle on the compass on my arm would point to the man at my side. It's pointing to you. You're my North Star, Elliot."

The men kissed again in front of The Mocambo Grill's open glass doors. They didn't hear Claudio shout from behind the bar, "Get a room."

The Block Party

Simon didn't want to go to the exhibit today. He was emotionally drained. It had taken so much energy to stay focused on his kids' project. He lay in his bed staring up at the ceiling fan that sliced at the warm, early morning air with casual precision.

The motor's hum tempered his anxiety while the blades pushed like Sisyphus against the heat, only to return again and again to the task. Occasionally, the fan let out a small, high-pitched "wee!" from the effort. It reminded him of the sound a drunk he had sat next to once in a dive bar in Greenwich Village made every ten minutes. Simon had spent most of that night talking to a writer named Davie, who reminded him of Michael.

Simon had taken Davie back to his hotel room that evening. They exchanged numbers. Neither called. Simon was flying home to California the next day. A few months later, Simon read that Davie died. Alone.

He bought Davie's final book. It didn't sell well. Critics found it too serious and sad. They wanted Davie to give them more clever one-liners.

Simon found an interview online given by Davie before the book came out. He said he felt he had been condemned to write funny; readers expected that he would deliver joke after joke, book after book, never getting anywhere that mattered. He felt he was condemned to a life of forced hilarity. In dying, Davie finally did tragedy well.

The ceiling fan emitted a "wee!" as Simon rolled over on his side to look at the time on his phone charging on the small table next to his bed. It was 7:30. He had to get up, go to the gym, shower, shave, and be at the hall by eleven. The kids depended on him.

He went into the bathroom, brushed his teeth, ran some water over his face, and went back into the bedroom. He put on gym shorts and a T-shirt, stuffed some clean clothes into his gym bag, and left his apartment. He would change at the gym and go to the parish hall directly from there.

Saint Thomas Episcopal Church was displaying eighty panels of the AIDS Quilt in its parish hall, in addition to the panel just completed by the parish LGBTQ youth group. The teens wanted to undertake a service activity that connected them to the history of gay rights. They decided on making a panel for someone from the community who had died during the height of the AIDS epidemic—someone who had died with few friends. Someone who was not so much forgotten but who had never been known.

It was a daunting task to be sure: Identify someone who had died more than twenty years earlier, learn about them, and then make a panel. It was the work of missionaries and detectives. Simon's hesitation about going to the exhibit was not because he didn't care about the display or the service project. He had been the group's mentor for the past five years. It was that he needed some space from the memories. The last twelve months working with these teens had bled him. It took him back to a place he had forgotten, back when he was coming out. He didn't like that man.

Simon remembered spending a weekend with a former college friend and her then-husband. They had a beautiful home near the water. Her husband was a contractor, and he was talking about a new client he met with earlier that week. The client was gay. It was the mid-80s. The college friend's husband said he told his assistant after the gay client had left his office, "Burn the cup."

Simon was not out to many people then. Certainly, not to them. He didn't agree or nod. He didn't object. He said nothing. The shame of it still burned. Like Peter in Gethsemane, he had failed the moral test. How do you castigate Ronald Reagan for doing nothing when so many people were content doing nothing as well? Simon asked himself that question for many years. One inaction does not excuse the other, but like most things in the past, it informs the present.

Eventually, Simon did take his place in the parade. He marched. Signed petitions. Wrote elected officials. Sent checks. As he grew older and became a seasoned educator, he worked to develop inclusive classroom curricula and mentored LGBTQ youth.

To the teens in the St. Thomas youth group, AIDS was *Angels in America* and *The Normal Heart*. Probing plays and films that, while riveting, couldn't literally expose a young audience to the actual fear of the times. There was no Angel Bethesda healing then, only angels of death striking down Simon's friends.

While the Bethesda Fountain in New York's Central Park makes for a dramatic ending, according to the Gospel of John, Bethesda only healed the first person to step into the waters after she touched it, so it was a mad rush for a cure even in old Jerusalem. Whenever Simon stumbled upon that passage in John, he imagined an assortment of the ailing and dying fighting to get into the water first, like they were the bargain-hunting shoppers his mother would describe back on Long Island where she grew up shoving to get inside the now-defunct discount clothing store Loehmann's for its "back room" sale.

Dark humor was how you survived the unimaginable. You had to try to find something absurd to hold onto, something that reminded you that you had only two choices: push the rock back up day after day or be crushed by it. How many stones had Simon seen where once stood men? Fields of stone marked by names, dates, and nothing more.

Simon admired his kids, who wanted to understand what it was like back then. He could point them in the right direction and listen to their questions, but he could not truly explain what it was like to be gay in the early 80s and 90s. There had been hope of general acceptance before AIDS. In places like San Francisco and New York, gay men could find pockets of safety to meet, hold hands, kiss, and cruise. The safety pockets were smaller than millennials realize. Gay bashing in metropolitan areas was not uncommon. Straight men screaming "faggot" from a passing car as gay couples walked down a street in a "safe" neighborhood was not uncommon. Being fearful those four or five men might run out of their car with baseball bats was not uncommon.

Then The Plague turned the man you were holding, kissing, and fucking into a loaded gun to the head. You tried to be careful. But who is careful 24/7? Who doesn't get caught up in a moment? Why should that poor decision result in death? In a horrible, socially ostracizing death?

The families of dying gay men often abandoned them. Funeral homes didn't want to bury them. Even friends, at least in the early days when no one understood exactly how HIV was spread, were wary about hugging or kissing a friend who was already in the clutches of an angel of death. These winged envoys sent by an inscrutable god swooped down upon Simon's generation, leaving 3' by 8' holes in the ground where men once stood and played.

Simon couldn't explain that to LGBTQ teens who just wanted to do some good. He could not overwhelm them with pain because pain was the price his generation had been destined to pay. The Plague killed millions, but it also united millions more. Gay-rights activists found men and women who once were unlikely to leave their closets standing shoulder to shoulder with them on marches and at protests because even worse than living in a closet was dying in one.

Unity is fleeting. It comes most often out of a profound collective fear of losing that which is most basic to the human condition—freedom. Freedom can be applied to different concepts, but it comes down to the right to be who you are, who you want to be, who you could be. The growing number of deaths brought the last vestiges of the genteel gay-rights movement that was white, male, and looked like corporate America together with the activists who threw things, desecrated the eucharist inside churches, and staged protests, marches, and boycotts. The most powerful armies are not conscripted. They coalesce organically.

There is nothing more organic than death.

After his workout, Simon sat in the steam room of his gym. On another day, he might enjoy the cruisy vibe. It was the Bay area. Everybody was gay. Not today.

Simon leaned his head against the wet tiled wall, letting the steam wash over his face and body like water in a pool touched by the Angel Bethesda. There was no miracle. The water's power was gone. Three other men were there before him, sitting in the steam room. No matter. Simon closed his eyes and breathed slowly and deeply. He thought about his kids.

Just like Dorothy and her red pumps, the journey began with one yellow brick. Mateo, an earnest young man of seventeen, was the leader of the St. Thomas LGBTQ youth group. He was tall, confident, and fearless. Simon looked at Mateo with wonder. When he was seventeen, Simon would not have acknowledged to himself that he was gay, let alone lead a public group. Mateo was a pied piper, drawing in other peers. Some probably had a crush on the dark-skinned, broad-shouldered young man. If Mateo was dating any of them, Simon didn't know about it, and he probably would because all the kids looked up to Simon as a surrogate dad who they could confide in. That suited Simon fine. He had always wanted a family.

He was Mama Rose at the end of "Gypsy"—"I was born too soon and I started too late." The kids in the youth group became his kids. He'd offer advice when asked. Suggest options when he could. Mostly, he listened. That's what Simon did best. He liked listening so much more than talking, which seemed ironic because he taught English at a community college. But he wasn't talking to a class; he was teaching a class. There was a difference. Once Simon explained a concept, a theme, or a trope, he let his students explore. One yellow brick at a time.

His greatest joy came when students passed him on that brick road like he was running a 10-minute mile, and they, starting after him, were doing a 7-minute mile. Seemingly out of nowhere, they were at his side. They smiled that effortless smile of an athlete in the flush of youth, and then they were gone. First, Simon could see them ahead. Not out of sight but already out of reach. And then, gone. Unlike the friends of Simon's youth who were snatched up by angels of death, these youngsters had a full life ahead. Simon was merely a small character who exited early in their five-act play.

That was OK. It was a role Simon liked, not like Michael down in Los Angeles. Michael wanted to be in every goddamn scene. If he could, Michael would have starred in the intermission as well.

Simon hadn't thought about Michael in several years—or at least not consciously thought about him. But as the quilt project went on month after month, he found he missed Michael's endless conversations that were almost always about Michael even when they weren't. Simon enjoyed the banter with these teens, whose points of reference were often alien to him. But a conversation with Michael was like a hard game of racquetball—it was all out. Fast. Exhilarating. It was foreplay.

Simon wondered how Michael would react to his kids—whether it would bring out another part of his personality. Michael was extraordinary. That was the initial attraction when they met in a museum. There was something unique about him. But Michael was also like his perfect apartment—ordered, uncomfortable when something was out of place—be it a pillow, magazine, or his own emotions.

It had been so long ago, but the kids made Simon acutely aware of the passage of time. While Simon was rarely lonely, he felt he and Michael were still unfinished.

"Feels good, doesn't it?" a voice in the steam said.

Simon opened his eyes. An attractive man in his late twenties had entered the steam and sat down next to him. Another time. Another place.

"Yes," Simon replied as he stood and adjusted the towel around his almost trim waist. "Enjoy. I have to shower and shave. I've got to meet my kids at church." With that, Simon left the steam room, leaving the young man wondering whether Simon was a closet case or a married gay man with children. "An interesting choice," Simon muttered to himself as he opted not to pursue the young, attractive man and headed into the shower. There was no space for that kind of play today in Simon's brain.

He was three days short of sixty, a surrogate dad to an ever-changing cast of young gays and lesbians, and he had to be with them today.

When Mateo approached him about making a panel for the AIDS Quilt, Mateo had asked Simon where the youth group should go to find someone to memorialize. Simon suggested they come with him to a new LGBTQ center specifically for older gay men, men older than Simon. There, Simon knew, were people eager to talk about friends who had passed. Perhaps there was a wound to be healed. It was a place to start. One yellow brick at a time.

The center was called Last Blush, a gay name if ever there was one. Its meaning was like a drag queen's makeup—deep. An anonymous donor left the funds to create a community center for the over 75-year-old LGBTQ people living in this suburb of San Francisco. The name was a nod to makeup and to the final blush of life.

The center was open to anyone, but its mission was specific, and its clientele were gay men all over eighty. They shuffled. They grumbled. They pushed that rock every day up the hill, and as hard as that was, they could not rest. Death is inevitable. You cannot escape it. But to these valiant warriors clinging to memories and jars of foundation, you could not willingly surrender to it.

Simon was surprised at how comfortable he felt in the center. It was like going back in time to when he was in his twenties, and these men were the hot older guys, the men with the Tom of Finland mustaches or the gender-bending wardrobes of scarves, clutches, blouses, and short shorts. He could see through the façade of age to the youth that still lingered slightly on their skin like a strong cologne.

Henry was his favorite because Henry, like Davie and like any interesting man, reminded Simon of Michael. Henry was fastidious. He was still in pretty good shape. He was lonely.

And he liked to talk. Henry talked about being young in New York. About hotel bars and fancy cocktails that sometimes led to less fancy cocks. He was a writer. Like Davie. Like Michael. But not as successful as either. He moved west in the late 90s because all his friends in New York had died, and he wanted a new start. And even though San Francisco was under the same shadow of death, here he was a stranger. He would not feel the loss as acutely.

He was mistaken. Just as Simon saw Michael in every man who interested him, Henry saw old loves and friends in the faces of strangers. The idea that all gay men are really just one person looking for love should be enough. But you cannot kiss an idea. Hold it. Smell it. Touch it. Still, Henry pushed at his rock, knowing it soon would roll back on him. Not today. Not today. That's what he would say to Simon and to Mateo, who soon found a kinship with Henry as well.

The youth group made many friends at the center, but it was Mateo who found the person they were looking for—Timothy Talbott. He was a young friend of Henry's who died in 1993 at age thirty-four. Timothy Talbott, or T Squared, as Henry had nicknamed him, was also a writer, just starting to get his footing in New York. The two men had met in a bar, started talking, and became fast friends, never lovers. For Henry, it was the closest he had come to having a real relationship with someone.

There was a bond between the two men, emotional and intellectual, but not sexual. In a different time, they would have had decades of shared experiences. They had four years.

T Squared was from California, near Sacramento. His parents were evangelical Christians, and when they discovered Timothy was gay, they closed the door on him forever. Timothy could have found a safe haven in San Francisco or Los Angeles, but he was a writer and thought New York was the place for him to find himself. He made few friends in New York. The years of being told by his parents that he and men like himself were deviants kept him from enjoying his freedom. He couldn't leave the scab alone. The wound would not heal. It was difficult for Timothy to form close relationships with men—Henry was the exception—but Timothy enjoyed casual sex, and it was the wrong decade for that.

Henry met Timothy before he was HIV positive and would tell his young friend to be careful. Timothy would reply he always used protection. Henry knew he was lying. And when T Squared told him he had tested positive, while Henry was not surprised, he felt an equilibrium shift in the pit of his stomach, like he was on a rollercoaster that had just started to descend madly. It was the first time Henry had felt a pain so great it marked his soul like a sacrament.

Timothy had access to health care, but it was the early 90s—there was little that could be done. The rock was rolling back too fast, and it was so fucking large. Tens of thousands of Timothys did not stand a chance.

Both Henry and Timothy liked opera—that was part of the appeal to Henry of eventually moving to San Francisco—so Henry took his young friend to the Metropolitan Opera often, until such excursions were no longer possible. They had a picture taken by an operagoer they stopped in the plaza outside of the Met. The two men stood side by side. One older and healthy. One younger and dying. They smiled for the camera.

After several visits to Last Blush, Henry invited Simon and Mateo to his apartment and showed them the photo from Lincoln Center. Henry showed them other pictures of Timothy taken at restaurants and from the one time they traveled together to London. That was soon after the diagnosis. Timothy wanted to see London and wanted to hear an opera inside Covent Garden. It was "Der Rosenkavalier," an opera that ends with a wise older woman releasing her young lover to his true young love, recognizing all love has a time and place. The old gives way to the young—unless a plague changes the natural order of life.

T Squared and Henry looked good in that photo, both in tuxedos. Henry had old opera programs and matchbooks from New York restaurants as long gone as Ernie's was from San Francisco. There were snapshots of Timothy as a boy and a young man, as well. No one came when Timothy died, so it was up to Henry to sort through the things that were left in his apartment. The pieces of paper, the trinkets, and the photos that formed the shell of a man. Henry had called Timothy's parents twice before Timothy died and then once an hour after he had passed.

He left messages twice. There was never a reply. When he called after Timothy died and started the message with "I felt you should know your son died today..." the phone picked up. It was Timothy's father, or so Henry assumed. "Our son died years ago," he said and slammed down the receiver.

Henry was not surprised by the vitriol. Timothy told him often his parents were rigid in life and religion. "Absolute lunacy," Henry would tell Timothy, mocking the vodka ad campaign and suggesting a fantasy image of Anita Bryant, the former orange juice spokeswoman who went on a crusade against gays and lesbians. Henry would joke about Bryant being imprisoned in a large vodka bottle that was positioned opposite a sling in The Mineshaft, one of the most notorious and nasty gay clubs in New York, where she would be forced to witness men engaged in the dirtiest kinds of sex. Neither Henry nor Timothy had ever gone, but like many men, they reveled in the stories of other men more adventurous or creative in their storytelling than they.

Timothy's parents, Tod and Sue Anne Talbott were not abstract like an ad campaign. The Talbotts were the real deal, believing God created men and women a particular way, and deviation from that one way meant that person was, by definition, a deviate. There was no grey. It was all black and white, and their son was going to hell.

If they ever had loved Timothy, it was a conditional love, dependent on Timothy being who he was supposed to be, not who he actually was. The Talbotts saw Timothy's openness about being gay as an act of betrayal. There was no forgiveness. No reconciliation. For all their talk of Christianity, the Talbotts never got past the Old Testament.

Timothy's funeral arrangements fell on Henry. He had Timothy cremated. Henry kept the ashes in a box tucked in the back of a closet. He could not bring himself to put them into something more dignified, and he could not scatter them. He was not ready to let go. When Mateo suggested the quilt panel, Henry started to cry. At first both Mateo and Simon thought the idea was too much for the old man, but he embraced the idea. This would be as close to a memorial service for Timothy as possible so many years later. Henry's tears were of joy.

Over the next months, he told Mateo and some of the others in the youth group stories upon stories. Henry hadn't talked this much in years. The young people recorded the conversations looking for highlights of this man, Timothy Talbott, who had thirty-four years of life and thirty years of death.

The finished panel was a thing of beauty. Simon was impressed with not just the dedication his kids had in gathering information or that they have formed friendships with the senior gay men at Last Blush, but that Timothy's panel was truly a work of art.

It was to be exhibited separately from the eighty panels sent to the parish by the Names Project, which managed the AIDS Quilt. After the exhibit ended, Timothy's panel would be shipped to Atlanta, where the Names Project was based. There, the panel would be joined to seven other panels to form a 12' by 12' square block. While a group or organization could make eight panels, and those could be joined into a unified block, most blocks were formed from disparate panels that visually worked together.

Simon was not at the parish hall when the eighty panels arrived the day before. He was finishing last-minute paperwork at his office before the long summer break. Mateo had called him on his cell when the panels arrived and sent him a photo of the layout later. It looked amazing. Simon could not have been prouder of his kids. Emotional exhaustion aside, deep down Simon was looking forward to interacting with some of his kids' parents who were members of St. Thomas. Once he was at the parish, he knew he would be rejuvenated.

Despite offers of rides, Henry said he wanted to come to the exhibit on his own. "I can still manage," he said. "T Squared wouldn't want to see an old queen." Mateo, who had gained trust with Henry, liked to tease the older man who paid him back in full, said, "He's just going to have to settle for a middle-aged queen."

Simon, standing next to Mateo when he said that to Henry, smiled and added, "I'm not sure if that was directed at you or me or both of us?"

Timothy's panel was to be hung at the far end of the hall, against the base of the stage. The hall also served as an auditorium and gym. The eighty panels, ten blocks, were placed on the wooden floor in two rows of five blocks, with a wide aisle in the center and smaller walking spaces between the blocks.

When Simon pulled into the church lot, there were already quite a few cars. "Turnout is good," he said as he climbed out of the car and spotted one of his kid's parents. "You're amazing," they shouted across the walkway. "This is what Christian fellowship is supposed to be about," the mom said.

Simon smiled. He felt relaxed from the workout and knew the hard part was over. He wasn't sure how Henry would react to seeing the panel, but there was a large support group on hand. It would all go well. As he entered the hall, Mateo came up to him and gave him a huge hug. "We did it," he said.

"You did it, Mateo. Your mom must be so proud," he added, seeing her walking up to him. "Without your son, none of this would have been possible."

"Thank you," she said. "But I know you are the force behind them all. Mateo thinks of you as his dad. I'm grateful you came into our lives."

"I don't know what to say," Simon said, embarrassed but also pleased. Mateo's biological dad disappeared from the picture when Mateo was eight, so Simon filled a void for Mateo, as did Mateo for Simon.

"I'm going to take a walk through the panels," said Simon.

"May I join you?" Mateo asked.

"Sure. It's a very powerful experience, Mateo. Don't forget each panel was made by people like you. All that attention. All that love is imbued in each panel. Do the math. Each panel is a force unto itself. There is healing all around us, Mateo. You can feel it when you look at each one."

They walked slowly side by side. Father. Son. Brothers.

"I think they form a family. The panels once they become a block," Mateo said as they walked past the first row. "Look at those eight panels here," he grabbed Simon's arm and pulled him in front of a block. "The eight men in this block will be each other's family."

"That's a beautiful thought, Mateo. Thousands of families were created by these quilts. In early America, expert quilters could make fourteen stitches to an inch and quilts were three layers. A top, bottom, and then filler in the middle."

"That sounds perfect to me. A three-way."

"You got a mouth on you, young man," Simon replied, smiling at Mateo's uninhibited humor. "You know there is a form of poetry that is based on quilting. Cento poems. *Cento* is Latin for patchwork, and a cento poem is made up entirely of lines from other poems."

"That sounds like plagiarism."

"No, the sources are credited. It's using existing art as the building blocks for new art."

"Then a block in the AIDS Quilt is a cento poem because it takes eight different stories to make one new one. Each block is a poem, Simon."

"That's profound, Mateo. That's really profound." Simon turned toward Mateo and then stopped. He went white, and his knees started to buckle. Mateo grabbed him quickly and kept Simon from falling.

"What happened? You're scaring me. Are you OK?"

"I know him." Simon was pointing to a panel.

"Who?"

"Calvin Reed. The panel. Cal. We went to college together. Lost touch. Fuck. Look at that photo. That's me in the background."

Simon pointed to the top right panel. "Calvin 'Cal' Reed. July 29, 1959—August 4, 1994."

There were many pictures of a handsome, rugged young man. He must have been a musician because there was a piano made of felt in the middle of the panel. The artwork in the middle was whimsical because the piano lid was held open by a hockey stick. The top left corner of the panel showed Cal as a boy. A piano recital photo. Little League. Junior hockey. Next down were high school years. More of the same, but Cal was already a handsome man, physically mature for his age. Big, muscular, and hairy. The lower portion of the panel was of Cal performing in what looked like jazz clubs, and there were large musical notes made of fabric. Up on the middle right were party scenes and one from a picnic. At the top right was just Cal, smiling. "I was at that picnic. That's me. Look."

Mateo looked at the photo Simon was pointing too. There was a group of shirtless young men playing football and mugging for the camera. Cal was center front. Simon was two guys to the left, a little behind Cal.

"I lost touch with Cal, like you lose touch with a lot of the people you go to college with. I was at that picnic by chance. We didn't know we were going to see each other. It was just a random gathering of several tribes of gay men at a park on Long Island. I was out there with a boyfriend who was from Long Island, and we were going to Fire Island later that week. It was just a crazy thing seeing Cal there. I didn't even know if he was gay in college."

"You're kidding?" Mateo said.

"I didn't know I was gay. It was a different time."

"What happened when you saw each other?"

"We laughed about it. I think he said, 'I always suspected you were a friend of Dorothy's.' That was a more common expression back then about if someone were gay, they were a friend of Dorothy from the Wizard of Oz."

"I know where Dorothy is from. I wasn't born yesterday." Mateo added with a smile, trying to make Simon feel less upset.

"Close enough, Mateo. Close enough," Simon added for emphasis, knowing what the young man was trying to do for him. "Cal and I traded stories and rumors about the gay men we went to school with and the professors who had sex with them. It was a very innocent time—that whole afternoon. No one was sick. Or I don't think anyone was. We just laughed, played touch football, sweated in the sun, and appreciated that we were all good eye candy for one another.

"It was my last moment of freedom. It wasn't until later that year that my first close friend got sick. Then more. Then, people you don't know but are friends of a friend who gets sick, and everyone gets nervous about who they might have slept with and who might have slept with that sick person. It all got so fucked up—the mourning for the dead and the fear and guilt that it will be you next or it won't be you. My God, he was so young."

"How old was he in that picture?"

"He was thirty-two. We're—we were—the same age."

Mateo was still holding Simon's arm out of fear that Simon would collapse. He wasn't sure what he was supposed to do, so he did what Simon had told him a thousand times friends should do for other friends in distress—listen. Simon rambled through college and the picnic but kept coming back to Cal was dead.

"We were the same age," Simon repeated. "He would be sixty this year. I don't talk about birthdays. I'll be sixty in three days. I'll be sixty, and Cal is dead."

Simon stared at Cal's panel. The reality of the quilt was deafening. He could hear Cal talking. He could hear all the men in that photo from the picnic talking.

"Do you want to sit down?" Mateo asked. "We can go over to the chairs on the side."

"No, thank you. I want to stay here. My friends are here. Simon looked Mateo in the face when he said that, including the young man in that category. "In all the years I've seen pieces of the quilt, I never stumbled upon someone I knew. I guess it was a matter of time."

"Someone cared about Cal," Mateo said. "He made a panel for him. Maybe it was a lover. Or friends. Or a group of people like us at Saint Thomas. Cal will be remembered. That's what's important. Someone cared enough about him to make this beautiful tribute. I wonder if that person was at the picnic. Or if you two met. Or whether he's still alive or memorialized in a panel waiting to be joined with Timothy."

"You're an old soul, Mateo," said Simon, looking at the son he should have had. That he did have now. "How did you get so wise?"

"I had this amazing teacher. This old dude with a little bit of a gut."

Simon laughed. He needed to laugh. "I'm OK, Mateo. Really. Thank you for letting an old man ramble on. Let's go over to Timothy's panel."

The pair walked toward the stage area as Henry came into the auditorium. He was carrying a small brown bag. Simon immediately knew what Henry was carrying. He was carrying Timothy's ashes.

Henry walked slowly but deliberately toward the panel, taking it in from a distance and then up close. Simon and Mateo each took a side of Henry in case he needed physical support. The three generations of gay men stood in silence, looking at the panel. Henry put the bag with the box of Timothy's ashes on the floor at the foot of the panel. He left the box inside the bag because he was concerned people would be disturbed by it. "I just wanted T Squared to see what you and your friends did," Henry said to Mateo. "He would be very happy."

"This is what it is? These panels?" an elderly woman around Henry's age said from behind them. "I had to see for myself." The woman was soberly dressed in black and approached them. She wore a gold cross around her neck.

"Isn't it beautiful?" Simon asked the woman.

"No, it is not. It's shameful. How can you put his name on that thing? He deserved to die—it was his punishment."

"You can't believe that?" Simon replied as the woman moved closer to the group of three men. "If you think that, why did you come here?"

"I had to see for myself. There he is," she added, looking at Timothy's panel. "Timothy brought shame to our family. If that wasn't bad enough, now it's in public for everyone to see."

"He was family?" Henry asked.

"He was my son. Someone sent me an invitation to come today. They probably thought I would want to come for closure. They were right. I did want closure. I wasn't sure until now. When I got that invitation, I thought maybe there would be something here that would show me Timothy had repented, that Timothy knew he had sinned against God. And don't look at me like that," Sue Anne Talbott snapped at Simon. "It's not easy losing a son. It's even harder when you have to close the door yourself."

"No one forced you to close the door," Simon replied.

"The hand of God is strong," Sue Anne said. "My husband and I were simple people. We believe in what is written in the Bible. Leviticus: 'You shall not lie with a male as with a woman; it is an abomination.'"

"The Old Testament is filled with many hateful things—slavery, for example," Simon reasoned. He wanted to change this woman's mind, if not for himself, then for Henry and Mateo. "There's the New Testament. Luke said, 'Judge not, and ye shall not be judged: condemn not, and ye shall not be condemned: forgive, and ye shall be forgiven.'"

"Maybe Jesus will forgive him," Sue Anne replied. "I cannot forgive him. His father could not. Timothy didn't repent. There is no forgiveness without repentance. Timothy never admitted he had sinned against God. He was as wicked at the end as he was when he told my husband and me that he was gay. Gay? What kind of word is that? Some way of trying to hide over the sin, the abomination. Look at him up there! He's smiling. Mocking me!" Sue Anne lunged at the panel, trying to tear at it.

"Stop!" Henry shouted as if someone was trying to stab Timothy. Despite his age, Henry was still strong, and he grabbed Sue Anne by the arm, pulling her away from the panel. "I don't know why, but Timothy wanted you to care about him. I called you several times when he was dying. No one called back. I spoke to your husband the day Timothy died, and he hung up on me."

"That was you? You're the pervert who turned him into a homosexual?" Sue Anne shouted. She moved close to Henry, slapped him hard, and exclaimed, "Faggot!" As Sue Anne's hand hit Henry's face, all the quilt panels went silent.

The parish hall was quiet. The parishioners and visitors were stunned by the outburst and by a word they all knew and had heard but never had heard inside a sacred space. The sanctuary was no longer a sanctuary, just the outside encased in walls, a floor, and a ceiling.

Henry did not physically react to the slap or homophobic slur. He stood erect, looking at Timothy's panel, knowing Timothy was watching him. He would not give Sue Anne Talbott the enjoyment of believing she had caused him pain. Henry was not surprised that this parish hall was not immune from the likes of Sue Anne; he was surprised that he had almost thought it was possible that it could be.

Henry's face burned from the slap, but he did not feel pain. Rather, he felt a sense of unity with Timothy. They shared something now. Henry felt closer to Timothy than he had since he held his young friend's lifeless body in his arms decades ago. He had been there for Timothy, and now, Timothy was here for him.

"You have to leave," Simon said angrily, breaking the silence. "I don't care how you came. By car, taxi, or broom. You have to leave—now!" Sue Anne didn't move.

"This is my fault," Mateo said. "I sent the letter. I thought it would be a healing moment for Timothy's mom. I thought after so much time had passed, she would want to see that Timothy mattered. I'm so sorry, Henry."

"It's not your fault," Simon replied. Henry now was looking at Sue Anne who still had not moved an inch. "You wanted to do good," Simon continued. "This is what it was like, Mateo, in the 90s. Take a look at what hate looks like. I didn't want you to see it, but I guess you have to see it because it's still out there. There is no cure. Just like HIV, no cure. We can learn how to survive it, but it's out there—always."

Mateo had started to cry. His mother came over to his side and addressed Sue Anne. "This is my son. My son, who is caring, generous, loving, and gay. You don't have a son because you were never a mother."

"I raised my son to be a good Christian, not some pervert who was with men. I made sacrifices for Timothy and what does he do? He commits sin. It was unnatural; he was unnatural."

"Rejecting your son is what's unnatural," Mateo's mom said. "Being a mother means loving your son no matter what. If he's straight or gay, he's your son."

"That's not what the Bible says. There are consequences for sin. My conscience is clean. Timothy brought on his own death."

"Your son didn't choose to be gay any more than he chose to be your son. And AIDS was never a punishment from God. These young men— many barely adults—should have had long, rich lives. They should be here today, standing tall instead of lying on the floor, faces on fabric. Mothers have one responsibility—to love their children. You're the sinner, Mrs. Talbott, not Timothy."

"You're just like all the other sick people in this perverted city," Sue Anne replied. "You twist it all around. God is watching. God is watching. God is watching."

"I hope he is," Mateo's mom said. "I know he is. I know that he is looking down at my glorious gay son, blessing him, strengthening him, guiding him to become a good and compassionate man. Leave. You have no place here, no family here. Leave."

Sue Anne glared at her, then at Mateo, then at Simon. She walked close to Timothy's panel, and Henry, fearing she would try to tear at it again, moved toward her. Sue Anne stared at the images, her body still straight as a plank, her face inscrutable. Whether there was an internal battle waging in her heart to forgive and love her dead son was unclear. Simon wanted Sue Anne to forgive; he wanted the power of what his kids had done to transform her into the mother she should have been. Finally, Sue Anne shifted her weight. She leaned into the panel as if to kiss it and then spat at it, striking the photo of Timothy and Henry in the plaza at Lincoln Center.

Henry gasped as if she had spat on him. And he knew what that felt like, back when it was faggot season across much of America, and being spat upon was better than being beaten with a baseball bat.

Sue Anne turned and walked out of the auditorium, her hardened gaze locked on the people she passed. No one spoke. The only sounds now were of the eighty-one dead gay men memorialized on the quilt panels; they had reclaimed their voices. Sue Anne Talbott would never silence them again.

Mateo walked to Timothy's panel and using part of his shirt sleeve, wiped the saliva off the photo. He walked back to his mom, who hugged him. Simon turned to Henry and asked, "How's your face? Can I get you some ice? Or a chair?"

"No, Simon," Henry said kneeling on the floor to pick up the bag with Timothy's box of ashes. "I'm glad Timothy saw this. I'm glad that he finally knows there was no reason to feel guilty about losing a connection with his parents. Like you said," Henry added, looking at Mateo's mom, "that woman was never his mother. They weren't his family. We are. We are his family. You and Mateo and Simon and these people," the old man said pointing to the people in the parish hall, "this is family. This is what family looks like.

"We will send Timothy's panel to the Names Project, and they will join his panel with seven other panels. What an amazing thing you have done, Mateo. Be proud. You have given Timothy what he wanted most in life—a family," Henry said, echoing what Mateo had said earlier, leaving Simon wondering whether Henry and Mateo had discussed the concept before or whether these two men, generations apart, were really the same man, and if he, Simon, was not part of them as well.

Henry continued, "Whenever people see Timothy's panel, they will see his family. I know the joined panels are called a block because it is a 12' by 12' square, but it is a block like a neighborhood is a block. Look at the neighborhoods in this room. Look at them. Not just the eighty panels on the floor but the people standing in this space. You don't need to be dead from AIDS to join with other people. This is a block party. This is a celebration of who we were, who we want to be, and who we can be."

Simon looked at Henry, and he did not see an old man. He saw a man who still saw the promise ahead. It wasn't a rock to be pushed, but just a life to be lived. All around Simon was life. The disparate messages on each panel had formed a neighborhood, yes. They also formed a cento poem. Lines of poetry from different authors combined into something new, something glorious, something living.

"This may seem like an odd request," Henry said to Mateo's mother. "I want to go to New York. I want to spread Timothy's ashes in the places he loved. It is time for him to leave me. But I can't do the trip by myself. Would you let me take Mateo to New York? I'm sure he would like to see New York."

Mateo looked at his mother, who had no reservations about the request. It would soon be time for Mateo to leave and she understood that this trip was a step forward in that process.

"I think it is time for me to leave as well," said Simon, who suddenly had a moment of perfect clarity. "I won't go until the fall. I need to figure out a plan. But I need to finish something I left undone."

"What was that?" Mateo asked.

"My life. I love you like you were my son, Mateo. But I need to finish something. You'll come to visit."

"I don't want to lose you," Mateo said.

"You won't. We are joined together. You, me, Henry, Timothy, Cal, and whoever made Cal's panel."

"That's only six, two people short of a block."

"We're not finished, you and I, we're not finished. We will find partners. We will be complete. Believe me."

"Where are you going?" Mateo asked.

"To the City of Angels. To the City of Angels."

The Secretary

Hatton reached over to silence the alarm, grunting as he turned on his side. It was 6:30. He overslept. He had only twenty minutes to get ready. Grabbing hold of the headboard with one hand, he slid himself to the edge of the mattress, swung his legs over the side, and stood up quickly.

"Jesus, like ripping off a Band-Aid."

He steadied himself and slowly walked into the bathroom. He looked in the mirror.

"Fuck me."

The left side of his face was swollen, and the area around his left eye was dark and purple. There were a few light scrapes on his forehead. He stared at his chest and could see the discoloration along his left flank.

"Fuck me."

Hatton splashed warm water on his face and rubbed it into his beard. He didn't have time for a shower. He would shave and run a washcloth across his armpits and that would have to do for now. He moved quickly despite the pain.

Going back into the bedroom, he dressed and then carefully made his way down the stairs, through the hall to the back door, where he then went through a small corridor. He unlocked the door at the end of the corridor and entered the next room, where Sam was already waiting.

"Jesus, Mary, and St. Joseph!" Sam exclaimed. "What happened to you?"

"I was mugged," Hatton replied. "Help me get ready. There isn't much time. It's almost 7."

Sam helped Hatton, and they were off. As Hatton walked out of the sacristy to the altar, there was a gasp from the twenty or so morning communicants at the 7 a.m. Mass at St. Michael's Cathedral. Father Dorsett looked like he went eight rounds with a heavyweight boxer.

After Mass, Mrs. Grieg came up to him and said, "Father, what happened to you?"

"I was outside the rectory last night and I was jumped by some man. It was dark. Not really sure what happened. He took some cash. I suppose I was lucky. It could have been worse."

"Oh dear, me, yes," she said, holding her right hand up to her mouth, the rosary dangling against her wrist. "This neighborhood is so bad at night. I wouldn't come here unless I could park inside the gated lot."

"It's important that we don't hide," he said. "Men of God must be present to everyone."

"You're a saint, Father."

Hatton winced, but to Mrs. Grieg, who could never see anything up close well, it looked like a smile. He walked back into the sacristy with Sam.

"Does the bishop know?" Sam asked.

"Not yet. He's at a retreat in the mountains. I didn't see a reason to disturb him."

"But you're his secretary. He would want to know."

"Not when he's on retreat. I'll be fine."

"What did the police say?"

"I didn't call the police."

"That's not wise, Father. He could be out there."

"I don't want to cause trouble for anyone," Hatton said.

"Have it your way," Sam replied. "But I think the police should know the bishop's secretary was mugged outside his rectory."

Two hours later, Hatton was in the chancery. He was wearing sunglasses indoors, which made him look like an extra in a Martin Scorsese film. As fellow priests and staffers saw him, they all asked the same thing, "What happened?" He replied each time, "I was mugged."

All was well until he bumped into Ron Santos in a chancery hallway. Santos was a reporter from *The Tribune,* and he had an interview scheduled with Auxiliary Bishop Bucco about the annual bishop's appeal. When Santos saw Hatton, he asked the question du jour but was not satisfied by Hatton's response. "You should report this to the police," Santos said.

"I'll think about it," Hatton replied and quickly went to his office down the hall and shut the door. He did not want to discuss what happened with Santos or the police. By mid-day, that was no longer an option. Santos had posted a picture of Hatton on social media. Hatton wondered when Santos managed to snap a picture with his phone. He must not have been paying attention.

"Fuck me."

Under the picture: "Bishop's secretary mugged outside rectory." Hatton's desk phone rang. It was the bishop.

"Yes, bishop...I didn't know you were trying me on my cell. It was stolen. Wallet and watch, too...I was mugged...That's what I said, mugged...By the rectory...Why would you say that? ...I'm careful...I don't deserve this. I wasn't looking to get beaten up...I didn't go to the press. Santos was in the building...The story will go away. If we ignore it, no one will care...It will be forgotten by the time you return...Yes.... Yes...I know...Goodbye, bishop." Hatton hung up.

"Fuck me."

He stared at the phone. The bishop, or Kenny, as Hatton would refer to the bishop when he was out of earshot, was pissed. Hatton was not sure what he should do except go back to bed. He was in a great deal of pain. He probably should have gone to the emergency room last night, but he wanted to avoid publicity. Now he had the pain plus the publicity. He decided to go back to the rectory and rest.

Before he could leave, Sumner was at his office door. They had been in seminary together, so there were no secrets between them. Hatton immediately could tell that Sumner had seen the social media posts. Sumner had that look of concern and delight that used to get him a lot of attention back in seminary.

It was a club within a club. A large club. He, Sumner, and his classmates were not children of the 50s or 60s. They knew "what was what" before they entered seminary. As Hatton would say to Tom, his closest friend at that time, when they would skip out for a night at the bars, "We went in with our mouths wide open." The men of the club were careful in front of the older priests who would not tolerate any sexual misconduct. And they were friendly with the ones who did. Sumner was very friendly which explained his rise within the chancery structure.

"What really happened, Hatton?"

"I was mugged."

"Yeah, I've heard the story. You pushed the stone away from the tomb and three guys jumped you."

"This isn't a joke. I'm in pain."

"I'm sure you are. But we both know you weren't mugged in front of the rectory."

"Really?"

"Well, for starters, the rectory is locked up as tight as a drum. There's a gate around the whole thing. You wouldn't be outside late at night."

"I was."

"I'm sure you were outside, but not outside the rectory."

"Are you saying I made this up? Does this look like I made this up?"

"You were beaten up, all right. We all have our theories about how and where."

"All? Who is all?"

"Tom, Gary, George, Bob...pretty much our entire class. You've been the talk of the morning."

"I would think you have better things to do with your morning."

"And I would think you had better things to do with your nights."

"What do you want, Sumner?"

"The truth. Where were you?"

"You know where I was. Let's end the charade. I'm surprised I didn't see you there?"

"I was with John last night."

"John, is it? How ironic that his name is John. How is your John or should I say the monsignor?"

"Very well. We had dinner at The Mocambo Grill. Now, don't change the subject."

"I was in the park. You know the section, The Wilds."

"The Oscar Wildes, you mean. I haven't been in a very long time. I don't know why you still go there. What happened?"

"This hot Latino…"

"All Latinos are hot."

"Is this my story?"

"Just tell it, then."

"His name was Carlos, or so he said. Tall. Athletic. Clean shaven. Wearing a white T-shirt. He started a conversation. 'Nice night,' that kind of thing as he moved in a little closer. Then he kissed me. Hard. I was surprised. He put his hands on my hands, squeezed them, and kissed me again. Then he pushed my hands behind my back, never letting go while still kissing me. It was very hot. Then, I felt another set of hands on my wrists. Another guy had come out of the bushes or the dark, I don't know. It all is a blur. They were beating me, both of them. I couldn't get away. They took my wallet. My watch. My phone."

"Jesus, Hatton. You're lucky neither of them had a knife. You could have been killed."

"I know."

"How did you get back to the rectory? Did they steal your car?"

"I never drive to the park. Don't want anyone to see my car so I took a rideshare. I had to walk back."

"You're lucky no one else attacked you."

"I think it's like lightning; you don't get struck twice. And I looked like shit. I probably scared people away. There's an electronic code to get into the rectory, so I didn't need any keys. By the time I got back, it was almost dawn. I collapsed in bed."

"That's a story, Hatton."

"That's a story between us, Sumner. You can't tell anyone about this."

"I won't tell anyone about this, Hatton. It's our secret. I'll be as good a friend to you as you have been to me." That worried Hatton because Hatton had never been a good friend to anyone, but he was not going to telegraph that to Sumner. "But maybe you can put in a good word with me with the bishop?" Sumner continued. "I would like to be pastor at St. Agnes. I hear Rawlins is retiring. It's a much better parish than Our Lady of Consolation."

"You don't miss an opportunity, Sumner, do you? You have John. Isn't that a good enough connection?"

"This isn't chess, Hatton. In real life, a bishop is much better than a queen. Deal?"

"Deal."

"But there are a lot of guys in the club who will be thinking exactly what I was thinking about the mugging—trick or treat or get beat. You should be smarter than this, Hatton. The Wilds?"

"It's anonymous. Social media can be tracked—too many guys with too many smartphone cameras in bars. Even at The Mocambo Grill, you have to be careful what you do. There's something to be said for The Wilds."

"Yeah. Dangerous."

"Ha, ha, ha."

Sumner left, leaving Hatton to ponder his fate. He knew Sumner was right that other club members would put two and two together. Why hadn't he been more discreet like Sumner? Hooking up within the club was so much safer. But truth be told, Hatton liked excitement. He liked the thrill of the hunt in The Wilds. He was careful about what he did there and thought he could spot trouble, but it was really a numbers game. Eventually, you had to have a trick go bad as Sumner said, "Trick or treat or get beat."

Hatton left the chancery and headed back to the rectory. There were TV trucks everywhere. And he could see Santos smiling like a cat with dinner in its mouth. Hatton was the mouse.

"Fuck me."

He couldn't drive away. He had to face them. Double down on the story.

"Not sure of the time when it happened," Hatton said. "They took my watch."

"They? A woman at your morning Mass said you said it was one man when she spoke with you," Santos said. He had been asking around all morning and tracked down Mrs. Grieg.

"Maybe I didn't explain it clearly to her. I was in pain. It was two men. It all happened so fast."

"Exactly where did it happen? Can you show us?" a TV reporter asked.

Hatton started digging the hole deeper. He picked a spot at the far north corner of the rectory. "It was there. Or near there. I thought I heard someone crying in pain. I went outside to look."

"You heard someone crying?" Santos asked. "I'd think you would be asleep."

"I was reading in bed. The window was open. I should have called the police, but I thought someone was in trouble and I could help. I went downstairs to check it out."

Hatton was now a good 4-feet under. He went the full distance and filed a false police report later that day. The problem was his story didn't quite add up. He said he was in bed reading to the reporters, so if he was in bed, how could he have come outside with valuables to steal? Who keeps cash in pajamas or sweatpants? He had to fumble that he was reading on the bed, not in the bed, and was still dressed. Hatton at least had thought enough ahead to check on the surveillance cameras inside the rectory perimeter. He was lucky the system had been down for a week. The bishop had wanted it upgraded and arranged for that to happen while he was away on retreat. There would be no evidence that he didn't get mugged in front of the rectory. Each time he dodged a bullet, Hatton felt more empowered. Nothing could touch him.

◆ ◆ ◆

Sumner was sipping a vodka martini at The Mocambo Grill a week later. He was alone. John wasn't available for dinner, and Hatton was staying in, forced to be careful while the media frenzy continued around him. Claudio, the bartender, came over to his spot at the bar.

"I don't think I've ever seen you here alone," Claudio said in a seductive voice. Claudio, like all the bartenders and servers at The Mocambo Grill, could make anything sound like foreplay to the middle-aged men who drank martinis in too-loud shirts with equally loud drinking buddies. "I keep seeing your friend Hatton on the news. He probably won't be in here for months."

"Sooner than that, I'm sure," Sumner said, swirling the olives in the glass. "Hatton likes playing with fire," Sumner added, looking up at the bartender. "You know, Claudio, I don't really like vodka."

"Why do you always order it, then?"

"It seems easier with Hatton. If I had something else, he would make that into an issue."

"I know he's your friend, but I don't like him. Nobody here likes him."

"Funny, neither do I," Sumner said. "He's been a habit for so long, I've just gotten used to his style."

"Between us," Claudio said, moving closer to Sumner, "he's a real asshole. You can do better."

"He has his charms, Claudio. He wasn't always an asshole."

"Once an asshole, always an asshole."

"Did they teach you that in bartender school?"

"I'm not stupid. Just because I'm a bartender, I'm not stupid."

"I didn't mean it that way," Sumner said, truly apologetic. "I don't know why I said that. You've always been nice to me, patient with me and with Hatton. I'm really sorry I said that. I didn't use to be this way, you know? If you're smart and reasonably attractive, it's easy to fall into a pattern in my line of work."

"Apology accepted," Claudio said, extending his right hand to Sumner, who shook it and smiled. "Break the pattern. Let me make you something without vodka. Did you ever have a *Vieux Carre*?"

"What's in it?"

"It's like my old boyfriend—Southern, dark, boozy, and very high maintenance. Give it a try."

"The drink or your boyfriend?" Sumner asked, sounding for the first time in many years like a nice guy.

"You can't handle my old boyfriend," Claudio said. "Start with the drink," he said, turning away, but turned back to Sumner and added, "and make sure to swallow."

Sumner grinned widely. "I like you, Claudio."

"The jury is still out on you," Claudio replied with an equally wide grin that activated his dimples.

◆ ◆ ◆

The deeper Hatton dug in with his fake story of being assaulted, the more excited he became by the danger. The account, as weeks passed, became grander as he embellished it for reporters and anyone who would listen— Hatton had fought valiantly against his attackers, but after they left, and before he went inside, he had gotten up on his knees to pray for their forgiveness. Hatton went from fearing discovery to believing he was indestructible.

Then his wallet turned up in the park—not just in the park, but in The Wilds. Someone stumbled upon it. The money and credit cards were gone, but his license was still inside. That started some rumors outside of the club about whether he was where he said he was. There was gossip that he was gay.

Hatton continued on the offense: "It is sad that people try to make everything about sex. It's an attempt by people who disagree with the Church's position on sexuality to make this sordid. I don't know how my wallet ended up in the park. I expect the robbers ditched it after they took my money and credit cards."

The police were not convinced until they saw a surveillance tape on the corner across from the rectory. It was aimed at the entrance of a gated lot across the street, but the camera caught the activity on the corner near the alleged attack. At 2:31 a.m., two young men were seen walking around the corner, heading in the direction where Hatton had said he was mugged. The footage was posted online.

Hatton could not believe his good fortune. When he met with the bishop, he could not contain his glee.

"I told you, bishop, I was mugged."

"Hatton, you are a resourceful man. I admire your skills. But don't think I don't know what you were doing."

"I have no idea what you're talking about, bishop," Hatton responded. "The tape shows the two men."

"The tape shows two men. Do you want me to show you the file I have on you, Hatton? The reports of you in West Hollywood at bars? At clothing-optional resorts in Palm Springs? Of parish workers who claim they were approached by you?"

"That's all gossip. Lots of clerics are in West Hollywood and Palm Springs. I have never been with anyone underage. I've never forced myself on anyone."

"No, you're not a criminal, Hatton. You're just the most amoral priest I have ever known, and I studied in Rome," the bishop added for emphasis. "You got lucky this time. Take it as a warning—a warning in life and a warning from me. You are brilliant at what you do, but I don't need a liability at my side. Do you understand me, Hatton?"

"Yes, I do, bishop," Hatton replied. He left the bishop's office, not chastised but empowered to gain an upper hand. Hatton was a good secretary; he knew where everything was kept. He needed time, but he was sure he could find leverage with the bishop if he needed it in the future. With the tape of the alleged assailants circulating across the media, Hatton knew the tide had turned in his favor.

Two days later, the two men on the video were picked up. They had a long criminal history and no alibi. But Hatton had said multiple times that he didn't see his attackers clearly, so he could not identify them now—that part of his fake story could not change. While police could not charge the two men, in the court of public opinion, they were guilty. Hatton's story became credible.

"You got lucky, Hatton," Sumner said the next day as Hatton sat down next to him at the bar in the Hotel Capone, a Prohibition-style hotel with a deco bar that had become a secret gay gathering place outside of the traditional gay bar district. Hatton had wanted to avoid the bar at The Mocambo Grill and West Hollywood, so insisted that he and Sumner meet at the Hotel Capone. "Everyone in the club is jealous," Sumner added.

"I did get mugged, you know. But I must say it felt exciting getting all the attention. All sorts of people come up to me. Some very attractive ones."

"You don't feel guilty making all of this up? Those two men in the video didn't attack you."

"They're criminals. They deserve what they get."

"If people got what they deserved, you wouldn't be sitting here, Hatton."

"When did you get so high and mighty? You play the game as much as I. You're the new pastor at St. Agnes, aren't you?"

"It doesn't make me feel very superior."

"Well, Sumner, you're not superior. That's why I am Kenny's right-hand man."

"Kenny? I hear the bishop isn't too pleased with you."

"He needs me. He knows he needs me."

"You're a piece of work, Hatton. A real piece of work," Sumner added. "Here's to you." He raised his glass to Hatton. Sumner was drinking a *Vieux Carre.*

"What is that?" Hatton asked while signaling to the bartender.

"It's called a *Vieux Carre.*"

"When did you stop having vodka martinis?"

"A few weeks ago. I discovered I didn't like vodka."

"Ridiculous. Everyone likes vodka, just like everyone likes me," Hatton added as the bartender came over. "I want a really dirty vodka martini. Rub the olives somewhere nasty," Hatton said, pointing to the bartender's crotch.

"How about on your face," the bartender said, walking away.

Sumner laughed out loud, put down $25 on the bar, and left. He didn't even say goodbye to Hatton. He went to see Claudio at the bar at The Mocambo Grill. Hatton, who had never been slighted by any bartender, decided he needed a release after being careful for weeks. He went to The Wilds, where he saw a handsome man sitting on a bench talking with a Cocker Spaniel.

Hatton was feeling confident, invincible. The man looked up from his dog and smiled at him. Hatton smiled back. He went over to the man and sat down.

"It's a beautiful night," Hatton said.

"I was thinking the same thing," the man said. "Sometimes you have to come out and let it all soak in." The dog looked at Hatton as if he were sizing him up.

"You brought your dog," Hatton said.

"We come as a package," the handsome man said, smiling. He was wearing a tight T-shirt that showed off the definition in his arms. Hatton was transfixed. "Love me, love my dog," the man said, still smiling.

"I like dogs enough," Hatton said. "I like men more," he added, moving closer to the man. "Tonight's the kind of evening that shouldn't be experienced alone—if you know what I mean." He put his hand on the man's right thigh. "Strong legs."

"You have good legs, as well." The man put his hand on Hatton's left thigh and squeezed.

"Maybe we can go somewhere?" Hatton asked.

"I don't know. What do you have in mind?"

"I think you know."

"I'm not sure I do. I'm just sitting here with my dog."

"No one just sits in this section of the park, particularly a man as handsome as you."

"Thank you. Like I said before, what do you have in mind?"

"Maybe we can take a walk over there, behind those trees?"

The man was still hesitating, which led Hatton to ask, "Look, if you want money, that's OK."

"Not sure I understand you."

"I'd pay you for a blowjob."

"You would pay me, pay me to have sex with you?"

"I have $100, what will that get me?"

"At least one night in a holding cell," the man said. "You're under arrest for soliciting sex."

"Fuck me," Hatton muttered in disbelief.

"Not even for $100," the handsome cop said as his dog barked in agreement. As the cop cuffed Hatton, the Cocker Spaniel sniffed Hatton's left shoe and then peed on it. The dog barked again, almost sounding satisfied by what he had just done.

◆ ◆ ◆

"I'll have a *Vieux Carre*, Claudio," Sumner said as he settled into his seat at the bar. "I really like this drink."

"I'm glad," Claudio said. "You're much more pleasant without your friend."

"I agree. I think I will cut the cord. Now that Hatton has outfoxed everyone, there will be no dealing with him."

"Karma is a funny thing. It doesn't forget. It takes its own time, but your friend will have his moment of reckoning. I promise."

"I would love to be there to see it."

"Just be content knowing it will happen."

"You were right about the cocktail, Claudio."

"I'm right about many things. And just so you know, I decided I like you now that you are free of that asshole friend."

"To new friendships," Sumner said, going to raise a glass but realizing he still didn't have a cocktail.

"I can fix that," Claudio said. "I can fix that."

◆ ◆ ◆

After Hatton was booked, he was put in a holding cell. Shortly afterward, two men were put in the same cell with him. Hatton recognized the faces. They were the men from the surveillance video, picked up for a new crime. They recognized Hatton from television. The two men smiled at their luck.

"Look," one said to the other. "It's the famous secretary."

"So it is," the other man replied.

Hatton realized his charmed existence had come to an end. The bishop would not excuse the arrest, the media would pounce, and now, in a holding cell with his shoes smelling of dog pee, he could not escape his fate. The two men moved closer to Hatton, casting him in shadow.

If either had listened, they would have heard Hatton say as they closed in on their trapped prey, "Fuck, me."

Thanksgiving

Jim stared at the vacuum cleaner in the hall closet the way he used to look at a solitary guy across a bar at 1:30 in the morning: with resignation and the knowledge that they were destined to dance. Not for long, but long enough. There were no other options, no waiting for something better to come along. This was it. Do or dance. And so now, at sixty-four, on this cloudy Thanksgiving morning, it was vacuum or face the wrath of his husband.

Robby began asking Jim to vacuum at 10:00, a least an hour ago. Now, Robby was in full pre-dinner party mode. Pots were steaming. The kitchen sink overflowed with the detritus of mushrooms, celery, and onions. A shredded loaf of Wonder Bread soaked in milk in a large plastic bowl positioned precariously over smaller sisters on the counter.

Robby was muttering. Never a good sign. He had a pie to make, a turkey to stuff and there was the bread to get into the machine. All the while, their three dogs—LaVerne, Maxene, and Patty—ran underfoot, much like Jim, as Robby often would say in an exasperated voice that did little to conceal the love he had for his partner of thirty-nine years.

Their union was unique, not just for two men who met just before AIDS consumed many of their generation, but for most couples— straight or gay. They managed to stick it out through the disappointments and transformations that shaped partners in their inextricable journey from the heady days of twenty-one, drinking shots in a sweat-infused dance club, to the sober moments of sixty-four, holding hands in the sterile examining room of an oncologist.

It had taken much work to get to this place, this life, and as Jim looked down at the aging Electrolux, to this much dust on the living room floor.

"People will be getting here soon," Robby shouted from the kitchen. "I don't want you cleaning when Bill arrives. He's always early."

"It's only 11. You told everyone to come at 3."

"He'll be here by 2. He always comes too early."

"Do you know that from experience?"

"Ha, ha, ha, mister funnyman. Bad jokes aren't going to clean this house. I'm cooking dinner. All I ask of you is to run the vacuum. Geez, Louise."

"Language, mister man," Jim said in that voice that always took them to the same place. Jim abandoned the vacuum in the foyer. "Get out of my way, LaVerne, daddy is coming through." Jim shooed a dachshund from his path to the kitchen. "I'd rather be doing something else." He grabbed Robby from behind, pulling the robe away from his chest.

"These mushrooms won't get into the stuffing by themselves."

"Yes, dear. Anything you say, dear." Jim's hands were firmly around Robby's still-trim waist. His mouth was working his partner's neck. "You taste like butter."

"Honestly, what's gotten into you?"

"If we can get these damn dogs out of the way, you might be asking the same question about yourself in about three minutes." Jim ushered Robby into the bedroom. The vacuum was still in the hall.

◆ ◆ ◆

Michael stared at himself in the bathroom mirror, surveying his 59-year-old body. The brown chest hair was turning white. His beard already was grey, and the hair on his head—what was left of it—was salt and pepper. Michael didn't mind that his youth had receded, but the goddamn hair, well, there was no justice in the world.

He sucked in his stomach as if he were at the gym, walking into the steam room hoping to attract the attention of a younger man. That hardly ever happens, just like hurricanes in Hartford, Hereford, and Hampshire, Michael sighed.

Robby always said men over fifty become invisible to young gay men, except those few attracted to older men or to the twinks seeking a Daddy. Michael didn't reject the occasional attention from a twink, or whatever millennials call twinks, but he would intellectualize them into a hasty departure. They wanted a Daddy; he wanted a man.

So, Michael usually went home by himself, neither loved nor laid. Still, Michael thought, he looked damn good for his age. The belly was almost flat, the chest broad, and the stoop of advanced age had not yet set in, which for a man of only 5'6" offered him some comfort. Michael imagined himself as a curled-up curmudgeon at eighty-six, banging around Trader Joe's with a walker, looking for fibrous food.

"Oy!" he said, giving his belly a pat.

That was long from now, or at least long enough. Michael walked into the bedroom and pulled a pair of grey slacks, a crisp, blue-striped shirt, and black lace-ups from the closet. He tossed the pants and shirt on the already-made bed. Michael made the bed as soon as he woke up every morning, one of many quirks a partner would have corrected decades ago.

Michael went to the long dresser he bought when he was twenty-four and took out a pair of boxers and a striped pair of socks. From the tall dresser of equal vintage, he chose a cream cashmere pullover. "Yes, this will do nicely," he said aloud.

He had to look good for Thanksgiving at Robby and Jim's. Maybe there would be an extra man, as opposed to a leftover. That was how he described himself—a leftover. A man of a certain age without a partner or without the backstory of a long, committed relationship that ended in death was a leftover. Someone never chosen.

Michael's romantic life was an extension of 11th grade gym class and always being the last boy left when choosing sides for basketball at Cedarhaven High. If the humiliation of being picked by default wasn't bad enough, he would be put on the "skins" side and have to take off his shirt, exposing a mass of hairless white flesh and burgeoning breasts. That image of how he looked at sixteen haunted Michael still.

He could see the reality of how he looked at fifty-nine, but it was a façade. Under the hairy, personal trainer-toned veneer was "the faggot" of Cedarhaven High. There are words that cannot be unsaid. There are sacraments that cannot be undone. You cannot be un-baptized. You cannot be a grown man who was never called a faggot as a boy if you were called a faggot as a boy. It marks you. It mocks you.

Michael had his share of boyfriends, but they stuck like peel-off nametags at a convention: Hi, my name is Dave or Mark or Tim. Without even noticing when it happened, they weren't on your chest anymore but lost somewhere in a crowd of strangers.

Maybe it was him. Maybe it was his choices. But Michael remained optimistic that today would be different. There would be no basketball. No "skins" or "shirts." There would be singing, and Michael could sing.

Most guests at Robby and Jim's were expected to sing. Whether they did it for a living—and how many people make a living singing?—most had started out as singers or performers. Robby and Jim's living room was like playing the Carlyle in New York or the old Cinegrill at the Hollywood Roosevelt Hotel.

After dinner, they each took a turn with a song they had worked on with Robby many times before. As the years passed, guests—the singers and the ones who just listened—heard the same damn tunes over and over. Vocal ranges shrunk, testicles shriveled, and breasts dropped, but the joy of singing never diminished.

Robby was generous to a fault when it came to singers. An accomplished pianist beyond the talents of 90 percent of the performers he played for, Robby could make most anyone sound good. Singers were like the ingredients in Robby's homemade pies, thrown together seemingly without any thought, yet they came to the table as pure perfection.

Michael would sing today. He would dive head-first into a pool of Sondheim, Porter, or Berlin, the water pulsing against his skin as his body propelled him through lyrics and melody until he emerged at the song's end, dripping with contentment, letting the chill of the air mix with the warm smell of one of Robby's pies cooling in the kitchen.

◆ ◆ ◆

"Are you done vacuuming?"

"Is that what you call it now?" Jim said from the living room. "You used to call it making love."

"Don't 'making love' me, mister. I am way behind."

"It's a nice behind."

"Honestly."

The spouses bantered back and forth as Robby put dry and wet ingredients into the bread machine, assembled the stuffing, and got it into the turkey and a casserole dish. He would put the pie in the oven after the turkey came out.

"This house is still a mess," Robby said as he came out of the kitchen and surveyed the living room. "We have to dust, pull out a tablecloth, set the table…"

"Will you relax? It all comes together. It always comes together. John and Mary, Maggie, Sean, and Harris are bringing food. Michael's bringing the champagne. And you know Bill loves to set the table."

"He does, doesn't he?"

"I think he goes from neighborhood to neighborhood with plates, cutlery, and napkins and sneaks into people's homes and does up their dining rooms."

"He's a sweetheart, you know."

"I know. We all have our things. Some of us are obsessed with vacuuming."

"Are you mocking me, James Howard Wagner?"

"'James Howard Wagner. James Howard Wagner!' Them's fighting words."

"Get back. I have a spatula, and I know how to use it. What got into you?"

"It's the smell of turkey in the air."

"I just put the turkey in the oven. There's no turkey smell."

"Maybe it's you? Let me take a sniff. It is you. Yummy."

"Your mouth is writing checks your body cannot cash, mister. Now, just get away from me so I can get this house into shape. When you're done with the vacuum, clean the guest bathroom."

At 2:00, Patty started barking, which sent Maxime to the grey Art Deco lounge chair by the window. LaVerne quickly joined the trio. Jim went to the door to let Bill in as he shooed the dogs away.

"Happy Thanksgiving!"

"I know I'm a little early. I thought I could help set up," Bill said as he took his coat off in the foyer. The dogs were barking up a storm. "I'll just put Inspector Renault in the other room," Bill said as he walked into the guest bedroom and put his vintage coat on the bed. Like its owner, the coat has seen better times, but it was, again, like its owner, one of a kind.

The coat was a costume from a 40's movie and had been worn by Claude Rains. Bill had bought it at auction thirty years ago and trotted it out for special occasions. And although the coat was not made for *Casablanca*, Bill called it his "Inspector Renault."

Bill was older than Robby and Jim, nearing seventy-seven. Pencil thin, Bill was like a cherished Christmas ornament handed down for generations, surviving moves and hardships. While there was little frame to Bill, his smile was sturdy. Perhaps from decades of looking happy in chorus lines, his facial muscles had frozen into an upright position.

He had been a dancer on Broadway. The pinnacle of his career was dancing at the Palace Theater in *Applause,* starring Miss Lauren Bacall and then later, with Miss Anne Baxter. Bill embraced the affectation of putting "Miss" before stars' names because it made him feel as if he were raised in the South rather than on the South Shore of Long Island. As Bill grew older, his style of tap-dancing musicals became no longer commercially viable, so he moved West where the weather was kinder, but casting directors and choreographers were not. He was cast from time to time on some tribute show on television or old Hollywood benefit—which was where he first met Robby—but those jobs were far and few between. And by the time he hit forty-five, they did not exist. He found a job at an independent movie/theater bookshop where he became like the shop's resident cats, Ustinov and Wells, a fixture. *The Los Angeles Times* featured him in an article when the bookstore was sold and torn down to make way for a condominium complex. Now Bill lived on Social Security, memories, and StarKist.

"I brought a new song, Robby," Bill called out toward the kitchen. "I wanted to sing something no one has heard me do."

"You'll be wonderful no matter what you sing," Robby said, poking his head out of the kitchen. "Everybody loves you every year."

"That's kind, Robby, but I know who the singers are—Maggie, Harris, Michael. They really can sing."

"Making music is like flying a kite," Robby said. "It's less about talent and more about trusting nature to lift you up."

"That's easy for you to say because you play so well," Bill said, giving Robby a hug. "I don't catch the wind, I just pass it."

"Well, you're an amateur on that score compared to some," Robby said with a smile directed at Jim.

"I'll ignore that," Jim replied. "Did you hear that, girls?" he asked the dogs. "Your daddy just disrespected your other daddy." The dogs wagged their tails in agreement. "You see that? Who's your favorite daddy?"

"Honestly. This is what I have to live with, Bill."

"It looks very good to me," Bill said to the couple. "Happy Thanksgiving."

"Happy Thanksgiving," Robby and Jim said in unison.

"Jim, can you shut the guest bedroom door so the girls don't jump all over Inspector Renault?"

"Sure thing."

Robby grabbed Bill's arm, leading him toward the dining room. "Jim and I love having you on Thanksgiving. Who else is going to set the table?"

"I bet you haven't even ironed the tablecloth."

"You're right. Let me introduce you to the iron. Bill, meet Mr. Black and Decker."

◆ ◆ ◆

When Michael drove up to the house on Washington Street, there were already two extra cars in the driveway hanging past the sidewalk. He parked on the street and took out a cardboard box with four bottles of champagne and his folder with sheet music.

Michael had parked at a 7-Eleven nearby and gotten a coffee thirty minutes ago. By nature, he was always too early, so now Michael made a point of sitting in his car close to where he was going and waiting until it was the announced time. He could hear sounds from inside the house. The front door was slightly opened behind the screen door.

"Any gay people here?" Michael said as he tapped the unlocked door and entered the house. LaVerne, Maxene, and Patty were barking. Patty was particularly attentive to Michael, who immediately stooped to pet her.

"We're all in the closet waiting for the next general election," Jim shouted from the office.

The house smelled of Thanksgiving. There was turkey, fresh bread, and that mixed scent of too many gay men wearing cologne. Michael headed into the dining room and put the champagne next to bottles of wine, gin, scotch, and soda on the massive sideboard.

"Something smells great," Michael said as he entered the kitchen.

"It's Robby. He smells of butter," Jim said, coming through the other kitchen door and giving Michael a big hug.

"I'll take your word for that," Michael said.

"Happy Thanksgiving, little brother. Let me take your coat."

"Happy Thanksgiving," Michael responded, handing off the coat and then grabbing some chips from an open bag on the table in the breakfast room. Harris was already double-dipping in the guacamole.

"Happy Thanksgiving, Michael. You're looking fit," Harris said, giving Michael a hug.

Michael was pleased. His outfit did what it was supposed to do.

Harris was originally from Scotland and came to the States in the 70s and did voice-over work. He had made a little pile back in the 80s as the voice of an owl with a Love Jones for a particular single-malt scotch.

In his youth, Harris was a ginger. Now, while his hair was still thick all over—he sported a generous mustache—the once-vibrant red had gone dull brown to slightly white. He was wearing a Versace shirt opened to mid-chest, which exposed fur and an impossibly large pectoral cross.

The buttons on the shirt strained against the fabric and Harris's expanded girth. The pants were a wide windowpane on burgundy wool, and his shoes were black velour with gold tassels. Harris never wore socks, even in winter, so the red-brown hair on his ankles was clearly visible.

Harris, when younger, was irresistible to men and women. Even now, Harris wore his sexuality like his clothes—with wild abandon. Michael had gone out with Harris to concerts and for drinks after Harris had entered Robby and Jim's orbit seven years ago, but Harris and Michael had never clicked on a sexual level.

Harris was an amiable companion. He most always attracted a crowd of men, younger ones looking for a piece of Versace. But occasionally men closer to Michael and Harris's respective ages who recognized Harris's voice from the scotch commercials would come over and order said scotch until everyone sounded like a bad imitation of Harris. The bar would be transformed into a Brigadoon where every man would lean into another drunk man's face and say, "I dinna know you can come." After Harris realized he could live off the scotch royalties but no longer on the actual stuff, there were fewer of those trips. Harris had been sober for three years, seven months and sixteen days.

"What are you going to sing today?" Michael asked Harris.

"Not sure. I was thinking, "Why can't a woman be more like a man?""

"Because we don't have penises, sweetie," Maggie interrupted, joining the two men. She was Robby's oldest friend. They had met in college. Robby was a piano major and Maggie was a theater major. At twenty, she was tall, dark, and as Robby would say lovingly, smoked everything but salmon. Forty years of smoking and drinking later, her voice had acquired the patina of the wood in an old English pub, smooth and splintered, marked by the passage of lives well celebrated.

"Don't get me wrong, women like penises," Maggie said. "We just don't want to have to be swinging one 24/7."

"You don't know what you're missing, duckie," Harris said. "It can fire a missile at DefCon 1."

"My experience is that too many missiles fire long before the silo gets open," she said, grabbing a chip, dipping it extravagantly into the guacamole and stuffing it into her mouth.

"Impressive technique," Michael said to her.

"I give it a 9," Harris quipped. "I take off a point because there was no dismount."

"Hard audience," she replied.

"You have no idea, duckie."

"You're irresistible, Harris," Maggie said, smiling. "Why aren't you straight?"

"For the same reason a woman can't be more like a man."

"I'm going to play with your chest hair just for that."

"I like to call it Loveland."

Maggie ran her fingers over Harris' chest. "There's nothing like a man with chest hair."

"Agreed," rang out across the kitchen from Michael, Robby, Jim and Bill.

"This is why I am still single," Maggie said. "The only manly men I know are gay."

"It's proof of a vengeful God," Michael said. "He's still making Eve pay for the garden of Eden. She only tempted Adam with the apple because he was paying too much attention to Steve."

"None of that religion stuff, Michael," Bill said. "I want tonight to be happy. It always gets ugly when you start with religion jokes."

"I'm just saying God created Adam, Eve, and Steve."

"Steve and Evie," Harris suggested.

"None of that," Bill said. "Remember Boris."

"Boris. That little unpleasant man. How can I forget him?" Harris asked.

"We all did," Michael said, starting to laugh. "How many years ago was that? Eight? Nine?"

"Seven," Bill said. "Boris came with Sarah. What happened to her?"

"One story at a time, duckie. First, Boris. Where's he these days?"

"Probably still down the block in her car," Michael said which sent everyone laughing.

"It's Thanksgiving," Robby shouted from his vantage point over the stove. "That was a sad Thanksgiving. He and Sarah got into that huge fight because she wouldn't sing that Cole Porter song about keeping pets. He wouldn't let it go and she said he was acting like a child, and he stormed off..."

"Except he had come in Sarah's car, so he couldn't go home," Bill said, grabbing a chip.

"And poor thing Sarah was drinking up a storm," Robby added. "She was so upset she kept drinking and drinking and eventually passed out in the den. She had parked a couple blocks away, so we forgot about Boris still in her car. We figured he would either come back here or call a cab."

"But he didn't," Jim said, rubbing Robby's shoulders. "No, that angry little queen sat inside that car all night long. He was so pissed at Sarah when she stumbled out of here the next morning."

"Serves him right," Harris said. "Disagreeable people deserve what comes to them. But Michael, duckie, it wasn't just the song. The song was the *coup de foie gras*."

"I don't think that's the correct phrase," Bill suggested.

"I don't like plain *gras*. I love *frois gras*. And that was a yummy event—the *coup de frois gras*, duckie. Michael primed the pump. He got Boris all hot and lathered when he started at dinner about Pope Benedict wearing $600 red shoes and that the pope, when alone, would tap them like Judy's sequined pumps. 'There's no place like Rome. There's no place like Rome. There's no place like Rome.' Boris turned purple."

"I think plum," Jim said.

"Eggplant," Robby interrupted.

"Amethyst," Maggie added.

"Ducky, there was nothing semi-precious about Boris. Purple."

"And it was my fault that he went off like a firecracker?" Michael asked mockingly.

"Wipe that smirk off your face, ducky. You enjoyed every minute."

"How was I supposed to know he was going to stay pissed when we moved to the piano portion of the evening?"

"You poked the bear, duckie. You poked that little Russian bear, Boris."

"I have never poked a bear," Michael said.

"That's not what I heard, duckie. You have poked many a bear." The men all laughed.

"There is a lady present," Maggie said. "Have you no boundaries?"

"Duckie, if you want a wall, you're in the wrong party."

"Tushy, Harris. Tushy."

"Don't you mean touché, Bill?" Maggie asked.

"No, I do not. Miss Carol Channing as Lorelei Lee in *Lorelei*, a 1974 reworking of *Gentlemen Prefer Blondes*, a production in which I danced in, would retort, 'tushy, tushy,' instead of touché. It got a huge laugh."

"That's what I love about you, Bill. You aren't a window into old Broadway. You're the whole friggin' stage," Robby said from the kitchen. Robby never cursed. Bill blushed.

"Well, this is all very nice, but what about Sarah?" Maggie asked. "That was how this whole conversation started."

"It got started with Bill asking Michael to refrain from talking about religion, which is a very good idea," Robby said, waving a celery stalk at Michael like a weapon. And as for Sarah, I heard she found a man, got married, and moved to Camarillo."

"Damn," Michael, Harris and Bill said.

"It isn't fair," Bill added.

"Which brings me back to 'why can't a woman be more like a man?'" Harris said.

"Come on, you," Maggie said playfully to Harris. "I'll buy you a ginger ale in the dining room. Bring Loveland. I want to take my manicure out for another spin."

Harris and Maggie went into the dining room as the doorbell rang. LaVerne and Maxene ran to the door barking. Michael captured Patty's attention. It was John and Mary at the door. Mary worked with Robby at Santa Monica Community College, where she taught art.

A short, squat woman, Mary was Earth Mother to the group, although the youngest. She was from an old New England family, who, according to Robby, had some connection to the frozen seafood industry. Harris used to call Mary "Mrs. Paul's" when he was drunk in the old days, not because it annoyed Mary, who found it funny, but because it really ticked off her husband John. That gave Harris great pleasure.

John Bayer was tall and pale, with a scraggly beard and angular beak. Seen in a profile, the bird-shaped proboscis leaned into the beard as a bird stretched its head from a nest. He had a decent build, which might have been what attracted Mary to him. That remained a mystery to Robby, Jim, and the circle.

What made John so annoying was he ejaculated opinions like a hustler passes on a treatable STD, with little concern as to the consequences and the belief that an hour spent with him was so pleasurable an experience, a little subsequent urination pain was hardly of note. He was an attorney specializing in probate law. And he was said to be very good, often by John himself. Which explains why Harris would refer to John when he was not in earshot as Manure Man.

"Manure Man has arrived, duckie."

"Be good, Harris. It's Thanksgiving," Maggie said, barely containing her laugh.

"Hey guys, you're all here," John said, walking into the dining room. Mary was behind with a casserole dish.

"We're late," she said. "It's all my fault. John was ready on time, but I didn't time the casserole right."

"I tell her, just read through the recipe thoroughly before starting, but she never listens," John said as Mary smiled.

"Maybe you should do the cooking, then?" Harris said. Jim, Michael, and Maggie looked concerned. Bill quickly poured a glass of ginger ale and handed it to Harris as Robby came dashing from the kitchen, taking the casserole from Mary.

"No worries," Robby said. "We're not all here. We're still waiting for Sean and Simon."

"Who's Sean?" Maggie asked.

"Maybe he's this year's Boris, duckie?" Harris said, sipping the ginger ale.

"You're an evil, furry man," Maggie replied, walking next to Harris. She was determined to keep Harris in check. She played with the large pectoral cross around his neck.

"And I thought Simon was up north," Michael interrupted.

"Sean just joined the Vivaldi Singers," Robby said looking directly at Harris with a "don't start with me, mister, look" that would have sent Jim running for cover. "He's a wonderful singer. He had no place to go on Thanksgiving, and no one should be alone on Thanksgiving, so I invited him. And yes, Michael, Simon was living up north, but he moved back at the beginning of October. I told him to come home to us for Thanksgiving."

The bell rang again. The dogs went flying. It was both Sean and Simon. They had arrived at the same time. Sean was tall, blond and no more than thirty—in age and waist size. Harris, Michael, Bill, and Jim exchanged looks.

"Jesus," Bill said.

"Indeed, duckie. He could be my savior anytime this week."

"Goodness," Maggie said. "I think we are about to have a missile launch."

"There's no military hostilities," John said. "No one's launching missiles on Thanksgiving."

"It was a phrase, John," Mary said. "Maggie wasn't talking about actual missiles."

"Then why did she say that?" John asked.

"And why can't a woman be more like a man?" Harris said.

Robby interrupted them. "Everyone, this is Sean. And some of you know Simon. He's an old friend. Everyone introduce yourselves while I get dinner finished."

Simon was a good friend of Robby and Jim's, but Michael had met him first at LACMA, staring at an early Picasso. They started talking and went for coffee. From there, they went to a diner and then after that to Simon's. It was an uncharacteristic encounter for Michael. Completely spontaneous. They dated for two years. Michael eventually brought Simon to Robby and Jim's who were delighted that Michael had met someone. But while there was a real connection between the two men, it needed work on both sides. There was never a break-up or a fight. Over time, Michael had put Simon on the side, not forgotten, but not remembered enough. Eventually, he and Simon slipped into a casual friendship. They hadn't had sex in years when Simon left to take a teaching job in San Francisco. Michael couldn't remember how long ago that was.

Back then, Simon looked like he played professional baseball. He was tall, broad, and muscular. If Michael had a fantasy type, it was Simon. But Michael, being Michael, never told Simon that in exactly those words. Now, years later, Simon still looked good. Not as lean, but still handsome.

"You look fantastic," Michael said, shaking Simon's hand.

"I want a hug," Simon said and pulled Michael into him. Simon's scent was familiar and intoxicating. "You look damn good, yourself."

"Let me have some of that," Harris said coming over to Simon. As the two men also hugged, Michael walked over to Sean. "I'm Michael."

"Sean," he extended his hand to Michael. The grip was firm and confident. It distracted Michael, who had wanted to go over to Simon, but Sean was new and shiny, and Michael, for all his pretentions of being evolved, was still a gay man on the hunt. "Let me get you a drink, Sean," he said, shepherding the younger man to the sideboard. Simon mingled with Harris, Bill, and Maggie. Tom had cornered Jim in the living room, wanting to talk about estate planning, while Mary was helping Robby in the kitchen.

◆ ◆ ◆

Robby and Jim had made several promises to one another over their nearly forty years. One was they would never forget how important companionship was. As gay men, they had seen too many people they knew die without family. It wasn't just AIDS or the 80s and 90s, although AIDS had thinned out their particular herd of men born in the 1950s and early 60s.

There were so many "leftovers," as Michael would impoliticly say; the men and women not chosen by either side to play in the game who ended up assigned by default. Robby and Jim made a promise that on Thanksgiving there would be no "leftovers"—everyone was chosen.

Robby and Jim were not particularly religious, but they believed God was found wherever two or more people gathered in love. Their well-worn home was a sanctuary for anyone needing to feel wanted, chosen, and not assigned by default to a team because everyone else had been picked.

A key part of the Thanksgiving tradition at their home was the breaking of warm, freshly baked bread, which Robby would explain was not a Christian or Jewish tradition—but a human one.

Bread was a staple of life; to share it was to share life itself. Before the Thanksgiving meal began, a basket of roughly sliced bread was passed among the dinner guests. And rather than proclaim "the body of Christ," as Jim had done throughout his childhood as a Catholic, the communicant would proclaim an expression of thanks, whatever they felt at that moment.

The guests had found their chairs, and the chatter stopped when Robby entered the dining room with the linen-lined basket. The smell of warm bread filled the room and brought with it a deep silence. Robby handed the basket to Jim and then took his seat opposite his husband at the other end of the table.

Jim broke off a piece of bread. "I give thanks for my friends, for this wonderful meal we will soon eat, and for my husband who challenges me to enjoy each and every moment." Jim looked at Robby, who understood what was not said, and passed the basket to Mary at his right.

"I give thanks for this meal, for these friends," she said, handing the basket to her husband.

"I give thanks that Robby is such a great cook, so I get one fantastic meal each year," John said, passing to Sean.

"I give thanks for this invitation, and for new friends," Sean said as he turned to Maggie on his right, who took the basket and gave his hand a gentle squeeze as she smiled.

Michael noticed the gesture and thought to himself, "Maggie, you deserve so much more than you have."

"I give thanks for this family that chose me, for Robby and Jim, for all of you. This is the best day of the year," she added with a smile."

Maggie handed the basket to Robby at the head of the table. "I also give thanks to all of you for the joy of being able to gather again this year. I give thanks to all who sit here today and for having known so many others who are no longer here in person but in spirit, in our hearts. I'm not a formal prayer person, but let's think of those friends who have passed…And most of all, I give thanks for my husband, the love of my life." Robby and Jim looked across the table at one other. Jim's eyes were watering slightly. No one noticed but Robby who passed the basket to Michael.

"I give thanks for this day, for old friends and for new ones, for the possibilities that both provide," Michael said.

"I may cry," Maggie said, looking at Michael. "Someone, please, say something funny."

"I give thanks that Boris is not here," Harris volunteered.

"Who?" asked John.

"Mood officially changed," Maggie said.

Michael passed the basket to Simon on his right. "I give thanks for a Thanksgiving with true friends, people I have not seen in years who I feel

I never really left. This means so much to me—you all mean so much to me." Simon looked at Michael as he passed the basket to Harris, but Michael was looking at Sean and did not notice.

"Well, I give thanks that I still have my looks, my hair, not like some of you," Harris began. "I give thanks that this aging old Scot has a nest he can return to whenever he needs one. I give thanks that in this house, it is always Thanksgiving. I give thanks for Robby and Jim."

"Amen to that," Bill said, who took the basket from Harris. "I give thanks for finding Robby first and then Jim. I give thanks for all the memories that I still can savor. For the years enjoyed and for the moment that is now, I give thanks."

Bill handed the basket to Jim, who placed it on the table. "Now, all join hands," Jim said. "For the meal we are about to enjoy, we thank thee, God." There was a slight squeeze of hands as they embraced, not as "leftovers' but as the chosen. "Now, let's get at Mr. Turkey."

"He's not very thankful today," Mary said. "Tom Turkey is dead."

"Another straight male bites the dust," Maggie chimed in.

After dessert, the guests moved into the living room, some carrying coffee, others their wine glasses. Bill had taken another piece of pie and put it down on the coffee table, artfully keeping it out of reach from LaVerene, Maxene, and Patty, who shamelessly were playing to the crowd.

Robby went to the piano and said, "Who's going to start?"

"I will," Maggie said. "You men all want to stare at each other, so I'll get out of the way quickly," she added as she walked to the grand piano.

"Duckie, we will do that whether you go first or last."

"Harris, you are evil," she replied with added drama.

"Compliments might get you another trip to Loveland."

"Promises. Promises. I'm going to sing a song most of you know. It's a bit of cliché, but then again, look at us."

Maggie proceeded to sing "I'm Still Here," a song from *Follies* that is an anthem to survival. It is as ubiquitous to gay men as are glass bowls filled with condoms at the end of a bar in a club. What Maggie lacked in voice, she had ten-fold in commitment. She was the song even though the references to former fame or post-World War II America did apply to her generation. The song was about reveling in the now, not because you regretted the past, but because it was *your* past and you lived every goddamned minute of it. When Maggie finished, everyone applauded. As she walked back to her seat, she looked at Harris and said, "Top that, duckie."

"At my age, duckie, I would be happy to top anything."

Harris proceeded to sing, "Why can't a woman be more than a man," from *My Fair Lady*, the song he was promoting throughout the party. His Scottish accent added to the flavor of the song. He was no Henry Higgins. He was Harris, and that was impressive enough. As he went through each verse, his face reddened, almost like when he was drunk, but this time, it was excitement pushing the blood to the cheeks. When he finished, Sean stood up, clapping. "You were amazing. Just amazing. I'm going to sing from the same show. 'On the street where you live.'"

Sean was exactly as advertised. He had a beautiful, clear tenor voice. He conveyed the buoyant optimism of the ballad, even if the character who sings it in *My Fair Lady* is a weak-willed dolt incapable of winning and keeping a strong-willed Eliza. Listening to Sean, the men in the room were taken back in time—hearing him sing, looking at the sturdy chest expand with breath, the middle-aged men felt the tug of their youth in their hearts, and to the surprise of some, a tug in their briefs. In truth, Sean could have sung "Mary had a little lamb," and at least three of the men listening and watching would have become moist.

When Sean finished, everyone applauded and asked for another song. Sean declined which elevated him in Michael's eyes immediately. Despite his youth, Sean had it together at such a young age. He clearly didn't need to push what was already well out there.

Bill always went last. That was his spot, so it fell upon Michael to be the penultimate performer. He gave Sean's arm a squeeze as they passed one another near the piano.

"I'm going to sing something new," Michael said, handing sheet music to Robby.

"I hope it's from *Hamilton*, duckie. I just see you in *Hamilton*."

"Is that because you traveled to New York with him," Michael replied, not quite as humorously as he should have. Michael didn't like being the butt of any joke.

"Someone's testicles are in a twist," Maggie said.

"Girls, girls," Jim said. "Let's hear what Michael is going to sing. I'm hoping for hip-hop."

"Maybe hip-hoppy, like 'Peter Cottontail,'" Simon added, looking straight at Michael. The quip had the right effect. Simon had known how to get Michael to loosen up and Michael chuckled and said, "OK, I had that coming. No, this is not a song from *Hamilton* or about a character from Mr. McGregor's garden. It's a song about fathers and sons, about getting old, about legacies."

Michael sang "If I Sing," a song from *Closer than Ever*, a musical revue about grappling with middle age. The song describes a grown man coming to grips with his father's advanced aging while realizing the shared bond they have is music. It's a song written for a man about ten years younger than Michael, and his voice was more forced at the top than it would have been when he was still in his forties, but he still had the notes, and his delivery was honest. There was something in the air that Thanksgiving, or maybe in Robby's pie, that was changing what usually was a fun, campy, semi-serious entertainment into something more powerful. Truth.

Michael felt good about how he sang. Simon's eyes were watering, and so were Sean's. Michael was not sure whose approval mattered more at the moment. He was still more in his own head than anywhere else.

Maggie broke the mood. "Damn, that was so good. I can't even fathom what you would do with Peter Cottontail."

"There's a porn movie, duckie..."

"None of that," Robby interrupted. "Michael sang beautifully. Now let us hear from Bill, who also has a new song."

Bill walked up to the piano and put his hand on the lid. "I usually sing funny songs. Novelty songs. But the more I thought about this Thanksgiving, the more I thought about a Thanksgiving I spent when I was as young as you, Sean. And cuter. Well, maybe not cuter, but I had a certain something back then. Every openly gay man in New York City in the late seventies had that something. We were invincible, daring people to frown at our clothes and mannerisms. It was a special time if you were out and, in the dance community and you were a chorus boy, you had to be gay. It was on your resume. Age, height, weight, homosexuality. These were boxes that had to be checked—and not a word from you, Harris."

"I wasn't going to say anything about checked boxes, duckie. Maybe about a particular Czech's box, but never mind."

"As I was saying," Bill continued, unfazed. "It was a glorious time. I had three close friends. We had all danced in shows together—Dean, Sam and Tom. Since we all had moved to New York from other places, we became our own family. There was this one Thanksgiving when we had nowhere to go, and none of us could cook and you really can't do much with a turkey on a hot plate, anyway, so we went to this old man's gay bar. It wasn't officially a gay bar, but it had a piano, and the crowd was somewhere between King Lear and the ghost of Hamlet's father. We were all drunk. We were always drunk back then if we weren't in a show or had the day off. There we were, three sheets to the wind, and this old, old guy—probably around seventy—which was really old back then, got up and sang this song. We started to snigger when he got up, but there was something about him that made us respect who he was, where he had been, and where he would soon be going. He was so comfortable with who he was.

"We didn't have that kind of self-confidence. And on that Thanksgiving, we were all a mess—part from drink and part from being silly homosexuals. It's funny, when you're twenty-seven, being silly can be considered sexy. When you're seventy-two, being silly is seen as comic, but not in a good way. No, not in a good way.

"That was the last Thanksgiving we were all together. We were in different road companies, or someone had a performance, or two of us were in New York while the other two were not and then it was suddenly 1983. Sam died in March. Dean that July. Tom didn't pass until '87. I still don't know why I didn't. There were so many funerals. So many memorial services.

"It's funny AIDS never really had a song—something that gave people hope through it all. There were attempts to find one, but you can't force those things like making famous actors wear red ribbons on award shows so everyone feels like they have accomplished something.

Anyway, I've been thinking a lot about that last Thanksgiving with Dean, Sam, and Tom and the song that old queen sang.

"I wanted to sing that song today. That queen didn't sing from the heart; he sang from his soul. It moves me still. So today, the torch has been passed from one old queen to another. It's an old Cole Porter song.

"I guess there are no new Cole Porter songs," Bill added for a slight comic effect. "This is for you—Dean, Sam, Tom, and for that old queen in a dingy piano bar."

Bill closed his eyes as Robby began playing.

"Every time we say goodbye, I die a little. Every time we say goodbye, I wonder why a little..."

Bill spoke the lyrics more than sang them. His delivery was slow, deliberative, and poetic, and Robby filled in the spaces from his Steinway. The assembled held on each word, and as Bill moved toward the song's closing lyrics—"how strange the change from major to minor," it forced everyone, except Sean, who was too young, to reflect on that very change in their lives. Imperceptible as you live it, but somehow, in moments like this, the changes are understood in the linear journey of life. The major chords of youth. The more complex minor chords of later years. Michael sat transfixed, no longer in himself. He had poured out all his substantial vocal power into a beautiful song, but it was his voice that carried the song.

With Bill, it was not his voice, or his heart, but just like the old queen in Bill's story, Bill now sung from his soul. It filled the room, and when Bill finished singing, there was complete silence. It was not a joyous quiet. It was not sad. It was as if God—if indeed there is a God—had found a way inside each man and woman in that living room, pulled away the stone in front of the proverbial tomb, and exclaimed, "Rejoice!" They did. They each gave thanks to one another. All in the silence of a moment.

Harris was first to speak with a quip. "Duckie, flush those comic tunes down the loo. That was stupendous."

Bill was engulfed with praise. Everyone got up to applaud and celebrate him. Maggie got a glass from the dining room, poured some champagne into the flute, and handed it to Bill. "Let us all raise a glass to the best singer of the evening."

Everyone found a glass and said, "To Bill," who breathed it all in like clear air on a mountaintop. Bill was crying. "I don't know what to say," he began and then looked confused for a split second like he was trying to find a word. And then, Bill was on the floor. The glass had flown out of his hand, shattering under the piano. The dogs, frightened, started barking, and Jim was first to get to his friend, who was not moving.

"I think he had a stroke. Call 911!"

For the next five minutes, there was another silence. This one was terrible. Bill still had a pulse. Maggie grabbed pillows to put under his head. As John started to say something while they all waited for the ambulance, Mary turned to her husband and said firmly, "If you say one word right now, it's over." For once, John remained mute. Michael found himself involuntarily saying a "Hail Mary." He didn't notice Simon was doing the same thing. Robby held Bill's hand. Jim stood outside the house looking for the ambulance, which came quickly. When the EMTs rushed into the living room, so recently a site of thanksgiving, they found a group of mainly late-middle-aged men and women quietly huddled around Bill.

"He just collapsed," Jim said to the EMTs. "He was standing one minute and then he collapsed. Did he have a stroke?"

The EMTs assessed Bill and did not look optimistic as they placed him on a gurney while monitoring his vital signs. No one spoke as Bill was carried into the ambulance. Jim said, "I'll follow to the hospital." The sirens shrieked into the night, and then it and Bill were gone.

"Let's just clean up and wait until we hear from Jim," Robby said. "I think that right now, we should all be busy."

Maggie found a dustbin and swept up the glass. Mary dabbed at the beads of champagne from the floor. Michael, Simon, and John started collecting plates and glasses from the living and dining rooms, bringing them into the kitchen, where Robby was wrapping up leftovers.

Harris sat on the couch. He was sobbing. Sean sat next to him. "He'll be OK," he said to Harris, not believing it but feeling compelled to say it.

"It's horrible."

"I know. He's your friend."

"No, what's horrible is that I'm not crying for Bill. It's Nico."

"Who is Nico?"

"When I was a young man, a little younger than you, I lived in Greece for about a year. I met this young Greek, Nico. He was like a god, or at least that's how I choose to remember him. It was January when we first met. The feast of Epiphany. One of the Greek traditions is a large cross is thrown into the water and young men dive for it. If you retrieve the cross it's good luck. Nico dove with other young men into the cool water and came up with the cross. It was like he had found the Holy Grail and a 40-carat diamond at the same time. He was beaming. Our eyes met as he came out of the water, shivering slightly, his hairy chest glistening as the early morning sun hit the tanned skin. Later, we started talking. His English was very good. Before sunset, we had sex, sex like I have never had since. Passionate, raw, and tender. We were playing with fire in a room filled with gunpowder. Just because the Greeks invented being queer didn't mean they approved of it. It's one thing having homoerotic vases and another having a homo in your house. But we were young and too stupid to think about that.

"Nico was athletic. An adventurer. He did not know fear. All that summer, we would go diving off cliffs together. We'd find places where we could swim naked and have sex in hidden coves. Matches and gunpowder. There was this day when we had too much to drink, and Nico wanted to go diving. I said no, but not in a way that would have stopped anyone of his will. He dove off this cliff—not even a really high one—and he hit a rock. There I was in the middle of nowhere with the love of my life drowning before my eyes. I ran down to the shore as fast as I could. I was buck-naked. By the time I pulled him out of the water, he was gone. I tried to revive him, but he was bleeding, and he wasn't breathing. He lay there broken but still beautiful, still warm. This perfect, beautiful man died before my eyes.

"What happened later remains in this haze of events. It was deemed an accident, but I felt responsible. And now everyone knew our little dirty secret. They did not dare speak its name as the drama queens would say, but I had to leave. And I wanted to leave. Nico and I hadn't lived together, but he stayed in my rented room often. The one thing I have of his is that cross he brought up from the water. This cross," Harris said, fingering the large pectoral cross hanging from his neck. "He gave it to me the first night we met."

"I'm so sorry," Sean said, holding Harris' hand. "He must have been an amazing man."

"He was. I'm an old fool crying like this for a man who died before your parents were born. I haven't seen someone die in front of me since Nico. Bill is ..."

"Bill is getting the best attention he can," Sean said. "We don't know what's happening with him. Memories are odd things. Even I know that and I'm the youngster here. Memories come out of nowhere. One minute, it's all sunshine, and then something clicks, and it's twilight. It's OK to cry for Nico. You carry him with you. He's just as real today as he was then."

"I miss his touch. His scent. I can smell him. If I put this cross close enough to my face, I can remember how he smelled. I can remember the way he looked when he shot up from the water with the cross like he found the Holy Grail ..."

"And a 40-carat diamond. It's OK, Harris."

Harris leaned into Sean's chest and started to cry as Sean stroked his back slowly. Michael, Simon, and John came into the living room and didn't say anything. Michael and Simon out of respect and John out of fear that Mary had finally had enough and would leave no matter whether he spoke or not. Truth still filled that house on Washington Street. There was no escaping it.

"I'm making some hot tea," Robby said as he came from the kitchen. Mary and Maggie followed behind. Everyone found a seat. Robby went over to the piano and started to play "Every Time We Say Goodbye." Jim's car pulled into the driveway. The girls started barking and ran to the door. They all knew Jim was back too soon.

"He didn't make it to the hospital," Jim said as he came inside. "When I got to the hospital, the EMTs said he passed in the ambulance. I can't believe he's gone. We were all so happy and now this."

"I know I am the youngest guy here, and I don't know much about life," Sean began. "I don't know anything about death. But I know Bill was happy today. He was beaming when he finished singing, and you all came up to him and toasted him. Maybe at the moment he achieved the greatest happiness possible for him, he died. Isn't that the best way to die? Surrounded by people who love you and are telling you they love you?"

Harris, who had been holding Sean's hand while he spoke, said, "You're right, duckie. We don't know when we check out, but to be with people we love—a family who loves you because you're exactly who you are and not who they want you to be—that is a good ending."

No one else said anything. They remained quiet in search of an epiphany. Harris fingered the cross around his neck. Mary was the first to say that they should go. After she and John left, Simon got up. Michael wanted to follow him out to the car and suggest they get a coffee, but he didn't. Old habits are not like old friends. They rarely die on you.

Maggie left next. Followed by Harris and Sean, who clearly were not ready to say goodnight. Robby and Jim smiled at the two men—one old with the spirit of a child and one young with an old soul—who seemed to have found a connection. Maybe it would last. Maybe it would last just long enough, which really is all that matters.

Michael was the last to leave. He hugged his two brothers. "We should talk tomorrow. Did Bill have any family?"

"Yes," Robby said. "He had all of us. We'll take care of the arrangements. I'll call you tomorrow. Drive safe, Michael."

"I will," he replied, hugging them both and then crouching down, giving each dog at pat. He stopped at Patty and hugged the dachshund, who was most pleased with his show of affection.

"It will be all right, Michael," Jim said.

"I want to sing that song at his funeral," Michael said. "The torch passes to another old queen. I want people to know he mattered to us."

"They will, Michael," Robby said. "And Bill knew that. Get home safely."

"I will." Michael went to his car, and Jim and Robby stood at the door, more like parents than brothers, watching him drive off. It had started to rain. They locked the front door and turned off the porch light.

◆ ◆ ◆

Michael turned on the lights in the living room. It felt cold. He went over to the fireplace, turned on the gas, and lit the fire. He sat in the tufted chair to the left of the fireplace. The dark leather had warmed into honeyed brown after many years of use. Michael ran his fingers over the leather, letting his fingers dip into each tuft trying to remember every touch he ever felt.

It was raining hard now. He could hear it beat against the windows. "Like the drip, drip, drip of the raindrops when the summer shower is through," he sang low. "Damn that Cole Porter." It wasn't summer. Late autumn. How many songs are left? How many more Thanksgivings with Robby and Jim?

"Fuck!" Michael got up and took off his wet coat and hung it up in the hall closet. He walked back into the living room and fingered the keyboard of the Baldwin his parents gave him at graduation. He moved past the piano and poured himself a scotch from the Waterford decanter next to the Waterford tumblers. It was all so perfect. The living room. The glasses. There was no mess because there was no one but him in the house.

Not like the blessed chaos of Robby and Jim's, with dogs yapping and peeing on rugs never quite clean and dust in corners like children playing hide and seek, never completely concealed from the eye, and that was perfectly fine with everyone. The jumble of lives lived well and full, without apologies to anyone.

Michael thought of Bill and his song—*how strange the change from major to minor*. When did the harmonics in his life change, he wondered. Michael closed his eyes and remembered Bill standing in front of Robby's black Steinway, a piano as long as the box that would hold Bill for eternity. Michael wanted to cry for Bill. But Sean was right; there was nothing tragic about Bill in those last moments. Bill knew this was his swan song, the perfect song before death.

To die with friends. To die surrounded not by darkness or fear but in the fading glow of the lavender twilight. To die surrounded by people who, like you, had been chosen not by default but by Robby and Jim to be part of a family.

Michael sipped at his scotch as his fingers caressed the tufted indentations of his chair, looking for something lost.

◆ ◆ ◆

"Are you OK, Jim?"

"I need to clean all this up."

"No, you don't, honey. It will keep until tomorrow," Robby said as he put his arms around his husband. "It will all be here in the morning."

"Let me turn out the light in the guest room," Jim walked into the guest room and let out a loud cry. Robby ran to him.

"What happened?"

"Look. Look." Jim pointed to the only coat left on the bed. "Inspector Renault." He picked up the coat with great care as if Bill were still inside it. He started to cry uncontrollably. His chest heaved back and forth as he gasped for air.

"Sweetie, it's OK. I'm here."

"I'm afraid, Robby. I'm afraid of what's going to happen. I know we're going to die. I'm not ready."

"And I'm not ready for you to die. We'll beat this. You know that we will beat this."

"Maybe."

"No, maybe. I'll kick your ass if you don't pull it together. You're not leaving me with this house to clean by myself."

"I like it when you're in control."

"Sweetie, I'm always in control. I just let you think otherwise."

"We should do something with Inspector Renault."

"We will drape it over Bill's casket like an American flag. And every Thanksgiving we will take it out and put it on a chair at the dining table and toast Bill."

"Is that a little much, even for a couple of old queens?"

"The beauty of being an old queen is that everybody has to do what you want. Our house. Our kingdom."

"You're my king."

"And you are my queen." Robby held Jim close to him now. Jim had put the coat back on the guest bed. The two men kissed gently as their bodies began swaying slightly to a melody no one else could hear. They danced.

"I always liked this tune."

"Me too."

◆ ◆ ◆

The rain was heavy now. Michael stared at the fire. "How strange the change from major to minor," he sang out loud. He wanted to wallow in the moment, allow himself to be swept out to sea in a wave of self-pity as he had done countless times before. Yet, there was something different tonight. Truth.

So much had happened. Harris and Sean seemed to have found one another. An odd match, Michael thought, and then realized there were no odd matches. People come together when they are supposed to—the oddness is avoiding the natural connection. Finally, Michael understood. He took his phone out of his pocket.

"Hey, there. I wasn't sure this number was still good...Me too...Had the same number for the last twenty-two years...I know this is out of the blue. I should have said something earlier, and it's raining, and you're probably home...oh, you're not holding the phone...good, don't want you to get a ticket... Thinking about tonight...yeah, yeah...maybe, maybe you would like to come over?...I ...I've missed you...I'm glad you said that. It would have been awkward if you hadn't. You remember the place?...Ha, ha, ha, you can't see perfectly dimpled sofa pillows from the street...You're not going to see those dimples from the street, either...Why do you think I'm drinking a scotch? I'm not that predictable. OK, I am that predictable. That's part of my charm...You remember how to get here? ...That's right, yes, the fifth house on the left...Drive safe. See you soon."

Michael hung up the phone. He sipped the scotch, and chuckled, looking at the glass and that he was indeed a creature of habit. Well, not anymore—or at least not right now, he thought. He walked over to the sofa, picked up one of the "perfectly dimpled" pillows positioned into a crook of the couch, squashed out its perfection, and tossed it. Michael looked at the pillow lying on the floor across the room.

"Find yourself a new friend."

About the Author

Alfred P. Doblin has spent most of his professional career working as a journalist, most notably as the Editorial Page Editor of *The (Bergen) Record* in New Jersey. Writing a twice-weekly column and editorials, he has been recognized by numerous state and national journalism associations, including the American Society of News Editors (ASNE) award for excellence in editorial writing, the Society of the Silurians, NLGJA: The Association of LGBTQ+ Journalists, and was nominated four times for the GLAAD Media Award for Outstanding Newspaper Columnist. In February 2024, he was announced as a runner-up in the Saints and Sinners 2024 Fiction Contest, part of the Tennessee Williams & New Orleans Literary Festival. He is also the grandson of the German novelist Alfred Döblin. Currently working in communications, Doblin lives in Brooklyn, NY. This is his first published book.